Tindog Tacloban

Claire Morley

To Mally

Thank you for your support in buying my book. I hope you enjoy reading it.

Lots of love
Claire xx

Copyright © 2015 Claire Morley

The right of Claire Morley to be identified as the Author of the Work has been asserted by her in accordance with the Copyright, Designs and Patents Act 1988.

All rights reserved. You may not copy, distribute, transmit, reproduce or otherwise make available this publication (or any part of it) in any form, or by any means (including without limitation electronic, digital, optical, mechanical, photocopying, printing, recording or otherwise), without the prior written permission of the publisher. Any person who does any unauthorised act in relation to this publication may be liable to criminal prosecution and civil claims for damages

First published as an Ebook in August 2015

All characters in this publication are fictitious and any resemblance to real persons, living or dead, is purely coincidental.

ISBN 978-1535-492-35-5

Cover photograph © Claire Morley

Registered with the IP Rights Office Copyright Registration Service. Ref: 4135851266

ABOUT CLAIRE MORLEY

Claire Morley lives in North Cyprus with her dog, cat and partner, Steve.

In her previous life, she has been a marketer, a journalist and a wedding planner and currently works with authors to help with self-publishing and promoting their books.
www.myepublishbook.com

Tindog Tacloban is her first novel and was inspired by a trip to the Philippines as a volunteer to help after the devastating typhoon known locally as Yolanda hit Tacloban on 8 November, 2013 and sales from this book will go to benefit charities working to stop human trafficking and helping in disaster areas.

You can also find Claire at:

Twitter: clairemorley @clairemorley15

Facebook: https://www.facebook.com/clairemorleyauthor

ABOUT THE BOOK

In the aftermath of the fiercest typhoon on record to hit land, banners bearing the words Tindog Tacloban started to appear all over the city. Meaning Rise Up Tacloban, they were a testament to the determination and resilience of the Filipino people as they tried to rebuild their shattered lives.

For many, things would never be the same:

Izel Sombilon watched in horror as two of his children were ripped from his arms and swept away by the huge storm waves

Eleven year old Lika Faye was plunged into the sordid underworld of Webcam Child Sex Tourism.

For Helen Gable volunteering in the typhoon ravaged area was a chance for her to come to terms with her own personal tragedy.

For exploited children, everywhere.

Tindog Tacloban

CHAPTER ONE

Rain pounded on the corrugated iron above him and echoed around the kitchen. The wind sucked at the edges of the roof determined to pry under the metal sheets. He jumped as tree branches clawed at the window. Another flash of lightning streaked across the grey dawn sky. The house walls shuddered as a particularly malevolent gust assaulted the building. Outside the coconut palms bowed and twisted.

'Daddy?'

Izel Sombilon turned to the steps leading down into the kitchen and from where the scared young girl called to him. Tall for her eleven years, Lika Faye's big brown eyes were fixed on her father in fear. Her chin length bob of hair dishevelled by sleep, framed her pretty heart shaped face. She was still in her pink and white polka dot bed clothes, although she'd also put on her new pink trainers, he noticed.

Izel had been sitting at the table finishing his morning coffee. The kitchen was a large square room where his family spent most of their time together. Opposite him was a long white tiled unit with a sink and gas burner on which his mother and his wife prepared the family meals. In the corner stood an old cumbersome television; if they got a good price for their rice this year, he was hopeful they would be able to afford a new flat screen.

Behind him was the family Sari Sari store. Adelaida, his wife, managed the little shop the majority of the time. It ran the length of the kitchen and was a metre wide. The wooden hatch covering the metal grill which served to display items, while keeping them safe from sticky fingers, crashed noisily as the increasing wind snatched at it.

On his left two large windows faced the sea. Although only half a mile away, houses blocked a clear view of it. He was looking out at the wooden house in front of his; the family had wisely evacuated last night. It was already showing signs of weakening to the elements. It was half past five on the morning of November 8, 2013 and Yolanda, the category five super typhoon was gathering her strength.

Izel turned his attention to his daughter.

'It's okay, sweetheart,' a broad smile was quick to his lips, revealing a row of uneven white teeth under a broad nose, wrinkles creased at the corners of his eyes. 'This old house has seen off a lot of typhoons, we're safe here. We just need to sit tight and let her pass. Are Angelina and Ellijah still sleeping?'

Lika Faye nodded. Izel drained his coffee, stood and walked over to the sink unit, rinsed his cup and upended it on the white tiles. Lika Faye padded across the terracotta coloured concrete floor to his side and slipped a warm hand into his. He tugged at the sparse hairs sprouting from his chin.

'I don't think I'll be going to the farm today though.' It was as well he and his father had managed to harvest most of the rice over the past couple of weeks and get it into the storage sheds before this typhoon. As greater precaution before leaving last night they had helped the farm workers secure tarpaulins over the sacks. He hoped it would be enough to keep their stock safe from the driving rain. They had borrowed money this year to rent more land but it would be worth it for the extra income, even after they had settled the loan.

'Let's see what this storm is up to,' he smiled down at his daughter. Together they crossed the room to one of the kitchen windows. They peered out into the grey half-light and at the squall that was growing in strength by the second.

Debris swirled and danced in front of them before being whipped away. A powerful gust of wind smashed into the concrete wall causing it to reverberate. They both stepped back in alarm.

Izel could barely hear Adelaida over the raging weather as she appeared with their two younger children. Their eyes were wide and Ellijah's bottom lip was wobbling. They stood either side of their mother and clung tightly to her skirt.

'I won't get many customers this morning,' she was trying to keep calm as she nodded at the Sari Sari store and moved into the kitchen, Angelina and Ellijah in tow. Adelaida's Sari Sari store was one of the most popular of the corner shops in the San Roque district. Always greeting her customers with a wide smile, Adelaida's gentle countenance and soft voice made her a favourite with her neighbours. On her regular trips to the big Robinsons Mall in Tacloban city, she always tried to find something slightly different from her competitors. She also ensured she was well stocked with the usual calls for canned goods, cooking oils and sauces, cigarettes, beer, soft drinks and of course, sweets for the local kids.

The banging of the shutter increased in volume and frequency prompting her to continue: 'This one's a bad one, Izel. Maybe we should have evacuated after all. They kept talking about a storm surge, whatever that means, on the radio. I'm really worried,' her voice trembled slightly as she stared at the trees bowing manically outside.

The overhead florescent strip light flickered. Adelaida had put candles and a couple of storm lanterns on the kitchen table last night in preparation for the approaching typhoon. Although the sun had already risen, the thunderous black clouds and thrashing horizontal rain contradicted the fact. The light blinked on and off a few times more and died, leaving them in grey gloominess.

The two younger children screamed as a coconut smashed through a kitchen window, landing at Izel's feet. The sudden strength of the wind funnelled through the gaping hole forced Izel backwards into Lika Faye, knocking her to the ground. He grabbed at the child's elbow pulling her upright and thrust her towards his wife. Rain whipped in through the broken window, stinging at Izel's flesh. There was a sound of wrenching metal as the typhoon won its battle with the corrugated iron and sheets were ripped like paper from the kitchen roof. Others flapped threateningly, beating a fast, irregular rhythm on the eaves. Yolanda forced her way into their home, uninvited, the noise deafening.

Trying to make himself heard above the cacophony, Izel screamed at Adelaida, 'Take the children to my parents' room.'

Lika Faye looked up at her father, whimpering: 'What about you, daddy?'

'I'll be right behind you, go with your mother. Now!'

They scurried up the five steps leading to the bedrooms. The force of the swirling wind within the house caused them to stumble and it knocked Ellijah to his knees. Adelaida yanked the screaming five-year-old to his feet, fighting to keep upright herself. Izel stared wide-eyed at the scene before him; the speed at which the typhoon was escalating terrified him.

His earlier confidence had been shattered when the roof had been torn away. Above him he could make out sheets of iron, branches and other debris propelled by the force of the increasing wind. The tree in the garden was going to be uprooted any second if the battering continued. Izel debated whether to grab the television before retreating to the back of the house, abandoning the idea when he remembered the weight of it.

The elements were now whipped up into such a fury he couldn't make out the house in front of theirs. His jaw went slack as he realised why. He was looking at a wall of black water and it was coming straight at him. He stumbled backwards up the stairs, his eyes wide in disbelief. Time slowed and he watched in horror as the wave smashed into the wall of the house. The rest of the windows gave way under the pressure and shards of glass burst into the room quickly followed by sea water. He came to his senses and hurtled towards the back of the house. By the time he reached the bedroom door, the water was already up over the steps and rising fast.

Adelaida and the children were in the hallway frozen in terror as they watched the demolition of the kitchen. They hadn't made it to his parents' room and the door was closed; Izel could hear his father yelling but couldn't make out the words. He tugged at the door handle, but the water was rising and the force of it was pinning the bedroom door closed. He managed to open it a crack and got his fingers round the edge trying to wrench it open. He screamed as the pressure of the water against it pushed it back, crushing his hands.

'Dad, mum, push the door, my hands are trapped,' he screeched above the roaring storm. With Izel pulling and his parents, Rogelio and Lorna, putting all their strength against the door, the thin aluminium gave way and bent backwards. Izel fell into the swelling water as his hands were freed and his parents stumbled into the hallway. He got to his feet, the water now to his knees.

'Quickly,' he gasped. 'You three get into the bathroom.' He grabbed at his children, pushing them roughly towards the small room.

'Climb up on the toilet to keep above the water. Lika Faye, help the other two.'

The children were shaking and sobbing as the brackish water attempted to tug them off balance. The house was filled with the sound of gushing water as it threatened to engulf them. It had displaced their furniture, mattresses and upturned chairs spun in the current, the noise roaring round the house like a jet aeroplane taking off.

Adelaida's clothes were plastered to her body. She stood rigid with her parents-in-law in the churning water staring in horror, paralysed.

Izel forced his way through the water, holding his arm in front of his face to protect him from the hurricane force wind and stinging rain. He had to put his mouth to his father's ear to be heard above the din surrounding them.

'You need to get higher, above the water,' he gasped. 'Take mum and Adelaida and stay together, I'm going to get the children to safety.'

He fought his way back to the bathroom. The water was over the top of the toilet and the children were holding onto each other screaming. Their bed clothes were like a second skin on their trembling bodies, terror etched on their small faces as the water continued to advance.

The bathroom was a concrete box with space between its roof and the rafters. It was the highest platform in the house, two metres off the ground, two metres wide by three metres long, enough room for the four of them. Izel grabbed at each of the children in turn roughly hoisting them up into the raised area, hoping it would remain above the encroaching water. As he went to haul himself up beside them, the second wave crashed into the outside wall of the kitchen. The house shook violently before the water smashed through the concrete armed with debris dragged back by the first surge. Izel screamed in pain as a large chunk of wall caught by the churning water struck his left arm, splitting open the skin. He was now treading water and at face level with the children. Shock had stunned them into silence.

Izel realised their only hope was to try and stay afloat in the foul water swirling beneath him. He could feel the debris twisting and turning in the sea water as it eddied around his legs. Adrenaline kicked in and his only thought was how to save his family.

'Grab my neck,' he screamed to Lika Faye, hoping she could hear the words before they were swallowed by the howling winds.

He clutched the back of Ellijah's tee-shirt with his right hand and threaded his bleeding left arm under Angelina's arms, leaving his hand free to hang onto the rafters. Lika Faye gripped his neck and he kicked with his feet to try and keep them all afloat. The upsurge of water meant his head was already in line with the rafters. It wouldn't be long before they were against the ceiling. Izel started to panic, they had nowhere to go. The pressure of the water was pinning his body to the wall of the bathroom. He couldn't fight against it. Getting out through where the kitchen once stood wasn't a possibility.

He tried to get his bearings. Where were the doors and windows at the back of the house? Could he try to get the children to hold their breath and attempt to swim down and out? The water was black, he wouldn't be able to see anything underwater, he realised it wasn't an option either.

Before he could think any further a third wave caught the little group by surprise, spinning them away from the bathroom wall and into the centre of the room. Izel vaguely heard Ellijah's scream as a large plank of wood ripped the boy from his grasp and then punched into his own head, stunning him. He couldn't see anything. Salt water stung his eyes and filled his nostrils. He was underwater. He kicked frantically, hoping he was heading upward. He reached the surface and gasped for air, realising that a petrified Angelina was still clinging to him and fighting for breath. Ellijah and Lika Faye were gone.

The water sucked violently at him, dragging him under. He kicked desperately trying to keep them both afloat. When his head broke the surface, narrowly missing a jagged piece of corrugated iron, he hopelessly screamed out the names of his other two children. He swung his head round frantically straining to catch sight of them. He caught a glimpse of Lika Faye by the wall at the end of the house. She was thrashing her arms trying to keep her head above water. The eleven year old could manage a couple of strokes in a calm sea, but in these conditions, panicking, she had forgotten how to swim.

'Hold on tight,' Izel yelled in Angelina's ear. She obediently wrapped her arms round his neck and he started towards Lika Faye.

The water was littered with floating debris. One of Ellijah's toy cars bobbed sadly past, coconuts, corrugated iron threatening to lacerate flesh, plastic containers; a soup of household items and possessions hindered his progress.

Overhead the lightweight sheets of corrugated iron were no match for the screaming winds. The roof from the rest of the house was plucked into the sky and ripped away, leaving them totally vulnerable to the elements. He tried to call Lika Faye's name, get her attention, but the wind snatched the words from his lips. His face was being pricked by the driving rain and he had to squint against it. The cut on his temple stung from the salt water and the spray from the sea whipped against him making it almost impossible to see.

There was no sight of Ellijah, Adelaida, or his parents. Izel concentrated on trying to reach the place he'd last spotted Lika Faye. By some miracle, he spied the top of her head as she disappeared beneath the water's surface. He reached down, grasping in the black murkiness, desperate to connect with his daughter's body. He felt something brush against his outstretched fingers. He tightened his grip around it and yanked it free of the water.

He swore as he realised it was only a tee-shirt. He threw it away in disgust and resumed his search using his right arm in a sweeping motion, stretching as far around and below as his reach would allow. He felt something brush against his knuckles, was it hair? He grasped at a handful. This time he was successful. Lika Faye's face came into view, gulping at air as she was pulled from the clutches of a watery grave.

So focussed on pulling her to them, Izel wasn't aware of the leaden coconut tree until it rammed him. Pain exploded in his elbow causing him to loosen the grip on his eldest daughter and before he had a chance to grab her, she was sucked away from him. With no building left to contain her, within seconds the distance between them stretched beyond his reach and he watched in desperation as the current dragged her away.

He couldn't hear her calling him, but he could make out the words on her lips while she was still visible, words which would haunt his dreams.

'Daddy, daddy, help me, please....'

Izel gripped Angelina tighter to him, closed his eyes and howled as his beautiful daughter disappeared from view and he could do nothing to rescue her.

CHAPTER TWO

Lika Faye tasted salt, her head hurt and she couldn't move her legs. She closed her eyes and screwed up her face trying to make sense of what was happening. Was she having a nightmare again? She opened her eyes hoping to see the comforting sight of her bedroom, her brother and sister asleep in their beds next to hers. Instead she found herself face down, with strange objects all around her. Something was sticking into her left side and her legs were buried.

She remembered hearing somewhere if you could wiggle your toes, then your legs were okay. She concentrated really hard and squeezed her toes on one leg then the other. That seemed to be okay. Oh no. Her shoes. She couldn't feel her shoes on her feet. If she was outside, then she should have shoes on and they weren't there. Mum was going to be furious if she'd lost her shoes. They'd only bought them a couple of days ago. It had taken her ages to persuade her mother to buy the pink trainers rather than another pair of flip flops and now she'd lost them. Her bottom lip trembled and tears started to form in her eyes. Then another thought occurred to her. Where were mum and dad? She lifted her head and a throbbing pain made her cry out. She reached up behind her head to where it hurt with her one free arm and touched it gently, flinching as she did so. When she looked at her fingers they were crimson.

She tried to call out, but only a croak resulted. Her mouth was dry and she was very thirsty. She coughed and tried again.

'Mummy? Daddy?'

Nothing.

Where was everyone? It was so quiet.

She tried to recall what had happened. She had been in the kitchen with her dad and the wind had been really loud. She gasped as she recalled the water smashing the windows and pouring in. Then they had all been in the water, swirling around. Her dad had been trying to reach out to her as it got higher and then...she frowned. The next thing she could remember was waking up here. She wriggled her other arm loose of the debris and tried to roll over onto her back so she could better see. She could twist the top half of her body but her legs were pinned. She tried again.

'Mummy, daddy. Where are you?'

Looking around she could see she was on a pile of rubbish. How had she got here?

She could feel rain spitting on her face. She had to get free. She had to find her mum and dad. They would know what to do. They would make the pain in her head go away. She frantically twisted left and right. Something scratched painfully in her left side. She reached down with her hand. It felt rough, like a piece of wood. She grabbed the end where it was sticking in her ribs and tried to pull it free. It wouldn't move. She cried out in frustration. It was useless, she was stuck.

Lika Faye lifted her head as high as she could, ignoring the throbbing it caused. There must be someone who could help her. After a couple of moments she could see movement and a man came into view.

'Help me, please help me,' she called out.

The man turned his head, searching for where the voice had come from.

'I'm over here. Please help me, I can't get out.' She waved at him.

He turned away from her and called over his shoulder.

'Quick, over here, I've found one alive.'

Within moments three people came to her rescue. Clawing at the wooden planks, sodden clothing and corrugated iron that held her captive, they finally pulled her clear.

'Can you stand?' one of them asked. 'Are your legs okay?'

'Yes, yes I think so,' she said. 'I wriggled my toes before and they were okay.' She looked down. There were red lines where her legs had been scratched and they were covered in mud. She had been right her shoes were gone. She looked up at the three faces crowding round her.

'My shoes, they've gone. Mummy is going to be so angry, they were new.' Tears started and she turned to the pile she had been pulled from, tearing at the debris. 'I must find them.'

One of the women who had helped free her, gently took her arm.

'It's okay, sweetheart. Don't worry about your shoes. Your mum will just be happy you're okay. Do you know where your house was?'

Lika Faye looked at the woman, then looked around her. 'I…erm…I'm not sure.' She frowned, nothing looked familiar. 'Where's my mummy and daddy?'

'I'm sorry, sweetheart, I don't know. Where were you when the typhoon came? What's your name?'

'Lika Faye Sombilon,' she replied. 'I was at home and then the water came…I woke up here.' She pointed to the pile in front of her and shrugged.

'I'm sure your family will be looking for you, we're all looking for our lost ones,' the woman bowed her head, her voice breaking as she spoke. 'I'm sorry. I have to search for my boys. Stay here where they can see you, I'm sure they'll come soon. If they don't, do you know where your evacuation centre is?'

Lika Faye paused, thinking. 'Yes, it's the convent,' she said.

'Good, find your way there if they don't come, okay?'

She nodded and watched as the woman continued her search, calling her children's names as she rummaged through the debris.

She looked around her, her eyes stopping at the Metrobank. The sign was hanging off a bit, but she recognised it as the one she passed every day as she walked home from school. So if that was the bank, Kristina's house would be down there. Lika Faye turned and looked towards the turning she and her friend took each day. She thought she could make out where the narrow road had been. She looked again at the bank, trying to visualise how it had all looked yesterday. If she could find Kristina's house, they would be able to help her find mum and dad. She scrambled carefully over the debris to the other side of the road. A coconut tree lay across the gap between buildings where the road had been. She climbed over it and tried to see her friend's house. It was the third on the left, back from the main road. That can't be right, she thought and looked behind her to check she could see the bank, yes that was definitely it. She looked ahead once more. Where Kristina's house had stood yesterday was a mass of broken wood and bits of furniture. She clambered a bit closer. Kristina's dad's red scooter was lying on its side, the handlebars all twisted. There was no sign of her friend or her family.

Lika Faye bit her lip, unsure what to do next. Her head was throbbing. It had stopped bleeding but she had traced with her fingers a nasty gash about ten centimetres long. Her throat was burning. The salt water in her mouth had left her really thirsty. The Sari Sari shop next to Kristina's house was gone too. Not that she had any money to buy a drink, she thought. She flopped down onto a coconut tree trunk lying in the road. She hung her head and stared at the mangled objects on the ground. Tears started to run down her face, dripping from her chin.

She jumped as she heard a woman's scream nearby.

'Noooo, oh sweet Jesus, no, not my baby.' The bereft mother grasped a dead child to her chest, rocking him back and forth.

A shadow crossed in front of Lika Faye and stopped. The girl squinted to see a woman's smiling face.

'Hi. Are you okay?'

Lika Faye nodded. 'I'm thirsty.'

The woman thrust a bottle of Coke at her. She looked at it greedily, then snatched at it and drank, belching when she had quenched her thirst.

The woman moved to sit next to her on the tree trunk. 'What's your name?'

'Lika Faye,' she replied clutching the bottle tightly to her chest.
'Are you here on your own?'

She nodded. 'I was looking for Kristina. She lives here.' She pointed to the remains of the house.

'Did you live here too?'

'No. And I don't know where my mummy and daddy are.' Her eyes brimmed with tears.

'When did you last see them?'

'When the water came, my mum went with grandma and grandpa, daddy was trying to get us into the roof of the house, but the waves took me away and I woke up over there.' She pointed up the road. 'And I lost my shoes.'

'Well that's not good. Maybe I can help you. The house I'm staying in is up the road, I'm sure you're hungry. We can have something to eat and then look for your family.'

Lika Faye looked sideways at the woman. 'But I don't know you.'

'Well, my name is Rosela. And I live about a ten minute walk from here. I'm only trying to help.' She smiled at Lika Faye.

The idea of food made her stomach rumble. But she desperately wanted to look for her parents.

'Thank you,' she said remembering her manners. 'But I think I want to find my mum and dad.' She offered the bottle of Coke back to Rosela.

'Okay, no problem. Keep it. It might take you some time to find them.'

The woman stood up and wandered away. Lika Faye watched her leave. She glanced over her shoulder to smile at the girl before disappearing behind a building.

Lika Faye looked in the direction of her house then back towards the route the woman had taken. Should she have gone with her? She seemed kind. Lika Faye looked down at the Coke bottle in her hands, torn between looking for her family and going after the woman. She unscrewed the cap on the bottle and drank the warm fizzy liquid and made a decision. This was where the road to her house had been, if she followed it, she would find her home. She wanted her mum.

The sun had broken through the clouds and a heavy humidity filled the air. Lika Faye started to pick her way over the mounds of rubbish filling the road, but with one hand clamped tightly round the Coke bottle, she kept losing her balance and slipping. When she looked up, she didn't recognise anything and she wondered if she was on the right road after all.

Now she regretted not going with the woman; perhaps she should try and find the convent. Her feet were sore without shoes after climbing over the uneven surface. It wasn't fair, why was she here? Tears of frustration made tracks on her mud-streaked face as she stood still among the typhoon chaos.

More people were visible now, all searching through the clutter around them, some calling out names as they moved about. Lika Faye couldn't see anyone she recognised and she wrapped her arms around the Coke bottle. Finally the need to find a toilet spurred her to move and she headed back towards the main road.

'Hello again, Faye isn't it?' The woman from earlier appeared beside her.

'Lika Faye,' she corrected her.

'That's right. No luck finding your mum and dad yet?'

Lika Faye shook her head. 'I'm going to the evacuation centre. They'll come and find me.'

The woman stopped and put a hand on Lika Faye's shoulder. 'Oh, I wouldn't go there. I've just been,' she said shaking her head. 'It's all a mess. I think you would be better to come with me. We can go back when it's all calmed down and find them. I'm sure you must be hungry by now. We can have some rice and look for them afterwards. What do you say?' She leaned down and tucked some of Lika Faye's hair behind her ear and stroked her cheek. She held out her hand.

Lika Faye tilted her head on one side and looked up at the woman.

'Okay,' she said and took the offered hand. 'Then we can look for my mum and dad later. I will need some shoes,' she said looking down at her bare feet.

'I'm sure we can find something.'

They set off in the direction away from the Metrobank, picking their way carefully along what had once been the Pan-Philippine Highway.

'Can you speak English?' Rosela asked.

Lika Faye frowned at the strange question, then smiled. She was top of her class in school for English. She had even won a medal for it last term. She puffed out her chest with pride. Then answered in the foreign language: 'Yes, I speak English very good.'

'That's excellent, you are a clever girl,' Rosela said and smiled back.

CHAPTER THREE

Helen Gable pulled on her black linen trousers. She would need a belt, she decided. They had been a snug fit a month ago, now they swamped her. She sat heavily at her dressing room table and stared at the gaunt face in the mirror. Dark circles were smudged around unsmiling blue eyes. Her usually short auburn hair had erupted into curls where it had grown longer than normal. She sighed wearily and picked up a black eyeliner pencil twirling it between her thumb and fingers.

She had requested people attend the funeral in bright colours to celebrate Charlie's life rather than mourn his death, but she was going to wear black. The dark colour made her complexion appear even paler. She looked away from the stranger in front of her and put her head in her hands.

'Oh, Charlie. Give me the strength to get through today.'

'Helen?' A voice floated up the stairs, it was her best friend, Sarah. 'Are you okay? Do you want me to come up?'

Helen lifted her head and cleared her throat. Pull yourself together, she told her reflection.

'I'll be down in a minute.'

'Okay, no hurry, there's plenty of time before…' The unsaid words hung clumsily in the air between them.

Helen took a deep breath, applied the kohl under her eyes and added some waterproof mascara. It would have to do. Make-up had never been a priority with her and today nothing was going to improve how she looked. Her heart felt like a cold stone in her chest. A mother should never have to bury her son.

She pulled her black jacket off its hanger and shook her arms into it. A quick glance in the full length mirror revealed a tall, slim, forty-three year old woman. A deep sadness burned in her eyes. She looked away before the tears started.

As Helen appeared on the stairs, Sarah jumped up from the

kitchen table wringing her hands. Her long blond hair which usually flowed over her shoulders was pulled back into a chignon. She wore a navy skirt, fitted jacket and black boots. It was a sharp contrast to the usual informal attire of a woman with three young children. Her face was full of concern.

'Can I get you anything? A cup of tea? A whiskey? It'll be another ten minutes before the cars arrive.' She moved to the bottom of the stairs and enveloped Helen in her arms. The two stood in silence for several moments, locked together in their grief.

'Maybe a whiskey, for medicinal purposes of course,' Helen croaked with a faint smile on her pale lips.

Sarah took her friend's hands and nodded. 'Your hands are like ice blocks. Do you have gloves? It's cold out and the church will be freezing.'

'I think there's a pair in my coat in the kitchen,' Helen said absently.

Sarah poured them both a whiskey and they sipped it in silence.

They heard cars scrunch across the gravel of the unmade road outside the house. Helen's heart lurched and started to pound, she could sense its beat in her temple and behind her eyes. She felt short of breath, she reached out to steady herself against the kitchen table and fell into one of the chairs. She looked up to see David, Charlie's father, come in through the front door. He and Sarah seemed to be talking, their mouths were moving but she couldn't hear them properly. Their voices seemed to come from far away, distorted as if they were speaking underwater, as they moved closer to her. She felt a warm hand on her arm.

'Helen, Helen, would you like a drink, some water?' She could just about make out Sarah's words.

She blinked and looked into the concerned face of her friend. She realised she was trembling violently, her teeth chattering, her breathing was ragged. David crouched beside her, looking anxiously into her face.

'Helen, are you alright, can you hear me?' he said.

'It's a panic attack,' said Sarah. 'Helen. Look at me. Take a deep breath in through your nose and out through your mouth, with me now.' Sarah calmly took a breath, encouraging Helen to do the same. Helen copied her friend, getting her breathing under control. Hot tears raced silently down her cheeks as the shaking slowly subsided.

'I'm sorry.' She wiped at her running nose with her sleeve.

'It's okay, sweetheart,' Sarah said gently, handing her a tissue. 'This is a traumatic time for you. It's the shock of it all. It's not uncommon in these circumstances.'

'Hey, you had me really worried there for a minute,' David smiled and kneeling in front of her he wrapped his arms around her shoulders, stroking her back.

Helen and David had split up amicably ten years earlier, both realising they weren't each other's soul mates. Even without Charlie, they would most likely have remained good friends. However, their son had ensured they remained close, even after David had moved to the United States, married and had two children with Valerie.

He had been on the first flight to England when he had heard the news and had remained there since. His family, waiting in one of the cars outside, had arrived three days earlier for the funeral. Charlie's young half-brother, Henry, and sister, Isabel, were struggling to comprehend their big brother wouldn't be going to spend the summer with them.

He sat back on his haunches. 'Are you okay? I can ask the drivers to wait a minute or two.' David checked his watch. 'The service is due to start at two o'clock. What's the church from here Sarah? About five minutes?'

Sarah nodded.

Helen looked at the man crouched in front of her. Grey tinged the brown hair at his temples. Smile lines crinkled the skin around his eyes. He was still a handsome man. She noticed how many of his features had been evident in their son's face.

They had met working at Frisco Systems. He in sales, her in marketing. They had moved in together after six months and two years later, Charlie was on the way, not entirely planned, but not an accident either. Helen had stayed at home with him for the first six months, but missed the adrenaline rush of organising events, advertising campaigns, seminars and conferences in the fast paced IT industry. She had decided to set up as a freelance marketer. It offered a way she could work around being a mum to Charlie, but still maintain her independence and her sanity.

'Can you stand, Helen?'

'Yes, I think so.' She got slowly to her feet. Sarah helped her on with her coat and, with David, guided her out of the house towards the waiting cars. They walked past the hearse. The coffin in the back was buried under a rainbow of flowers and wreaths.

'I asked people to make a donation rather than buy flowers,' Helen said.

She climbed into the waiting car. It wasn't raining, she noticed as she stared out of the window, although it was grey. The clouds were skulking low in the sky and it was only a matter of time before they released their load. It should rain, she thought, tears from heaven for her beautiful boy.

By the time the procession pulled up outside St Peter's church the first spots started to fall. Large drops exploded as they hit the windscreen, beating out a slow rhythm to start, speeding up as the downpour started in earnest.

One of the undertakers opened Helen's door, an umbrella at the ready. He escorted her and Sarah to the church door then returned for David. They watched as the pallbearers shouldered the coffin and solemnly made their way inside. Six young men from Charlie's rugby team had been chosen to carry the casket into the church and they all wore the club blazer and tie. They had taken the responsibility very seriously and carefully delivered him to the front of the church before silently filing into one of the pews.

The mourners followed them in until the church was full to overflowing and some of the congregation spilled outside, standing in the rain for the service. Helen sat numbly through the words of the clergyman, her head bowed. She couldn't bear to look at the coffin. The idea of her son being inside made her feel nauseous. She and David had chosen favourite photographs to be displayed on either side of the altar and the sight of him smiling out at her was more than she could bear. She gripped the bench either side of her to stop herself from racing out of the church. The dark varnished wood was smooth against her palms. She had declined to give a reading, however David had agreed to do the eulogy. He brushed past her and put his hand on her shoulder as he made his way to the lectern.

'Where's daddy going?' Helen heard Henry ask his mother.

'Ssshhh, darling.' Valerie glanced apologetically at Helen. 'He's going to talk about Charlie,' she whispered. The five year old nodded gravely.

Tears dripped onto Helen's linen trousers as she heard David's words, telling how proud they were of their son and all his achievements in a life too short. Sarah pried her left hand away from the bench and clutched it tightly.

They stood to sing the hymn Jerusalem. Helen could hear the rugby boys belting it out at the top of their voices and a memory of taking Charlie to watch England against France at Twickenham for his birthday flashed through her mind. The same words had echoed through the stadium as England had scored a try and gone into the lead.

As the last notes floated up from the organ, the congregation sat and the sound of heels clacking down the aisle could be heard. Heads turned to watch a friend of Charlie's, Katie, make her way to the front of the church.

She was dressed head to toe in scarlet, including her outrageously high shoes. A wreath of red flowers was perched on her flowing blond hair. She stood red eyed at the lectern and took a deep breath.

'Emma, Rachel, Kayleigh and I have written a poem for Charlie. He was my best friend…' she paused briefly before continuing, the pitch of her voice rising as she spoke. 'And I miss him every minute of every day.' She stopped and composed herself before reciting An Ode To Charlie, lamenting the loss of their beautiful, gentle and loving friend. There wasn't a dry eye in the church as she finished. She wiped away her own tears, nodded to Helen and walked back to her seat. David put his arm around Helen's shoulders as she sobbed.

After the church service, the mourners went on to The Black Swan for the wake. Helen and David followed the hearse to the crematorium.

'There's been no more news from the police since we last spoke?' David asked as they waited for the urn to be brought to them.

Helen shook her head, not trusting herself to speak. David took hold of her hand. Feeling the warmth of his touch on her skin she closed her eyes and leaned her head back against the wall.

'I still can't make any sense of it, you know. Did he tell you he'd just set up a "Just Giving" page to raise money for the earthquake victims in…where was it now? The Philippines somewhere I think. He only did it about a week before…'

David squeezed her hand and they sat in silence for a few minutes.

'I, erm…' David started. He cleared his throat. 'I've told Valerie I'll return back home with them at the end of next week.'

'Of course you must. There's nothing more you can do here.' Helen opened her eyes and smiled faintly at him. 'It's been a great support having you here, David. But your family needs you too.'

'What will you do?'

She sighed. 'I'm not sure. I've still got some clients' projects I'm working on. Although to be honest not doing a good job at the moment. They've been pretty understanding but…'

David nodded.

'I've been working with a human trafficking organisation, A21 they're called, just doing some marketing bits and pieces for them. I was talking with them about volunteering more with them, while Char…' she closed her eyes, willing her voice to remain steady. 'While Charlie was going to be with you in the summer. Maybe I'll see if I can start earlier.'

'You always were one for your causes.' David smiled at her.

'Things are never going to be the same again are they?' Hot tears pricked at her eyes and slid quietly down her cheeks.

A door opened and the undertaker emerged, carefully holding the urn they had chosen for their son's ashes. Charlie had always been concerned with the environment, it seemed fitting their son's remains should echo their son's beliefs. Helen was handed the grey bio-degradable container with a picture of a tree on its side. She stared at it. Her head and heart ached with grief. She couldn't imagine a life where she would never see her son again. She'd never chastise him for his untidy room, see his boyish grin or hear his laughter. They'd never play tennis again. She wouldn't hug him goodnight or remind him to put out the rubbish bins. What she held in her hands was all that was left of her child.

The undertaker waited patiently by the exit of the crematorium for them, his head bowed, arms clasped behind his back. Helen gently cradled the urn in the crook of her right arm.

'I was thinking I would plant him in Nettlebed woods. He loved it there. Do you remember the time we took him after it snowed? It was like a winter wonderland.'

David smiled at the memory. 'He can't have been more than four or five. He was worried the deer would be cold in the snow.

'You didn't want to have him closer to you? In your garden?'

'I did think about it, but then if I move…I wouldn't want to uproot him. No, I think in the woods is the right place.'

'Okay. Maybe we can go together before I leave?'

'I'd like that.'

They left the crematorium to join friends and family at the pub. A sign outside announced The Black Swan was closed for a private function. Helen braced herself as she opened the door and entered. Inside a fire roared in the big open hearth. Half-empty plates of sandwiches, sausage rolls and finger cakes were set up on a table along one wall. Groups of people stood or sat, chattering, sharing stories of Charlie. Sarah spotted Helen and handing her youngest, Matt, to her husband, crossed the room. As she did so, Helen's three other closest friends, Nicole, Fiona and Anne, left their conversations and surrounded her in a group hug.

The next couple of hours were a blur to Helen as friends, family and well-wishers approached her offering their condolences or sharing a memory with her. She was shattered as she said goodbye to the last of mourners. It was dark outside, although the rain had stopped. Cold air snaked in as David escorted his children out to their hire car. They had been staying at the Holiday Inn since Valerie, Isabel and Henry had arrived.

'I'll call you tomorrow,' he called over his shoulder.

Valerie hugged her and kissed her cheek. 'If you need anything, Helen, call us.'

Helen nodded and waved them off before joining Sarah at the bar.

'Can I have a Famous Grouse, please,' she asked the barmaid.

'Rob has taken the kids home. We dropped my car here before I came to you this morning. I thought you might need some company tonight.'

Helen grabbed the tumbler of whiskey from the bar and raised her glass to the ceiling. 'Cheers, Charlie. Are you looking down on us, seeing how today went? I hope we did you proud.' She knocked back the amber liquid and felt the warmth of it slide down her throat.

'What am I going to do, Sarah?' she looked forlornly at her friend. 'There's such an empty space where he used to be.'

'One day at time, Helen. I know it may not seem like it now, but it will get easier. Come on, let's take you home. You look exhausted.'

'Tell Andrew I'll be in tomorrow to settle the bill,' Helen said to the barmaid.

'He said to tell you no hurry, come in when you're ready.'

Sarah handed Helen her coat and the two of them walked out into the cold night air.

CHAPTER FOUR

The water had started to subside. Izel was hugging a surviving concrete post with his right arm and clutching Angelina protectively with his left. Her teeth were chattering, other than that she was quiet. They were both reeling from the past couple of hours. It was still raining, but the wind had lessened.

The water sucked and slurped as it snaked its way back to the sea. When he was sure it wasn't going to return Izel left the safety of the post. The remaining water around him was jammed with objects. Some he identified as items from his own home. He was now able to see the full extent of Yolanda's wrath, nothing was recognisable. He was filled with despair as he realised his own home was little more than rubble. Wooden houses had been reduced to matchsticks and concrete dwellings to shells. Corrugated iron which had once adorned every roof, skulked dangerously in the black water.

He cautiously picked his way through the remains of the house. He realised the water had sucked his sandals from his feet at some point. His left arm and head throbbed. Angelina's pyjamas were smeared with his blood.

'Angelina, sweetie,' he spoke to her softly. 'Does anything hurt?'

The little girl shook her head. Izel tried to smile at the frightened child in his arms.

'You've been so brave,' his voice cracked and a sob rose up from his chest, as he thought of his other two children.

'Daddy?'

'It's okay, sweetie, we need to see if we can find mummy and grandpa and grandma.'

'And Lika Faye and Ellijah,' she reminded him.

'Yes, of course,' he replied with a confidence he didn't feel. He had to stay positive. They could have survived, although he was filled with doubt. He had to put his negative thoughts aside and keep a brave face for the child in front of him. He moved Angelina to his uninjured arm and tried to take stock of his surroundings.

At first he was completely disoriented. Nothing looked familiar. Everything was flattened. Coconut palms, the ones still standing, were bent at angles. Many were stripped bare of their leaves, only sad stalks remained as if a giant hand had plucked them. It was then Izel saw his first body. He didn't register it initially. It looked like a large rag doll hanging from the electricity cable. The retreating sea had abandoned it there. He gasped and looked at Angelina. The little girl was thankfully oblivious. Still in a state of shock, she wasn't aware of anything.

Now the sea had ebbed further, it was easier to move around the remains of their home. It was still slow going, he had to avoid floating objects and to feel his way with his feet. More than once he was thrown off balance as his leg went through the floor where the wood had been smashed and broken away. He reached the stone steps he had fled up only four hours earlier. Walls no longer hindered his view to the sea. Izel stared in silence. All that remained of their kitchen was the white tiled sink unit, now covered in mud and sand. Everything else had been obliterated.

Apart from the sound of the wind and gentle knocking as debris drifting in the water bumped into walls, there was an eerie stillness. No birdsong, no engines, no children playing, no normal sounds from a normal day.

Izel could see people starting to emerge from their hiding places. Many were injured, streaked with blood, their clothes torn and ragged. They had been shocked into silence by the devastation and the sights around them. The people of Tacloban had seen many typhoons. Nothing had prepared them for the cruelty of this one.

A cry pierced the air. Izel turned towards the sound to see a man frantically tearing at wood and iron sheets to free a child. A huge gash in his head meant there was no chance of reviving him.

Water was now ankle deep. Izel had managed to find two mismatched shoes floating in the black water. He chose not to ponder on what had become of the owners. He watched the survivors around him, shuffling like zombies towards the main road. No one spoke. They nodded grimly when they saw a neighbour. No one dared ask the question they all feared the answer to.

Those less fortunate could be seen scattered among the debris. Izel could see them, dangling from wires, propped against walls, limbs at awkward angles, gashes and ugly wounds lacerating their damaged bodies.

'This isn't real,' he said aloud.

'Daddy?'

'Sorry, Angelina, daddy was talking to himself.' He kissed her forehead, unsure of what to do next. He didn't know where to begin looking for his family. They could be anywhere, inland or dragged back to the sea. Partly to distract Angelina from the sights around them, but also because he couldn't remember he asked her: 'Can you remember what mummy was wearing this morning?'

Angelina frowned, shaking her head, then: 'A skirt?'

'It's okay.' He smiled at her, tucking a wet curl behind her ear.

He tried to remember if Adelaida or his parents had been dressed or had they still been in their night clothes. No image came to his mind. The enormity of it weighed like ice in his stomach and if he found them, what then? They had nothing, no home, no food, everything had gone.

His thoughts were interrupted by Angelina's hoarse whisperings.

'Daddy, I'm thirsty.'

Izel closed his eyes and shook his head. Where was he going to find something as simple as a drink for his little girl? Spurred into action by his child's needs, he began looking for provisions of any kind. Maybe some of the Sari Sari stock had survived. He found their fridge. It had been swept into what had been his parent's bedroom, and was on its back. He gently put Angelina down and attempted to open it. The heavy door wouldn't yield at first. He tried from several angles with no luck. Finally with a hefty yank the suction relented and he pushed it upwards, letting it drop open over its side.

The contents had been violently tossed around and scraps of food lay in a gravy of water, juice and Coke. Some of the cans were still intact and he leaned in snatching a couple. He opened one cautiously. It hissed and spurted over his hand. Once it had settled down he handed it to his daughter. He hadn't realised how thirsty he was and drank greedily from a second can.

'Stay here, Angelina. I'm going to see if there's anything else I can find.'

Her bottom lip trembled. 'I'm scared, daddy, please don't leave me.' Tears brimmed in her eyes as she stared at him.

He sighed heavily and picked her up, holding her small body to him. She nestled her wet face into his neck.

'Shhh, shhh it's okay,' he comforted her.

He sloshed slowly through the dirty water and scoured the remains of his house for anything of use. Lika Faye's pink polka dot backpack caught his eye. *Hello Kitty* stared up at him, now covered in mud. He remembered standing in Robinsons Mall for what seemed an eternity while she had deliberated over which bag to choose. He snatched it up angrily. He filled it with drink cans, tinned sardines and packs of crackers he found swimming in the remaining sea water. He discovered a sack of rice, but it was wet and of no use. He sat Angelina on the sink unit and they feasted on dry biscuits washed down by Coca Cola.

Sustained by food and sugar, Izel decided to start the search for his family. He hoisted Angelina on to his right hip and gingerly made his way through the clutter of his home and outside. Paths and roads were no longer evident. Every surface was strewn with debris. An assortment of colours and objects were littered around them, making it hard to move in any direction. Izel made a decision, he would try inland first. He warily picked his way through the disorder around him. It was painstakingly slow. Each foothold had to be carefully placed to stop him from overbalancing, the task made more difficult by carrying Angelina. He set her down.

'How about a piggyback, sweetie?'

She nodded absently and climbed onto his offered back.

'I need you to hold tight. It's difficult for daddy to keep his balance and I don't want you to fall.'

He felt her arms tighten round his neck and her heels squeeze into his ribs.

He stumbled several times as haphazard items gave way under foot. He winced as he used his injured arm to steady them. Neighbours had emerged and were calling out names of their loved ones, hoping they'd have found refuge from the wind, rain and sea.

Izel clambered over cupboard drawers and toys, tree stumps and clothing, drink crates, bicycle wheels, tables, chairs, television sets and corrugated iron as he headed towards the main road. Lifeless limbs protruded from the wreckage and he hoped they didn't belong to members of his family. He shook his head. How long would it take to recover all these bodies and bury them? He climbed over slumped electricity poles, cables snaked lifeless across the ground.

After half an hour he had only advanced a couple of hundred metres. The dark typhoon clouds had been blown on to other parts of the country. A fierce sun accompanied by energy-sapping humidity replaced them. Izel's tee-shirt dripped with sweat from the heat and he was panting from the exertion. He stopped in the shade of a concrete wall which had endured the morning's tragedy and sank to his haunches. He set Angelina down and sat in front of her. He opened another can of Coke to share.

Izel glanced around, nothing looked familiar. He couldn't believe the destruction surrounding them. The sheer horror of their circumstances was incomprehensible and he shivered despite the heat. His mind felt numb, as he re-shouldered the backpack and Angelina climbed on his back, unsure of his next move. All around them other searchers had the same expression of incredulity as they scrambled over the rubbish on their own private missions.

Looking down, concentrating on making his way through safely, Izel didn't hear his name being called at first. When he looked up he saw Adelaida standing and waving from the balcony of a two-storey house, the one owned by the soft drink distributor. What was his name? Reymond? No that wasn't it, he was sure it began with an R, Ramon, yes, Ramon.

Further back from the sea, it had withstood the beating better than their home. The windows were all smashed and debris had gouged out chunks of concrete from the walls, but it was still standing and his wife had made it. A surge of relief flooded through him.

'Look, Angelina, it's mummy,' he pointed to the balcony and his daughter's eyes followed. She was still in severe shock and only managed a hoarse 'mummy'. He carefully negotiated the last twenty metres to the house. The front door was slightly ajar, held in place by a mound of furniture washed against it during the storm. He could hear scraping from inside as people tried to clear space for them to enter. After a couple of minutes they succeeded, welcoming Izel inside. They led him to the steps, where a lone teddy bear perched, sodden. He gingerly stepped over it and went upstairs. Adelaida waited for them at the top and grabbed for her daughter. She clutched her tightly to her chest and stroked her hair. She turned to Izel, tears streaming down her face.

'Ellijah, Lika Faye?' The question hung heavily between them.

He shook his head and looked down. How could he tell his wife he hadn't been able to protect them and keep them safe, that they had been ripped from his grasp and washed away?

Adelaida dropped to her knees, grabbing Angelina even tighter. Wretched sobs escaped from her throat.

'Mummy, mummy, you're hurting me,' Angelina croaked.

Izel knelt beside them and gently eased Adelaida's grasp. He put his arms protectively around his little family.

Rogelio emerged from the small crowd surrounding them and put his hand on his son's shoulder.

'Dad, you're here too! And mum?'

'You're hurt son,' Rogelio nodded at the wound on Izel's left arm and bruised temple. 'Let's see if we can get that bandaged. I've been helping with the injured over there, let's take a look.' Izel stood and followed his father in a daze.

He gasped as he saw his mother looking so frail and fragile, her face ashen. Above a rough bandage she had a tourniquet on her left arm. He looked at his father, his eyebrows raised.

'It was a piece of corrugated iron,' he explained. 'We've managed to stop the bleeding, but she needs to see a doctor. The cut is very deep and in these conditions...' he trailed off and Izel nodded his understanding.

'How did you get here, dad?' Izel asked as his father took care of his injuries.

'That second wave smashed the window in our room and we were dragged through it with the water. Your mother was terrified. It was difficult to see anything. A piece of sheet metal came out of nowhere, I didn't have a chance to get her out of the way and it sliced into her arm,' he stopped and took a deep breath as he remembered her screams. 'I tried to get us up onto the roof of the house behind ours, then the third wave caught us. I don't know how we managed to stay together. We were swept along with it and ended up here,' he motioned at the house. 'The water was up to the balcony and they were reaching out to us and pulled us in. It was a miracle, Izel.'

He finished bandaging his son and stepped back. 'What happened to Ellijah and Lika Faye?' he asked quietly.

Izel shook his head. 'I don't know, dad. I had them all in my arms, I got hit on the head. It happened so fast. The water snatched them from me. I couldn't save them.' He broke off as a sob escaped from his chest.

'They could still be alive, son. We should be out there looking for them.'

Izel nodded. Maybe his father was right. He truly wanted to believe they could find his children safe and sound. On the other hand, he had already seen many who had lost their lives. What were the chances his children could have survived?

'Come on, son. We can't afford to delay.'

As they made their way across the room to re-join Adelaida and Angelina, Izel nodded at a couple of the other refugees who he recognised.

The two men explained their plans to a silent Adelaida. She nodded as she gently rocked her surviving child. They left her and started down the stairs with dread in their hearts. Standing outside they looked around at the devastation.

'We can cover more ground if we split up, dad. Although it's hard to know where to begin. I keep hoping Ellijah will be standing in front of me, his thumb in his mouth, holding Lika Faye's hand,' Izel swallowed hard.

Rogelio nodded, a frown creasing his forehead as he looked at his son.

Izel's chin dropped to his chest. Looking down he could see an adult's arm protruding from the debris. Nothing in his life had prepared him for this. Surely this person couldn't have survived; should he check? He couldn't absorb the enormity of the disaster Yolanda had brought. He didn't know how to react. He continued to stare at the arm. Finally he bent down. It was cold to the touch. There was nothing they could do here.

An elderly neighbour approached the men, asking if they had seen his wife. His face was streaked with blood and mud, his eyes pleaded at them to give him a positive answer.

'I'm so sorry, Federico, no we haven't. Have you seen Lika Faye or Ellijah,' he enquired of the desperate man.

'No, no I haven't…she was with me…but the water was too strong…I couldn't hold on to her…it dragged her away…why couldn't I have held on…she can't swim,' he managed between sobs. 'How will I find her in all this?' He waved a shaking arm at the rubble around them, before stumbling off calling her name.

Other neighbours appeared, asking if relatives had been seen and a small group formed. No one was sure of how to deal with the situation before them

'Perhaps we can all help each other if we know who we're looking for?' suggested Rogelio. 'If we form small groups with the names of who we're searching for we could cover more ground.'

They all nodded in agreement and called to others around them to join together and form search parties. Izel caught sight of another of his neighbours, Sheila Mae. They had been at school together. He realised her son was one of those he had recognised in Ramon's house. The boy had some cuts and bruises, but he was alive.

'Jericho is alive, Sheila Mae,' he shouted to her. 'I saw him not ten minutes ago in Ramon's house, you know, the soft drinks man?' He pointed to the house.

She put her hands together. 'Oh thank you. Sweet Jesus, thank you for saving my boy,' and made her way as fast as she could across the detritus to find her child.

The knowledge that one survivor had been found, lifted their spirits slightly. Maybe they'd also be fortunate enough to find the missing members of their family. They split into six groups, three or four in each and exchanged the names of the loved ones they were hoping to find. Rogelio and Izel were joined by a Sheenly, a mother looking for her teenage son and a young man, Ben, who had been separated from his younger brother. They trudged slowly inland in the direction of the main road.

The small search party spent three hours slowly trawling through the debris. Their minds became numb as the number of bodies they discovered grew. Some Izel identified as friends and neighbours, a lump coming to his throat. Others were unrecognisable due to the extent of their injuries. The children were the worst. He felt his heart pounding heavily every time they turned over another small corpse. He was filled with a sense of sorrow, feeling powerless against the circumstances they were facing. How will they ever recover from such disaster, he asked himself over and over again.

The small bodies had been battered, bruised and ripped apart by the wreckage which had been whipped up by Yolanda's fury. It was a harrowing morning. The scorching sun and draining humidity took its toll on the living and the dead. With no way of burying them or giving them any real dignity, they covered up the corpses as best they could with anything they could find, clothing, sheets or plastic bags.

The task of searching was mentally draining, the humidity exhausted them physically. Izel called time for a break.

'I think we could all do with a few moments rest. I've got some crackers and drinks, let's sit over there in the shade.'

'But we have to find them,' Ben was close to tears. 'I don't want to think of my little brother out here all alone. I want to know what's happened to him, even if it's the worst.' The young man had worked hard all morning, desperate in his mission.

'Son, it's like trying to find a needle in a haystack,' Rogelio moved to him and gently placed a hand on his shoulder. 'We can only do our best, but we all need a short break to gather our strength. We won't be any good to them if we can't function properly. Come on, let's sit.'

He steered Ben towards a shady spot. The four sat in silence as they chewed on the meagre provisions and gulped warm Coke.

'We need to find water and more food,' said Izel. 'I need to take some back for my family.'

The others nodded their agreement and looked to him for direction.

'We can start by checking these empty houses to see if anything was left behind, or we can try further up by the main road where there are more shops?' He looked around at the mud and tear streaked faces. Exhausted and emotional, they waited for guidance.

'Okay, let's start here and see what we can find,' he said.

They searched through the buildings, collecting packs of noodles, dry biscuits and cans of soft drink. Wiping off sand and mud which caked the packaging, they stuffed them into Izel's backpack until it bulged. They found other bags and filled them. Fresh water wasn't so easy to find. They decided to continue their search to the main road and see if they would have more luck there.

'I'm not sure how much more of this I can take,' said Sheenly. The weariness was etched on her face, her eyes dull and full of sadness. 'What if I never find Jerome?' She started to cry quietly as she mentioned her son's name.

They all felt the weight of the daunting task in front of them. They were all thinking the same. What if they couldn't find their missing family members? A nearby scream disturbed their thoughts. The little group exchanged glances and continued on their quest.

They reached the Pan-Philippine Highway. Not much of a highway at the moment, thought Izel. No cars would be able to get through here, although the buildings weren't as badly damaged. The Metrobank opposite him appeared relatively unscathed with only the sign hanging off. Larger numbers of people were searching along the road and some were already helping themselves from some of the stores, emerging with food and water. Izel couldn't tell if windows had been smashed by the storm or from desperation. He climbed over a pile of rubble outside a shop and in through the window. Perished goods were strewn across the floor, of no use to the hungry and thirsty. Everything edible had already gone.

Reappearing outside he shook his head at his fellow searchers. 'There's nothing left worth taking…' He trailed off and turned to look down the street as shouting broke out.

A band of people were wrestling with the metal shutters of a bottled water supplier company.

'It won't give.'

'Can someone find a piece of wood we can use?'

'This bit is loose, someone help me.'

They stumbled over rubbish to join the noisy and growing throng, frantic to ensure they wouldn't miss a chance of getting some water for themselves. By the time they got there four or five individuals were smashing at the shutter with wood they had been handed. They were trying to get some leverage under the buckling sheet of metal, urged on by the desperate crowd.

'C'mon, you can do it.'

'We need that water.'

'It's nearly there.'

'That corner's giving way.'

Finally the shutter crumpled under the hail of blows. The metal screeched as the men pulled it free, exposing about fifty nineteen-litre water bottles. The crowd yelled and surged forward. They pushed inwards and like locusts stripped the storage unit bare in seconds. Izel and Rogelio elbowed their way through the jeering mob and managed to grab a bottle each. They had to fight to keep their grip as frantic hands clawed at them. A skirmish broke out in the street as two men fought over a bottle.

'That's mine.'

'I got it first, get off, it's my bottle.'

Izel's group hurried away and started the journey back to Ramon's house. As they were about to leave the highway Izel saw another of his neighbours scouring the debris. Her clothes were ripped and blood was seeping from a nasty gash on her thigh.

'Maria?' he called out to her.

She turned and studied him for a moment, screwing up her eyes.

'Izel? Izel is that you? I'm looking for Felipe. The waters took him, have you seen him?' Her voice trembled.

'I'm so sorry, Maria, we haven't come across him. I'm looking for Lika Faye and Ellijah, they got taken too. I don't suppose…'

'Yes, yes, I saw her, I'm sure it was her.'

Rogelio moved closer. He dropped his bottle to his feet as he followed the conversation.

'When, where?' Izel's heart raced. He lowered his bottle from his shoulder, his attention fixated on the woman in front of him. 'Where did you see her Maria, was she…' he swallowed hard. 'Was she…alive?'

'Yes, she was standing over there.' She pointed beyond the bank.

He squared up to the woman and gripped her shoulders.

'Are you sure? It was definitely her?'

Startled by his touch, Maria hesitated, then stuttered, 'I…I…I think it was her. She was talking to a woman.'

His arms dropped to his sides. His little girl was alive. He looked at his father, relief flooding his face. He turned back to Maria.

'Where did she go? Who was the woman? Was Lika Faye injured?'

The confusion crossed Maria's face as the questions rained down on her

'I…I think it was her, I wasn't so close and I lost my glasses, but it looked like her.' She bit at her lower lip. 'I thought it was her.'

Izel grabbed her again and started shaking her.

'Think, Maria, think. Where did she go?'

Izel watched the colour drain from Maria's face and she cried out.

'Let her go, son,' his father's voice demanded. 'You're frightening her. Come on now, we've all been through a traumatic time, stop scaring the poor woman.'

He pulled Izel back from Maria and spoke softly to the quaking woman.

'Are you alright, Maria?' He patted her arm. 'He didn't mean you any harm.'

She nodded and took a deep breath.

'I'm sorry, Rogelio, I can't be sure. I thought it was her, but…I only saw her for a couple of seconds, when I looked again she was gone.'

'It's okay, thank you anyway. I hope you find Felipe, he's a good man.' He closed his eyes and looked down as he walked away.

'It could have been her, dad.'

'Maybe, but maybe not. Don't get your hopes up too much, Izel. I want to find her as much as you. We can only hope it was her and she's safe. She's a bright girl, if it was her, she'll get the woman to take her to the convent.'

The men shouldered the water bottles and with Ben and Sheenly in tow, carefully picked their way back to Ramon's house. They collected empty containers from the waste around them as they walked.

It was now mid-afternoon. In the heat and humidity, flies filled the air. They were already finding laying places in the pale grey cadavers. Izel tried not to think of his son amongst them. In his mind Lika Faye was very much alive. Since they had met Maria, he had become certain she had survived, no matter what anyone said.

When they arrived back to the house, fifteen of the others they had split from earlier were sat in the shade, discussing their successes and failures. Some had found relatives injured but alive and were chatting, exchanging survival stories. In sharp contrast, a couple sobbed and rocked back and forth beside two small bundles. The group fell silent and gazed up as the four of them approached.

Izel surveyed the scene. His eyes rested momentarily on the covered bodies before turning to the grieving pair: 'I'm so sorry for your loss.' His mind filled with thoughts that it could so easily be him in the same situation.

'We found some water,' he said quietly and lowered his bottle to the ground. The group got to their feet and gathered round. Izel tore at the plastic guard at the neck, ripped it off and carefully started to fill the empty containers Sheenly and Ben had found. As they handed them out, Rogelio carried on into the house with his bottle.

Sheenly handed some water to the unmoving mourners, while the rest of the group exchanged their findings. None of the survivors they had encountered had answered to any of the names provided by Izel, Ben or Sheenly. As they discussed their next course of action, Izel followed his father into the house to tell Adelaida about their day. She was sitting next to Lorna, holding a cup to her pale lips. The older woman sat impassive and unresponsive. Rogelio was speaking softly to her, encouraging her to drink.

Izel smiled at Angelina and picked her up. The little girl was quiet, but not as withdrawn as when he'd left. She managed a thin smile back, twisting some strands of her hair round her small fingers and he clutched her tightly to him.

'Has dad told you?' he asked Adelaida. 'Maria thinks she saw Lika Faye.'

Adelaida snapped her head round to her father-in-law, Rogelio shook his head.

'My dear, Maria only thinks she saw her. She had lost her glasses in the typhoon, she couldn't be sure.'

'It was her, I can feel it in my bones,' said Izel.

Adelaida ignored him. 'And Ellijah, no news? Nothing?' her jaw slack, her lips trembling.

'I'm sorry,' Izel hung his head. 'It's chaos out there. We saw many bodies, but not our boy.'

Rogelio took the cup of water from Adelaida as tears ran silently down her face. She folded her hands in her lap, stared at the floor and started to pray quietly.

Izel watched his wife and was once again overwhelmed with guilt. If only he had been able to hold onto his children, they would be here with them now. How could he have let them go? His heart ached.

'Are you hungry?' He remembered the backpack full of biscuits and noodles and handed out salty crackers.

Handing Angelina back to his wife, Izel went in search of the house owner, Ramon. He found him downstairs staring at the turmoil in his living room. Furniture was upturned and waterlogged, kitchen utensils strewn around the floor. Piles of sodden clothes, cushions and children's toys filled one corner.

Izel stood beside him.

'Thank you for rescuing my parents and wife,' he put out his hand and Ramon shook it.

'It was a nightmare, so many people, we couldn't reach some of them. I pray to God for them,' he said, a solemn look on his face. 'I don't know where to begin,' he waved his hand at the chaos in front of them.

'I brought back some food and water. Are we able to heat water to cook noodles? Most people won't have eaten today. There must be twenty of us left upstairs. We can share it.'

They located the gas burner, a gas bottle and some pots and took them upstairs. Izel emptied out his backpack while others hunted downstairs to retrieve surviving plates, cutlery and tinned goods. Adelaida and a couple of the other women grateful for the distraction, set to work making food for everyone before darkness fell. They used as little of their prized water supply as possible to boil the noodles and opened cans of sardines to share between the sixteen adults and five children. They ate in silence, relishing each morsel of their meagre dinner, each deep in thought about the day's events.

By half past five the sun had set and they organised the sleeping arrangements in the gloom. Exhaustion soon overcame some of Yolanda's survivors. Yet for others, despite fatigue, sleep would not rescue them from the terrors of the day. Izel's eyes remained open, his thoughts wandering to the whereabouts of his daughter. He was haunted by her face as she had been snatched from him. Had it only been that morning? It seemed a lifetime ago. Where was she? Who was the woman she had been seen talking to? There was no doubt now in his mind she was alive and he wasn't going to stop until he found her. He blinked back tears as he recalled the sight of her being dragged away from him by the rising water. 'Don't worry, my angel, daddy will keep searching until he finds you,' he mouthed the words silently. He did not feel the same certainty about Ellijah and sadness filled his heart as he mourned his young son.

***

At sunrise the next morning Izel and Rogelio reviewed their options.

'We can't stay here. There's no food left and the water won't last long,' said Rogelio.

'I think we should get to the convent in Tanauan, that was the evacuation centre. It's where Lika Faye will go,' said Izel. Then seeing his father's face, rushed on: 'And we might get food and water there, of course.'

'I'm hoping there might be someone who can look at your mother. She's in a lot of pain and I think her wound might be infected, it's not looking good, Izel.'

Izel had heard his mother moaning through the night. His father looked exhausted, he was right. They needed to get medical help as soon as possible.

A heated argument outside disturbed their discussion. They rushed to the glassless window to see two young men shouting at Ramon. The storage cage for his soft drinks was locked. The contents had been awash in the storm surge water and many of the plastic bottles had split, but other crates still contained Coke, Sprite and Royal-Tru. The desperate men were trying to get Ramon to unlock the padlock. He was trying to explain the key had been lost in the typhoon, but they clearly didn't believe him. The shouting became more aggressive and knives were being waved in Ramon's face. His wife hovered nervously behind him, pleading with the young men not to hurt her husband.

Feeling a sense of duty towards the family who had saved his parents and wife, and given them all shelter, Izel raced downstairs to try to help the situation. He approached the men carefully.

'There's no need for anyone to get hurt here. We are all in the same situation. Put the knives down, guys, we can sort something out.'

Izel looked into their faces, their eyes were wild, their clothes in tatters. They were only teenagers and clearly brothers. They brandished the kitchen knives with a courage they clearly didn't feel.

'You're hungry and thirsty. We have water, why don't you have a drink and we'll see if we can find a way to open the gate.' Izel looked at Ramon who nodded his agreement. 'There's been enough death and injury, we need to work together, help each other. What are your names?'

The smaller of the two boys sunk to the ground and started sobbing.

'We've lost everything,' the older boy said. 'Our parents are dead, we've had nothing to eat or drink since the typhoon came, I'm sorry.' He hung his head in shame. 'We saw all the bottles, we were desperate.' He dropped his knife, his face a mask of despair.

They ushered the boys, Martee and Patrick, inside and offered them some of their dwindling water supply.

Ramon pulled Izel to one side. 'There will be others. We need to find a way of opening it so people can help themselves. I don't want to go through that again.'

'Do you have any tools anywhere in the house?'

Ramon thought for a moment. He started wrenching open kitchen cupboards trying to find something they could use to prise the gate open. Izel looked around the living space, his gaze was drawn to something metal half buried under some wet clothes. He pulled it free and held a crowbar up to Ramon.

'What about this, any good?'

They returned to the storage cage and levered off the chain. They picked up a couple of crates each to take into the house and left it open for survivors to help themselves.

It took three hours for the Sombilon family to cover the seven kilometres to the evacuation centre. They carefully picked their way through the chaos in stifling humidity. Lorna needed assistance and constant encouragement to put one foot in front of the other. They rationed the water they had taken from the house. The warm, sticky soft drinks didn't quench their thirst, but it was still liquid and they had left with a backpack full of bottles. People crowded the streets looking for family members, food and water. Looting had left most shops with smashed windows and ripped shutters where frantic groups had turned to desperate measures.

It was eleven o'clock when they reached the convent to find it brimming with people. The adjacent church had opened its doors to give more shelter to the homeless. A priest welcomed them in and pointed them to an empty pew at the front.

'You're welcome to stay here as long as you need,' he said. 'But we have no food or water. There's no news of when relief might arrive, I'm sorry to say. Some of the survivors here have small radios and we've been listening to the news. The reception is quite poor, but we've heard the airport was severely damaged and they can't land in Tacloban.' He shook his head as he delivered this information and wandered off to speak to more new arrivals.

The little group shuffled to the designated pew and sat heavily. They reviewed the sorry throng around them. Voices echoed around the building and up into the high roof, which even God hadn't been able to protect from the wrath of Yolanda. Izel could see patches of blue sky where corrugated sheets had been wrenched away. The church reeked of sweat and fear. It had been thirty hours since Yolanda had ripped into Tacloban. Every one of its population had been affected in some way. The people occupying the evacuation centres had lost more than most. They were equipped only with the clothes on their backs and a few items they had snatched from their homes as they made their escape. Izel shook his head and sighed, it was no good brooding. He needed to find food and water to keep his family alive.

A group of men were talking in hushed voices at the back of the church. Izel recognised one of them.

'What news, Joshua? Are your family okay?' he asked.

'Hi, Izel, yes we all managed to get out in time. The house is gone though. We were just discussing the rice warehouse on Real Street?'

'The one near the public market?'

Joshua nodded. 'We're going to see if we can get in and bring some rice back. Do you want to come?'

Izel agreed without hesitation. He told his father the plan and rejected his offer to join them.

'You stay and take care of mum. See if there is anyone who can look at her arm. There's enough of us going already.' He pointed to the group of six men waiting for him at the church doors.

'Take care, son. We saw looting yesterday, people will be even more desperate today.' Rogelio patted Izel's shoulder and watched him leave.

The seven men set off in the direction of the public market. After a day and a half in the sun and humidity, the dead had started the process of putrefaction. Swollen with gases, the rotting produced foul-smelling vapours which now pervaded the air. Izel pulled his tee-shirt up over his mouth and nose, trying not to retch. Everyone on the street had something covering their face, trying not to breath in the repulsive odour.

It was obvious as they got close to Real Street they weren't the only ones with the idea of storming the rice warehouse. Men stumbling to carry the heavy fifty kilogram bags of rice passed them on the road. When they reached the gates, they found them already smashed open and the buildings being ransacked. Successful individuals had to fight their way out as others poured into the courtyard. Seawater-soaked bags on the lower level of the buildings had been forsaken for the drier ones higher up. In time even they would be greedily salvaged as hunger gripped the more desperate, but for now there were still unspoiled bags on offer for Izel and his band of foragers.

'C'mon, we need to get up to the dry bags up there,' said Joshua. 'Hurry before they all go.'

The men scrambled up to the next level. Hitching a bag each on their backs, they forced their way back through the incoming throng of yelling men. Grunting from the effort of carrying such a heavy load, desperation and adrenaline gave them the strength necessary to get free of the warehouse gates.

'We're never going to be able to carry these all the way back to the church, Joshua,' said Izel panting as he set down his sack.

'Yeah. Erm, okay, you guys stay here,' Joshua pointed to the other five men. 'Come with me, Izel, there must be something around we can use to transport them on.'

Both men stripped off their shirts and tied them round the bottom half of their faces to give them two hands to work through the debris. After half an hour of searching Joshua called to Izel: 'I think I've found just the thing, come and help me dig it out.'

It was a half-buried pedicab. The front wheel was buckled but if they could wrestle it free, they might be able to use the three-wheeled bike taxi to get the rice home. It took them fifteen minutes to pull it out and stand it up. The framework was badly twisted, however it was better than trying to carry the heavy sacks. Pushing it back to the other men proved a challenge as the damaged front wheel worked in opposition to the rest of the vehicle. It would be a slow process, but worth it.

With the bags loaded into the passenger seat, the men took it in turns to push and re-direct the pedicab. They cleared the path where it wasn't wide enough to get through. After a lot of grunting, cursing and sweat, they arrived back at the church mid-afternoon. A scene of frenzied activity ensued as the idea of food spurred the church occupants into action. Glad of a distraction, people rushed about finding dry wood, burnable items and containers to boil the rice in or use as plates. The sticky rice was carefully rationed out. The remaining water kept, cooled and fed to the babies.

A little before sunset, Ben, one of Izel's search party from the day before, came looking for him.

'Izel, we think we may have found Ellijah,' he said.

CHAPTER FIVE

Helen stared unseeing at her computer screen. Her head throbbed and her mouth was dry. She knew she was drinking too much. The wine helped her forget her pain. It helped her fall into a comatose sleep, rather than toss and turn all night, with thoughts of Charlie running through her head.

She was finding it difficult to concentrate on her client contracts. Her attention span was only about five minutes. Coffee didn't help. Her heart was racing and her brain buzzing from caffeine overload.

'Oh no, not that song again,' she moaned and prodded angrily at the radio off switch. Too late. The tears were already streaming down her face as soon as Katy Perry's Roar had started to play. Every time she heard it, memories of the day Charlie died came flooding back. In all truth, it wasn't the only song which had this effect, although it was probably the worst. The first song she'd heard on that fateful day.

Once David and his family had returned to their life in America, the cloak of depression had slowly wrapped itself tighter around Helen. It dragged her into a dark abyss. She couldn't sleep, then she couldn't wake up and when she did her brain was foggy and numb. Wine became her friend. On more than one occasion she had managed to smoke a whole packet of cigarettes – not having touched them for sixteen years – in one evening. Then she felt guilty and disgusted with herself the next day, only to repeat the pattern several days later. Her friends took it in turns to call and invite themselves round to see her, when she refused to go to them. They sat patiently listening to her repeated tales of Charlie and her increasingly drunken ramblings of how she had nothing left to live for.

There was no doubt they were worried about her. They subtly tried to get her to see her doctor or a counsellor. Helen knew she was teetering on the edge between depression and survival. Somehow the dark clutches of misery had the greatest appeal. She felt safe there. It understood her. She could lose herself to the despair, it didn't judge her. It welcomed her. It pulled her closer in and down further and further. She was spiralling into the deep, black well of hopelessness and melancholy. She stayed up late into the early hours of the morning. She mindlessly watched anything on television until the alcohol blurred the screen. She'd often wake slumped on the sofa as day broke, drag herself upstairs and collapse into bed. She would wake in the afternoon, with only a couple of hours before it would be acceptable to start drinking again. A tiny thought would nag at her to break the cycle, but she shook it aside.

She started lying to her friends. She said she was going out when they suggested visiting, or she didn't answer their calls at all. Sarah turned up unannounced one afternoon, determined to check on her friend. Helen had managed to maintain a false cheeriness until her friend had to leave to pick up her children from school.

'You're looking so thin, Helen. Please look after yourself. I wish there was something I could do to help.'

Helen had nodded her head and wrapped her arms around herself. As she'd waved her friend off, red-eyed, heavy sobs racked her body.

Her mobile rang interrupting her thoughts. It was one of her clients. She sighed. She knew she hadn't been giving them the attention they expected from her. She was barely managing a couple of hours work a day. Several of her clients had started chasing her for deadlines.

'Hi Bill.' She tried to sound cheery. 'How are you?'

'Erm, yes, hi, Helen. Yeah fine, I erm, well, we were hoping you could come to the office for a meeting tomorrow?'

Helen's heart sank, she knew from the tone of Bill's voice it wouldn't be good news and part of her had been expecting something like this.

'Sure, Bill. When would you like me there?'

They agreed a time and Helen ended the call. She sat with her head in her hands. She had always been meticulous when it came to her work. She had prided herself on her attention to details and meeting deadlines. None of it seemed important any more. She felt as if she was wading through treacle. Tasks she hadn't given a second thought to before seemed impossible. There would be no point trying to defend herself, she had no argument left in her.

Helen took the train to London the next morning. Her head foggy from too much wine and not enough sleep. She sat through the meeting barely hearing the words from Bill's mouth. He said they were sorry for her loss and thought perhaps she should take some time off to grieve. However, they needed their marketing programme back on track. He apologised and gently told Helen they were replacing her. She nodded dully. She thanked him and agreed to send her replacement everything she had been working on.

On auto-pilot she took the tube to Paddington and the train back to Reading. At the station she went to hail a taxi, but changed her mind. She walked through the drizzle until she found a wine bar, one where she knew no one and could be anonymous. It was four in the afternoon. She ordered a bottle of Merlot, sat at the bar and played with the plate of peanuts the bartender had put in front of her. He opened the bottle and poured her a glass. She drank deeply of the ruby red liquid, feeling its warm glow as it entered her blood stream.

The bar started to fill as people finished work and joined their colleagues in a couple of glasses of wine before the commute home. Voices and laughter echoed round the trendy wine bar. The sole barman had morphed into four, shadows of black and white as they opened bottles, poured wine and laughed at their customer's jokes.

It was half way into her second bottle when her tears started silently dripping onto the bar. An embarrassed barman thrust some napkins at her.

'Ma'am, maybe you would be more comfortable at one of the tables?' he mumbled pointing to an empty one in a corner, worried that an emotional woman at the bar would dampen his customer's spirits and therefore their tips.

Helen shouldered her bag, clutched her glass and the bottle and stumbled to the corner, sitting heavily. She watched the suited and booted office workers around her laughing, talking and drinking. She felt so incredibly alone, disconnected from the happenings around her. She didn't belong here, but the lead in her heart weighed her down and she couldn't move.

'Hey there, are you okay?'

Helen looked up from the table at the barmaid standing beside her.

'My colleague over there is a little worried he'd been a bit unkind earlier.'

Helen followed where she was looking to see the barman who had asked her to move to the table. He nodded at her.

'I'm on my break now and he asked if I would come over and check on you. You know what men are like.' She smiled at Helen and sat opposite her. 'Is there anything I can do?'

'I'm fine,' mumbled Helen, wishing the woman would go away.

'I don't know what's wrong, and you don't have to tell me, but you look so sad. Would you like to talk about it? I'm not due back at work for half an hour.'

Helen looked at her glass of wine, twisting the stem between her finger and thumb.

'I've just had a bad day.'

'Sometimes it helps to offload, especially to a stranger.'

Helen looked at the girl. She wasn't much older than Charlie probably late teens or early twenties. Her face was full of concern.

'That's very kind of you, but I'm sure you have better things to do during your break,' she said.

'Not really,' she smiled. 'Most of them go round the back for a fag, but I don't smoke.'

Helen nodded and took a drink of wine. 'Do you work here full time?'

'No. I'm studying at Reading university. Business Studies.'

They chatted about the girl's course and where she was from until her break was over.

'I'm sorry, I have to get back to work now,' she said as she stood up from the table. 'It's been nice talking to you. I hope you feel better soon.'

Helen grabbed the girl's arm as she started to walk away.

'Thank you.'

'I didn't do anything.' She shook her head.

'You did more than you realise,' she smiled up at the girl. 'Good luck with your studies.'

For the first time in over a month, Helen felt a little of the gloom lifting. It was as if someone had opened a curtain a tiny crack and a ray of sunshine had shone in. A few moments of kindness from a complete stranger had ever so slightly loosened the stranglehold that depression had over her. She began to feel she might have a future.

Fuzzy-headed, the next morning she made a doctor's appointment. Due to a cancellation he was able to see her the following day. She spent the morning applying herself to her working life. She made some phone calls to her clients and prioritised her workload. It wasn't long before her mind wandered back to Charlie and the sickness in her stomach returned.

She made her way to the kitchen and put on the kettle to make tea. She switched on the small television set to distract her. Images of the destruction in the Philippines filled the screen. There was still no clear figure on the numbers of people dead or displaced. She hadn't paid much attention to the disaster which had happened on the other side of the world, she had been so wrapped up with her own grief. She listened properly to the news report for the first time.

'I had no idea,' she said out loud and thought of Charlie's Just-Giving page. 'Maybe there are some things of Charlie's I can send out there.'

She had been reluctant to touch anything in Charlie's room since his death. She felt if she disturbed it, she would lose part of him. But these people had suffered so much, perhaps some of his clothes would be okay. She would have a look tomorrow. It seemed too overwhelming to try now.

CHAPTER SIX

Lika Faye woke up. Her head felt heavy and as if it was stuffed with cotton wool. She screwed up her eyes and shook her head, trying to chase the drowsy feeling away. She was lying on a bare mattress in a small room. This wasn't her room. Nothing looked familiar. Where were Angelina and Ellijah? There were no windows. Sunlight seeped under a door providing enough light to make out a bucket in the corner and a bottle of water on the floor beside her.

She sat up, grabbed the water bottle, unscrewed the lid and took a long drink. Where was she? She needed to get out of here. Her head throbbed and protested even more as she tried to stand. She swayed as she got to her feet, but after a few moments the dizziness passed. She stumbled towards the door and tried the handle. It wouldn't open. The effort was too much and she slid down to the floor. Fragments of memory swam around in her mind. She looked down at her feet. She had lost her new pink shoes. She had woken up in the street. Kristina's house had gone and then she had met a woman. What had she said her name was? Lika Faye closed her eyes in concentration. She'd given her a bottle of Coke. They'd walked back to the woman's house. She'd cooked some rice and they had eaten it with sardines. It was the last thing she remembered. Rosela, that was it. Rosela had promised they would look for her parents.

Tears started to trickle down Lika Faye's cheeks. Where were mum and dad? She had tried to look for her house, but it had been too difficult. Why hadn't they come to look for her? But they wouldn't know to look in this room for her. She had to get out. She turned her attention back to the door, pulled herself up with the handle and started hammering frantically on it. She started to feel very scared, what if she was trapped. What if she couldn't get out? She pulled on the handle. The door wouldn't move.

'Is anyone there? Help me! Help me! I can't get out.' Her voice rose hysterically. She wrenched the handle up and down as her yells turned to screams.

She was so distraught she didn't hear the key scrape in the lock. She was knocked backwards on to the ground as the door swung violently open.

The room flooded with light, blinding her.

'Hey, hey. It's okay, calm down,' a voice said.

Lika Faye blinked as her eyes adjusted to the light. It was the woman, Rosela. Lika Faye stared up at the thin women in front of her. Her hair was dragged fiercely back into a ponytail, emphasising her sharp pointed nose and she could see a vein pulsated in her neck as the woman bent down towards her.

'What's all the screaming about? You're safe here.'

'I woke up and I couldn't remember where I was and the door was locked,' she cried.

Rosela helped her to her feet.

'Ssshhh, it's okay. I'm here now. I'm sorry I had to lock the door. You've not been well. You were delirious. I don't suppose you remember.'

'No,' Lika Faye sniffed.

'It was for your own safety. If you'd have got out in your state, who knows where you'd have ended up? It's so dangerous out there. Don't worry, I'm here now,' she smiled.

Lika Faye felt hands guide her back to the mattress.

'Sorry the conditions aren't better. It's the only space in the house available. You know after the typhoon and everything. Now sit here. I expect your head is hurting.'

Lika Faye nodded.

'I'll bring you some rice and some medicine. It'll help you sleep. You need all your strength for when we look for your mum and dad.'

'When can we look? I want my mum.' Lika Faye could feel tears welling up. She didn't want to cry in front of the woman but she missed her mum and dad. She wanted to hear their voices. She wanted to hug her dad and feel the hairs on his chin tickle her cheek.

'Well, while you've been ill, I've been making enquiries. So far I haven't been able to find any news. Now, will you sit here quietly for me? I'll be back in a minute.'

Lika Faye's stomach growled. She was so hungry. She nodded. She would feel better after some rice. Perhaps they could go and look once she'd eaten.

Rosela returned with a bowl of rice and a spoon. She stood over Lika Faye as she scooped the cold, sticky rice into her mouth.

'Someone's hungry. Sorry there's nothing more. Since the typhoon, no food has been coming in, so we're having to ration. Do you know what that is?'

Lika Faye nodded and handed back the bowl. 'Thank you. Can we go and look for my mum and dad now?'

'No, dear. Not now.'

Lika Faye felt disappointed. The woman seemed nice enough, but there was no time to lose. They should go and look.

'Why not?'

'I told you already, it's very dangerous out there at the moment.'

'Why?'

'People are fighting for food. Your mum and dad wouldn't want you to get hurt now, would they?' Rosela said.

Lika Faye pouted. She supposed the woman was right. 'When then? When can we go and find them?'

Rosela smiled at her and pulled a bottle out of her pocket. 'Take your medicine, like a good girl and we will start looking as soon as it's safe. Okay?'

The brown liquid tasted horrible and she nearly gagged. Rosela handed her the bottle of water.

'I need the toilet.'

'You'll have to use the bucket. The typhoon destroyed the bathroom.' Rosela pointed to the corner. 'Try and get some sleep. I'll check on you later.'

The room was plunged into darkness. Lika Faye groped her way to the bucket. By the time she'd finished, her head had started to feel heavy and she could barely keep her eyes open. She crawled back to the mattress and collapsed into a deep sleep. The next few of days passed in a blur. Lika Faye spent most of the time sleeping or so drowsy she couldn't get off the mattress apart from to use the bucket, take a mouthful of water or some rice when Rosela brought some for her. Her limbs felt heavy and her head was so fuzzy she couldn't think straight.

Lika Faye could feel hands shaking her. She tried to shrug them off, the drowsiness pulling her back under. The shaking increased and she could hear her voice being called from far away.

'Mummy?' she croaked. Her eyelids felt heavy as she tried to open her eyes. Finally she clawed her way up into wakefulness. It was dark. Rosela's hands were on her shoulders urging her to get up. She was pulled to a sitting position. She was too sleepy to protest as the pink, stained vest she'd been wearing when the typhoon came was hauled over her head and replaced with a pale blue tee-shirt. She was yanked to her feet and her shorts changed, the new ones tightened with a belt to stop them from falling down. Rosela thrust a pair of scruffy trainers at her. She sat back on the mattress and slowly put them on, trying to remember how to tie laces through her sleepiness.

'Come on, Lika Faye, that's it now.' Rosela pulled her to her feet. Lika Faye shuffled out of the room in a stupor. She followed the woman downstairs and into a kitchen where she watched as her old clothes were thrust into a plastic bag. The woman took the handle of a wheeled suitcase and bumped it down three steps onto the road outside into the grey light of early dawn.

'Where are we going?' she mumbled

'To the airport, planes are arriving. We need to get out of here.'

Lika Faye screwed up her eyes as she tried to make sense of what she was being told. They were leaving? Going to the airport.

'But what about my mum and dad?'

Lika Faye retched as the stench of rotting cadavers hit her nose. Rosela pulled a cloth from a pocket in her case and held it out to her.

'Here, cover your face with this and breathe through your mouth. Come on now. We have no time to lose.'

She clasped another cloth to her own face and prodded Lika Faye in the shoulders to urge her on ahead while bouncing her case behind her.

Her thoughts temporarily halted by the smells and sights around her, Lika Faye did as she was told. To their right, the wispy clouds on the horizon turned orange and bright rays stretched up into the sky. She watched the brilliant sun chase away the last of the night.

She stopped suddenly and turned causing Rosela to bump into her.

'What about my mum and dad,' she repeated, mumbling through the cloth over her mouth.

Rosela sighed. 'You've been unwell all this time. They're already making their way to Cebu, we're meeting them there.'

'You spoke to them?' Lika Faye's eyes were wide.

'Well, not exactly, but that's what they told me at the convent. Now let's get moving or we'll miss the plane.'

A new sound made Lika Faye look skyward. She shaded her eyes with her free hand and saw the underbelly of a huge aircraft as it made its approach into the airport at San Jose. As they walked the fog started to clear from Lika Faye's brain and she bombarded Rosela with questions.

'Why are they going to Cebu? Did they say all my family are going? Ellijah and Angelina are okay? And my grandparents are they were going too? Why would they go without me?'

'Lika Faye,' Rosela said irritably. 'I have told you what I know. Your family are going to Cebu. We will find them there. Now hush child, save your energy for the walk.'

Lika Faye narrowed her eyes and stared at Rosela. 'How do you know it was my family, you don't know their name.'

'I told you, you were ill most of the time, you won't remember you told me.'

'So what are their names?'

'That's enough Lika Faye, we don't have time for this. Walk, now!' Rosela refused to answer any more questions.

As they turned into another street, Lika Faye watched as Rosela thrust the plastic bag with her old clothes in it at a woman and her daughter.

'Here,' she mumbled. 'These should fit your girl. My daughter has no use for them anymore.'

'But I'm not your…'

'Come on, Lika Faye,' said Rosela as she took the girl's hand. 'We need to get a move on.'

Lika Faye turned to say something to the woman and child, but they had already moved away.

CHAPTER SEVEN

The news wasn't good. Ben and several of Izel's neighbours had resumed their search further along the Pan-Philippine Highway towards Tacloban.

'I'm so sorry, Izel,' said Ben looking at the ground and shuffling his feet. 'One of your neighbours thinks one of the bodies we saw was your Ellijah.' He looked up into Izel's face; anguish twisted his features. Ben rushed on. 'It may not be him. He said he wasn't one hundred percent sure. He sent me to come and find you. I went to the soft drinks man's house…'

'Ramon,' Izel interrupted.

'Yes, yes, Ramon's house. He said you had gone to the convent, but no one there knew you. It's taken me ages to find you.' The young man fell silent.

After several moments Izel found his voice. 'Thank you, Ben. Where…erm….where is…' he cleared his throat. 'Where is the boy you found?'

'I can take you to him.' He pulled at Izel's arm, keen to get moving, the distress of delivering the news obviously weighing heavily on him.

'Okay, let me speak to my family first and we'll go.'

Rogelio was tending to Lorna, her condition had deteriorated. She was delirious and unable to keep liquid down. The skin around her injury had started to turn black. Izel approached his parents, he felt totally wretched. It was obvious his mother needed urgent medical treatment or she could soon become another Yolanda victim. They wouldn't be able to get her to a Tacloban hospital today. It would soon be dark and the roads would be treacherous without any light. There were rumours that the nearest hospital, Leyte Provincial in Palo had been badly damaged along with many of the other medical facilities. They would have to take the chance tomorrow and try to find somewhere she could be treated. He shook the thoughts from his head as he reached his father.

'Dad?'

Rogelio looked up, his eyes bloodshot, weariness lining his face. Izel beckoned to him, moving out of earshot of the others.

'Ben just turned up at the church, he…erm…he,' Izel's voice cracked.

'Ellijah?'

Izel nodded. 'They think it might be him. Ben has come to take me to the…to the body.'

Rogelio nodded solemnly. They both turned as Lorna started groaning. Adelaida sat rigid on the bench beside her mother-in-law, her hands pressed together in prayer. Angelina sat beside her mother, copying her actions. The sight of them brought tears to Izel's eyes, he brushed them roughly away.

'I better go, dad. Ben is waiting.'

'Okay, son. I'll pray it's not our Ellijah.' He walked back to Lorna.

Izel joined Ben at the door and the men hurried out of the church. They covered their mouths and noses with their shirts and headed towards the highway to the place Ben and the searchers had found the body. It took them half an hour to get there. The light would soon be gone, but Izel couldn't bear to leave it until the next day to know the truth. They arrived at the small bundle. It was partly covered by a muddy curtain, the legs hidden under corrugated iron. Izel's mouth went dry. His heart pounded as he moved closer. Silently he chanted 'Please Lord not Ellijah, please spare him.' He took a deep breath and gently lifted the material. The body was bloated and discoloured, but there was no doubt it was his son. He looked up to Ben and closing his eyes, nodded. He gently pulled the small frame free of the rubble and cradled the boy in his arms.

'I'm so sorry, Izel,' Ben said breaking the silence.

'What do I do with him now?' croaked Izel. 'I can't leave him here.'

'I...erm....I heard they are taking bodies to the Plaza in Tanauan,' Ben said. 'Would you like me to come with you?'

Izel shook his head. 'Thank you for finding him and bringing me. I know you have your own family to search for. I hope you find them safe.'

Ben nodded and watched as the distraught man headed back to Tanauan. Small limbs dangled from his arms. Tears streamed down Izel's cheeks and onto the small corpse. Bloodless gashes crisscrossed Ellijah's torso. His clothes had been ripped from him. Izel hoped the large injury to his head had rendered his son unconscious or had been fatal. He couldn't cope with thoughts of his child suffering. Guilt consumed him anew.

Ben had been right. Izel arrived at the Plaza, the stench of death increasing as he approached. Bodies covered the once green public area. With no electricity there was nowhere to keep the cadavers from decaying, although Izel doubted things would have been much improved with power. So many dead. There must be over two hundred here, he thought to himself. There was nothing more he could do for his son. He gently laid him next to the body of a young girl. He gazed down at the small battered body.

'I'm so sorry, Ellijah. Rest in peace, son, daddy loves you.' Through tears, he offered up a silent prayer, then walked slowly back to the church.

Despite two restless nights, he was still unable to sleep. He was lying on the floor in the church. Angelina was next to him, Adelaida on the pew above them. Izel couldn't tell if she had cried herself to sleep or if she had exhausted the tears and now lay quiet and still, thinking of her son. She had been inconsolable when he broke the news of Ellijah.

Rogelio was sitting next to a moaning Lorna, lovingly mopping her brow with his shirt. The rice sacks from the day before were empty. There had been enough for them all to have a few mouthfuls that evening, washed down with sickly warm Coke. Water was in even shorter supply than the rice. Tomorrow they would need to find medical help for his mother and supplies to keep them alive.

***

As soon as the sky showed the first grey signs of dawn, Izel went to find the priest. He thanked him for his kindness and explained his daughter was missing.

'She knows the convent was the evacuation centre, so if she turns up, can you ask her to wait here and I will come back for her.'

'Of course, Izel,' replied the priest. 'What's her name?'

'Lika Faye, Lika Faye Sombilon.'

The priest made a note in the book of names he was making of the living, the dead and the missing.

Izel and Rogelio went in search of a means to transport Lorna into Tacloban City. As they were returning with a door they could use as a stretcher, they heard excited voices.

'Army, army, the army are on the highway. They're clearing the roads.'

'Help is coming, thank the Lord.'

'Are they bringing food and water?'

People ran into the street, anxious for news of help. Izel had heard helicopters buzzing around in the skies yesterday but hadn't seen any land. The only news they had heard had been on the radio. On the trip to the rice storage depot, they had seen fights break out as people frantically tried to find water and scraps of food. The feeling of panic and desperation was everywhere. Izel hoped this was a sign help was finally on its way. He turned back to the task in hand and helped gently to lift his mother onto the door. Izel estimated under normal conditions it would take them about two hours to cover the distance from the church to Leyte Provincial Hospital. Today it would take them more than double that. He and Rogelio tied Lorna to the door with rope to stop her falling off in her delirious state and set off. Angelina and Adelaida, rags tied over their faces, walked silently beside her. Izel had wanted them to stay at the church, but his wife had insisted they weren't to be separated. She also wanted to see if they could find news of her family. They lived in the Anibong district, another coastal area, on the other side of the city.

Once at the highway, they saw signs the army were arriving. Progress was slow due to the amount of debris cluttering the roads. They learned from a scouting party that bulldozers were making their way up from the south, clearing a pathway for relief aid vehicles to get through. The army captain told Izel that Tacloban airport had been completely devastated. Army personnel had been dropped in by helicopter to help clear the runways to allow planes, ready and waiting in Cebu, to land with supplies.

They arrived at the hospital mid-morning. There were hordes of screaming children and traumatised people begging to be seen by the exhausted medical staff.

'We have a triage area over there,' an exhausted nurse tried to make herself heard over the din. Her uniform was streaked with blood, her face pale and drawn. She pointed to an area at the entrance of the hospital. 'Most of our medical supplies have now run out and all our beds are full. Unless your injuries are minor, you will need to make your way to the City Hospital in Barangay eighty, or try one of the other hospitals.'

The disappointed crowd barraged her with questions and beseeches to help them.

'My little girl, please…'

'You must help us…'

She looked close to tears as she shook her head at the pleas. 'I'm so sorry there is nothing we can do for you here. Please try one of the other hospitals.'

Realising there was no point in pleading with the nurse, Izel and Rogelio took up their positions at either end of the door and headed north into the city. Adelaida carried a fretful Angelina, all of them parched in the midday sun. The scenes at the City hospital were no better. Moaning and crying filled the air. Everywhere around them the injured begged for help or lay silently, their energy zapped by loss of blood and the humidity. Adelaida found an umbrella in the debris; she and Angelina sat shading Lorna as best they could. After two hours they reached the front of the queue. A young medic who clearly hadn't slept for the past two days examined Lorna's arm.

'The wound has become infected. She has gangrene,' he said wearily. 'It'll need to be amputated.' He pulled a syringe and a small bottle from his pocket, drew some of the clear liquid and inserted the needle into Lorna's shoulder.

'That will help with the pain for the time being. You need to join the queue over there.' He pointed to a long line of people snaking out of the emergency doors and into the littered hospital car park, before moving onto the next patient.

Izel left the others in the queue and went to see what was happening inside the hospital. He passed a bank of noisy generators and squeezed his way in through the mass of people. The corridors were littered with bodies waiting their turn. Moans of pain mixed with screams and sobbing. Nurses, their uniforms soaked with blood and sweat, scurried between operating rooms ignoring calls from the waiting wounded.

Izel carefully picked his way back through a makeshift donor area set up in a nurses' station, for relatives to provide blood for their injured family members. Further along, surgeons snatched a couple of hours sleep on chairs. Everywhere was pandemonium. He found his way out to the car park.

'It's madness in there, so many people…' he faltered. 'Impossible to say how long we could be waiting.'

He handed out the last of the dry biscuits and bottles of Seven Up from his backpack while they discussed their options.

'I want to see my parents, Izel,' pleaded Adelaida. 'Make sure they're…that they're okay.'

He nodded.

'There's nothing you can do here, son. We'll be in this line for hours if not days. Go to Anibong and look for Felipe and Elena. They'll be worried about Adelaida too. I'll look after your mother, don't worry,' Rogelio smiled thinly at Izel.

Reluctantly he and Adelaida left his parents in the hospital car park among the injured and the typhoon debris. Izel carried the grizzling and hungry Angelina. Twenty minutes later they drew close to Robinsons Mall. There was a bustle of activity surrounding the shops as people dashed in and out of the damaged shopping centre, collecting whatever they could carry.

Izel handed Angelina to his wife. 'Stay here, I'm going to see what I can salvage,' he said.

'Be careful, Izel.'

He nodded and followed the stream of people in through the smashed doors. Shelves were being picked clean of foodstuffs, clothes, even electrical goods, much to Izel's amazement. The floors were littered with glass and plastic. Flood water had displaced the children's play area. The ride-on cars were heaped together at the bottom of the motionless escalators. Izel snatched at tinned goods, biscuits and drinks along with the other desperate survivors. He made his way back outside to Adelaida and Angelina, emptying his plunder in front of them. He handed the girl a bag of sweets and bottle of water. They used the towels he had taken to tie around their faces to protect them from the stink of rotting, bloated corpses.

The scenes in downtown Tacloban were identical to the other areas they had passed. Debris piled high, houses destroyed, desperate people taking desperate measures to find food, clothing and water. Suddenly everyone stopped what they were doing. Eyes turned skywards as the droning of the first C130 Hercules vibrated through the air. Above the engine noise cheers and yells could be heard as people waved at the plane.

'Here, we need food and water here.'

'At last, help is arriving.'

'Thank God, finally.'

'They must have cleared the runways,' said Izel. He offered a silent prayer heavenward.

By the time they reached the far end of downtown Tacloban it was mid-afternoon. It was two and a half days since Typhoon Yolanda had ripped the Philippines apart. It had been like something from a disaster movie, a destroyed city, dead bodies, loss of their son, their daughter missing. None of that prepared them for the scene which awaited them as they approached Barangay 69, the Anibong region. It had been flattened. Once a highly populated area, no houses remained. In their place a mass of wood and corrugated iron, household goods, clothes, bodies and seven container ships. Borne up on the massive waves that had struck the coastline, they had been dumped among the detritus where Adelaida's parents had lived. They stood in silence, staring in disbelief at the sight in front of them. Adelaida's knees buckled beneath her, she dropped to the ground and was violently sick.

CHAPTER EIGHT

The doctor had prescribed Helen with anti-depressants. She was reluctant to resort to taking drugs, but she also accepted she needed help. Since the afternoon spent with the barmaid in the wine bar, she had started to feel a little hope. She realised she didn't want to remain in the abyss she had fallen into. She also knew she couldn't manage to get out alone.

'Hi, Sarah,' Helen phoned her best friend.

'Helen. It's so good to hear from you. How are you holding up?'

'Yeah, I'm okay. I've been to the doctor and he prescribed anti-depressants.'

'Good, because you looked terrible when I saw you last week.'

'Thanks,' Helen replied sarcastically. 'Actually, I was wondering if you would help me with something,' she took a deep breath. 'I want to send some of Charlie's clothes to those poor people in the Philippines. Would you help me sort through them? I don't think I can manage it on my own,' her voice cracked as she finished the sentence.

'Of course. When do you want to do it?'

'Would tomorrow be okay with you, about ten o'clock?'

'I'll see you then.'

Helen signed heavily as she ended the call, tears brimmed in her eyes. It was a big step and she wondered if she was taking it too soon. She hadn't touched anything in Charlie's room since she had chosen his funeral outfit. She stood in the doorway most nights, saying a few words to his ghost. Letting him know she was thinking of him and missed him terribly. She knew she wouldn't be able to sort through his clothes without Sarah.

Returning to her computer, she did a couple of hours work. She had neglected her clients for too long, she was determined to make an effort. Once her concentration started to wander again, she returned to the internet, but this time to see where she should send

Charlie's clothes. There were hundreds of organisations vying for donations, it was difficult to decide. Helen was a bit cynical when it came to charities. There had been so many stories about where the money actually went. But, she chided herself, I'm giving clothes, surely they will get to the people who need them.

Scrolling through the pages of websites looking for inspiration, she came across a small organisation, World Disaster Response. Nursing a cup of coffee, she idly clicked on the link and read about them. They were raising money for projects in Tacloban. They were also looking for volunteers to join them in the Philippines. They weren't requesting donations of clothes. Helen was about to close the web page, but impulsively added it to her bookmark favourites.

'I can't make a decision now,' she absently muttered to the computer. 'I'll decide tomorrow with Sarah.' And she turned back to her work.

Sarah arrived the next morning with fresh croissants from the baker. They were still warm and the smell encouraged Helen to try one with a cup of coffee. They exchanged niceties for a couple of minutes, but it didn't take long for Sarah to get to point.

'What's made you decide to do this now, Helen?' She wiped flakes of pastry from her mouth.

'I don't know. Part of me is scared of doing it. I feel I'll lose part of Charlie. But then the more logical part of me says it's only clothes. Those desperate people in Tacloban have a greater need. I know if Charlie was here…' her voice faltered as she said his name. She took a deep breath. 'If he were here, he would have already set up another 'Just Giving' page to raise money for them.'

Sarah put her hand on Helen's. 'You're right. He would've been sorting through his things, deciding what would be most useful to send,' she smiled at her friend. 'I'm so proud of you. He would be too. He's probably looking down on us now asking why it's taken so long.'

Helen nodded, wiping her tears away and reaching for a tissue to blow her nose. 'It isn't going to be easy, be prepared for lots of tears this morning.'

'I've brought tissues. Come on, let's get started.'

They spent a couple of emotional hours packing up shorts, tee-shirts and sandals, pausing every now and again to share a memory.

'I'm starving,' said Sarah at half past one. 'It must be time for some lunch.'

They left Charlie's room and the bags full of clothes and went downstairs.

'There's not much in the fridge. I've not been shopping much recently,' Helen said apologetically.

'I'm sure we'll find something,' said Sarah as she rummaged through cupboards. 'Here, put this soup on to heat up. I've got some fresh bread in the car.'

They shared a tin of tomato soup and a French baguette.

'Which charity are you giving Charlie's things to?'

'I don't know. I thought you might have some ideas. There are so many, I couldn't decide.'

'Matt's school are asking all the kids to bring in some things to send out there. I'll add it to that if you like?'

Helen nodded. 'Perfect. I'm finding decisions a little difficult these days. Have you been following what's happening out there?'

'To be honest, I saw it on the news when it first happened, but other than that, I only know what the kids have said about the school collection.'

'It was the same day as Charlie's funeral,' said Helen.

'I know, lovey.'

'I feel a weird connection to it somehow. At first I couldn't bear to think about it. Now I've become a bit obsessed,' she admitted.

'Maybe it helps. Knowing you're not alone with your loss?'

'Something like that. It puts it a little bit into perspective, I guess. It's helping me cope.'

Sarah stayed until it was time to pick up her children. It was the first time since Charlie's death Helen had been able to talk about her feelings, her anger and her frustration. When Sarah left, she felt exhausted, but somehow more at peace than she had since she'd lost her son.

Over the next couple of days Helen continued to make progress. She was sleeping a lot, the anti-depressants made her drowsy and a bit sluggish. It was taking time, but she felt she was making headway on her work contracts. She felt a slight detachment from the world around her, as if she were on the outside watching herself. The doctor had confirmed after their first consultation since taking the tablets that it wasn't an uncommon side effect. She quite liked it, it took away the pain.

Taking a break from work one afternoon three days later, she clicked on the World Disaster Response icon she had saved. Flicking through the web pages she found herself on their volunteer registration page. It wasn't really a conscious thought, but she started filling in her details. She reached the end of the questions. The cursor blinked over the send button.

'Well, if they did accept me, I'm not obligated to do anything,' she justified to herself. She took a deep breath and clicked the mouse. 'I probably won't hear from them anyway,' she laughed at herself. She closed the website and went back to work.

To her surprise the next morning an email from World Disaster Response was sitting in her inbox. Her heart quickened. She was unsure how she felt about it. If they were interested in her joining them, she would be forced to make a decision. On the other hand if they rejected her application, she would be very disappointed. She felt this email held her future in its message. She stared at it, thoughts zinging in her brain. Finally curiosity got the better of her and she double clicked on it. She could feel her heart pumping in her chest as she skim read it. She laughed aloud. 'Of course they wouldn't offer a place that simply, what was I thinking. How silly of me to get so worked up.'

The CEO of World Disaster Response, Ian Tait had replied: 'Thank you for registering with WDR. I read your application with interest, based on your skills and experience. We're currently looking for people to support local relief efforts with a view to scaling up our overall work and taking on more volunteers. I'll be honest with you and say we are not sure what to expect or how things will progress until we arrive in Tacloban and can assess how WDR can best be of use. If you feel this is something which you would like to be involved with, I would very much like to arrange a time to call you to discuss further.'

Helen sat back. Should she call this Ian? She had a conversation in her brain. So if I'm thinking about calling him, do I want to go? I don't know. But you were going to be disappointed if they didn't want you. She tried to analyse her feelings. What harm would a phone call do? She could find out more, she didn't have to make an immediate decision. As she looked at her mobile, it rang, making her jump. It was Sarah.

'I just wanted to see how you're doing? The school wanted me to thank you for Charlie's things.'

'I'm okay. Thanks for taking them in.'

'You sound distracted, is this a bad time.'

'No, no it's fine. I was in the middle of something.'

'Anything I can help with?'

'Actually, no, it's okay I think I've got it sorted. Sorry, Sarah, I have to go.'

'You know where I am if you need me. Speak soon.'

Before she had time to think any more, Helen dialled the number in the email. She spent an hour talking to Ian Tait. A bubble of excitement swelled inside her. She felt she might be a little crazy, but maybe this challenge was what she needed. She had told David at the crematorium she thought a sabbatical could be what she needed. She laughed out loud. This wasn't quite what she had meant.

The first wave of the WDR team was leaving in a week. Ian had offered her a place with them if she was interested and could make a decision quickly. She had briefly explained her situation and that she was on medication to help her deal with the circumstances.

'Sometimes we need something else to focus on, to help us put things into some sort of perspective,' he had said. 'When I lost my wife in the 2004 Tsunami, I found helping to rebuild Khao Lak helped me. I won't lie to you. Things won't be pretty in Tacloban, Helen. Only you can decide if it is something you want to do and if you feel you can cope with it.'

She had requested twenty-four hours to think about it, but asked him to send her the list of items she would be required to take, should she decide it was for her.

She spent the rest of the day arguing the case for going against the case for staying. Still undecided, she drew a cross on a sheet of A4 paper and wrote 'Tacloban' at the top on the left and 'Staying' on the right, then listed the pros and cons of each. Frustrated she still couldn't reach a decision she threw the pen across the room and watched it clatter against the wall and fall to the floor. Eventually she gave up, shut the door to her office, made herself a sandwich and poured a glass of wine. She spent the evening curled up on the sofa, watching inane television until bedtime.

She woke with a start. It was dark. She listened intently, what was it that had woken her? She couldn't hear anything, the house was silent. She lay back against the pillows. The dream. She had been dreaming about Charlie. It was the sound of him calling her that had woken her up. She focussed and his words came back to her.

'You can do it, mum. What have you got to lose? It will be an adventure.'

He had been standing on the top of a hill, smiling and beckoning to her, the wind ruffling his hair.

Tears slid down her cheeks as she remembered it. Had he been referring to her indecision about going to the Philippines?

'Are you telling me I should go, Charlie?' she said out loud.

'You're right, what do I have to lose?'

She smiled. Her mind was made up. If she didn't like it, she could always come back. It was better than wallowing in self-pity here. She turned over and tried to get back to sleep, but thoughts of what she needed to do filled her head and in the end she threw on jogging bottoms and a rugby shirt. She sat at the kitchen table with a cup of coffee and started drawing up lists.

Over the next couple of days she went shopping for mosquito nets, drugs, steel capped boots and everything else on the list Ian had sent her. She had a sense of purpose. In quiet moments she also had a sense of terror. What the hell was she doing?

She phoned her closest friends and invited them for dinner. It had been some time since the five of them had been together, so the conversations at the table buzzed as they exchanged news. It was once she had served coffee that Helen got everyone's attention.

'Thank you, you guys. I know you've all been worried about me and it means so much to me to know I have such good friends to be there for me.'

They all started to respond.

'That's what friends do....'

'You would do the same for any one of us...'

'We're just relieved you're okay...'

Helen took a deep breath before she continued, saying her news out loud meant no going back. She would be committed to it.

'Sooooo...' her friends stopped talking. Leaning forward and looking at her when they heard her tone. 'I wanted you to be the first to know of my decision. I'm leaving next week to go and volunteer in the Philippines.'

There was total silence for a couple of seconds, before they all started talking at once, but the meanings were all the same: 'You're doing what?'

Tears glistened in Helen's eyes.

'I can't stay here. Everything I do, everywhere I go there are memories of Charlie…'

'Yes but…' interrupted Sarah.

'Please, let me say what I need to say.' She took Sarah's hand and smiled at her. 'It's not that I want to forget Charlie. He'll always be in my heart and my memories, but staying here…it's not good for me, I'm so unhappy. If I go there, I can put things into some kind of perspective. Those people out there, they have lost so much more, maybe we can help each other. I need to do this for my sanity.'

'Your work?' asked Anne softly.

'I've talked to all my clients. I've agreed to tie up loose ends before I leave. They were all pretty understanding actually and I haven't been doing a good job since Charlie…so I think some may have been rather relieved.'

'How long are you going for?' asked Nicole.

'I don't know. I've decided to rent my house out for six months. We'll see what happens then.'

'What happens if you don't like it out there? Renting your house out, that's pretty drastic,' said Anne.

'It just seems the right thing to do.'

'Bloody hell, Helen, you were never one to hang about once you'd made a decision,' said Sarah, her eyes brimming with tears. 'You be careful, you hear me? What about vaccinations, are you up-to-date on everything?'

'Always the practical one, Sarah. Yes I checked, remember I went to Vietnam? I'm still covered from then.'

There was silence for a few moments as they all took in the enormity of the news Helen had shared.

'So what will you be doing out there?' asked Fiona.

'Well I've signed up with World Disaster Response – WDR. They're a small organisation. They're just deploying out there and they're interested in me helping set up their volunteer programme. I won't know much until we arrive there and see what needs to be done. I've spoken with them a couple of times and four of us are flying out together. That's about all I know.'

They spent the next couple of hours talking about Helen's trip. They discussed what they had seen on television about the typhoon and whether it was something they would want to do. Her friends left at half past eleven. They made Helen promise to keep in touch as much as possible, even if it was just an occasional text to one of them, and to stay safe.

Sarah held back as the others waved their goodbyes.

'Are you sure about this? It's pretty extreme. I mean, there's been looting and they're still finding bodies...' she trailed off.

Helen hugged her dearest friend.

'It's the right thing for me,' she whispered in her ear.

'Okay then,' Sarah said trying to hold back her tears. 'You just be careful and don't take any unnecessary risks.'

'Yes, mum.' They smiled at each other and Helen watched from the door as her friend drove away.

***

A week later, with a rucksack and very large holdall, Helen waited beside the Emirates check-in desk for her fellow travellers. Finally three people approached her asking if she was Helen.

'I'm so sorry we're late,' panted Ian as he introduced himself and the couple with him.

'This is Ruth Bradbury and Neil Keys, they're volunteers like you, but have been deployed in previous disaster areas. They'll be the project managers. Ruth, Neil, this is Helen Gable. As I was telling you, she's going to run the volunteer programme, once we've got ourselves somewhere to house them.'

They checked in and used the six hour flight to Dubai, two hour transit time and eight hour flight to Manila to get acquainted. They arrived, exhausted, at Ninoy Aquino International Airport. They spent the night in a cheap hotel in the city. Even the groaning air conditioning unit and street noises couldn't stop Helen falling into a deep sleep as soon as her head hit the pillow. When she arrived for breakfast the next morning Ruth and Neil were already eating.

'Ian's gone out to pick up last minute supplies and buy Filipino SIM cards for us,' said Neil between mouthfuls of mango. 'Once he's back, we'll be getting a taxi to the domestic terminal. Dig in while you can. Who knows what culinary delights await us in Leyte.'

Four hours later The Philippine Airlines plane began its descent into Tacloban. Helen had her first sight of the damage caused by Yolanda. She couldn't stop staring at the decimated landscape beneath her. The news footage hadn't begun to portray the enormity of the destruction. She sat with her hand over her mouth, shaking her head in disbelief.

Bags were unloaded and dumped beside the plane for people to claim their own. Tarpaulin covered parts of the terminal building, or what was left of it. They collected their baggage and emerged into the debris strewn car park. People were clamouring to get past guards and into the terminal, desperate to flee the ongoing devastation and death. Several barged into Helen, causing her to stumble. She felt dizzy and started to hyperventilate. The jet lag, shouting, heat from the sun and the humidity were making her anxious and she wondered what on earth had made her come here. Suddenly a 4x4 jeep pulled up beside them. A large man leapt from the passenger seat and boomed in an American accent at Ian. 'Welcome to Tacloban, my friend.'

Ian shook his hand and turned to the other three. 'Let me introduce you to Hank. He has kindly offered us somewhere to stay.'

Hank's driver relieved them of their bags and put them in the boot. Helen, Ruth and Neil slid into the cool air conditioned comfort of the back seat. Ian, his American friend and the driver climbed into the front and they pulled away from the airport.

CHAPTER NINE

'Look, granddad,' Angelina said smiling and pointing towards a red and blue cargo ship. It was stranded aground and surrounded by the wood, concrete and household goods it had destroyed as it was carried ashore.

Adelaida looked up and followed the outstretched arm. People were sifting through the debris trying to find fragments of their life before Yolanda. Where his house once stood was Felipe, her father. She got to her feet and called out to him, then carefully picked her way toward him. Tears of relief ran down her cheeks as she embraced him. Izel, carrying Angelina joined them and the four of them hugged.

'Felipe, you're safe,' said Izel when the group separated. 'And the rest of the family?' He bit his lip as he asked, fearing bad news.

'We're fine, we're all fine,' he said frowning. 'Where's Lika Faye and Ellijah? What about your parents, Izel?'

'They're gone. My children are gone,' sobbed Adelaida.

Izel explained the last couple of days to his stricken father-in-law.

'Do you think it's possible Maria actually saw Lika Faye?' Felipe said at last.

'No!' said Adelaida. 'Izel is mistaken, she's gone. Thinking otherwise is madness and will drive us crazy. If she was alive, she would have come to the convent, she's a bright girl. She knew it was the evacuation centre.'

'We don't know that, she...'

'Enough, Izel,' whispered Adelaida shaking her head. 'Enough! You don't think I want her back as much as you? This thinking will tear you apart. You have to accept the reality.'

Izel stared out across the sea. She was wrong, he knew it, but there was no point arguing with his wife. He changed the subject.

'How did you survive this, Felipe, there's nothing left.'

The man went on to tell his own story. He and Elena had insisted

Adelaida's sister, Marjorie, her husband, Brian and their children see out the typhoon with Brian's family in town. To protect their house from possible looters, Felipe and Elena had stayed behind.

'When the first storm surge came, we ran. We ran out of the house so fast. The wind was so strong it pushed us up the hill. It was as if we were weightless. I had hold of your mother's hand,' he looked at Adelaida. 'And we ran up the hill as fast as we could. We were lucky. Many others weren't.' He shook his head at the memory. 'We sheltered behind that wall,' he pointed to the remains of a concrete wall halfway up the hill. 'Then the second wave came, the water was so strong and the wall was crumbling.' He shook his head at the memory. 'We kept moving up, to try and get away. It was terrifying.'

Once the waters had started to subside and the wind dropped, they realised just how lucky they had been. A cargo ship was in the place of their home. They had managed to walk into town and to their son-in-law's parents' house.

'The water went up to the second floor in their house when the storm surges came, but they were all okay. We've been staying there, they have food. Have you eaten? We should go back there now, show your mother you're okay.' He swallowed and looked at the ground. 'And tell her about Ellijah and Lika Faye. She's been worried half to death.'

They made their way into the city. At the house they were greeted with tears of joy, then tears of sorrow as they told the family their news.

'Those poor babies,' said Elena as she wept over her lost grandchildren. 'God rest their souls.'

Marjorie and Brian found clean clothes for the three of them. Over a meal of rice, the families discussed their possibilities for the future.

'You're welcome to stay here as long as you need,' said Brian's father.

'Thank you. But I think now the planes have started to arrive our best option will be to get out of Tacloban. We've lost everything here. My sister and her husband are in Cebu, they'll be able to help us get back on our feet. We can stay with them until things get better here,' Felipe said.

Adelaida looked from her father to Izel. 'We'll go with them. Won't we, Izel?' A frown creased her forehead. Izel could see she was desperate to get away. Away from the place which had taken her son, and as far as she was concerned, their eldest daughter.

'We have nothing left. I need to get away from this place. I don't want to stay here,' she begged.

Izel nodded, but said nothing. If he left how would he find his missing daughter? If he stayed Adelaida would never forgive him. She didn't understand the belief he had of Lika Faye being alive. She had convinced herself their daughter had perished in the typhoon and nothing he said was going to change her mind, she had made that very clear to him. He felt torn. He knew his mother wouldn't be capable of making the journey in her state.

'We need to think about going to the airport soon. We won't be the only ones trying to leave,' said Felipe. 'What about your parents, Izel, will they come?'

'My mother's condition wasn't looking good. I don't think she will be able to travel. I'll have to go back to the hospital and find out what's happening there. When are you thinking of leaving?'

'The first planes came earlier. It will be dark soon and too risky to go tonight. I've heard the army have now set a curfew after all the looting. We should make our way there tomorrow.'

'I'll go straight to the hospital at daybreak and see my parents. We can meet up at the convention centre, then go on to the airport,' said Izel.

They agreed to meet up at ten o'clock the next morning. It would give Izel a chance to see how his mother was and to let his parents know of the plan to go to Cebu. As night fell, it started to rain. Izel lay in the darkness listening to it beating on the corrugated iron roof, wondering where Lika Faye was hearing it. He couldn't understand why after three days she still hadn't made it to the evacuation centre. Or maybe she had arrived there now. How would he know if they left? He could only hope she would stay safe until he managed to find her. He was worried about leaving for Cebu without her.

He loved his wife, but she was wrong about their daughter. If only he could persuade her to see things his way. He fell asleep with images of Lika Faye racing through his head. His dreams were filled with her playing in their garden, chasing her younger brother and sister, the three of them giggling in the sunlight.

***

The chaos at the hospital was no better than the day before. It took him over an hour to locate his father. The smell of disinfectant assaulted Izel's nostrils. He slowly made his way past the patients on makeshift beds filling every conceivable space. Moaning and screaming echoed around the walls. Exhausted doctors and nurses shuffled from one injury to the next, staring at Izel blankly as he made enquiries. Finally he spotted Rogelio leaning against a wall. Fatigue gave him the appearance of a man ten years older. His eyes lit up when he saw his son approaching. The men embraced.

'How is she?' asked Izel.

'Resting. Oh, Izel, they had to amputate her arm.' He looked away.

'Dad, there was nothing more you could have done. She's alive, that's the main thing. How long did you have to wait?'

'Actually, we were incredibly lucky. You remember the young nurse I was helping at Ramon's house? She works here. She helped us get to theatre ahead of some of the others.'

Lorna would have to stay in hospital for a few days so they could keep an eye on the wound and change the dressing regularly. The biggest problem was supplies were becoming dangerously low. Staff were praying medical stocks would make it through soon.

Izel filled his father in on finding Adelaida's family and their plans to get aboard one of the planes later in the day.

'I don't know what to do, dad. I don't want to leave you and mum like this.' He pointed at the bedlam around him. 'I honestly believe Lika Faye is out there somewhere. If I leave I can't search for her.' He looked at his father. 'I know you don't agree with me, dad, but it's something I need to believe. What if she is out there and I don't look for her? I have already let her down once. Adelaida is desperate to get out of here as fast as possible.' He shook his head in despair.

'Don't worry about us. Your mother will be fine and if Lika Faye does turn up, we're here. Your family needs you, Izel. This has been a terrible thing for us all, they need your support. Go and be with them.' Rogelio smiled at his son.

They agreed that father and son would make the trip to the airport, meeting the others as discussed at the Convention Centre. Rogelio would try and get provisions for him and Lorna from the relief planes getting in.

'I'll see if they'll let me have any medical supplies I can bring back here,' said Rogelio.

They returned to the corridor where Lorna was recovering on a mattress.

'Mum.' Izel knelt beside her. 'How're you feeling?'

She nodded and managed a weak smile. 'Izel,' she croaked drowsily.

He lifted her head and held a bottle of water to her lips.

'Lorna, can you hear me?' Rogelio took her hand. 'I'm going with Izel to the airport. I won't be long, okay?'

She nodded feebly and her eyes closed as she drifted back to sleep.

Rogelio stroked her hair before the two of them made their way out of the hospital and to the Convention Centre. Half an hour later,

Felipe, Elena, Adelaida and Angelina arrived and the six of them started their journey to the airport. They joined the exodus converging on the peninsula, desperate to flee the city. Despite the number of people, there was an eerie silence. Dressed in tatters, their meagre possessions clutched tightly, the survivors of Yolanda shuffled towards what they hoped was an escape from the horrors around them. Two planes had thundered overhead as they walked. As they approached the airport a handful of soldiers and police struggled to keep order. Hungry and thirsty people were desperate to get to the supplies being unloaded from the Philippine Air Force C-130s sitting on the runway.

'We need water...'

'My children are sick...'

'Please, let us have some food...'

The air was filled with shouts and screams as supplies emerged from the remains of the terminal building. Hundreds of outstretched arms clawed at the aid hysterically. Others sat quietly sheltering from the sun under colourful umbrellas sprouting splintered spikes.

Izel mopped his forehead on the arm of his tee-shirt. The high humidity was causing even greater dehydration, his tongue stuck to the roof of his mouth.

'I doubt we're going to get on any of those planes today, there are hundreds of people in front of us. I'll see if we can get some food and water.' He handed Angelina to his wife and grabbing his father, followed the swarming throng to where the relief aid boxes were being stacked.

He felt elbows in his ribs and nearly stumbled as people tried to push past him. He saw his father fall and rushed to pull him to his feet before he was trampled underfoot. Shouts and yells came from the anarchic crowd surrounding them, pushing their way forward.

Suddenly two shots cracked through the air above them. An army officer, gun pointing skywards stood on the tailgate of an army truck waiting to load up with supplies. All heads turned as one and apart from a few screaming babies, silence fell.

'Form a queue and we'll hand out food and water from the trucks, but we have to get it unloaded first from the planes. We know you're hungry and thirsty. Please be patient for a little longer. Now stand back and let my men do their job.'

A young, armed soldier stood in front of the crowd. Voices blended as people jostled to get their place in line. Behind them the first plane emptied her belly and the last of the boxes were dragged down the tailgate. Those nearest the tarmac broke through the scant string of police and surged across the blistering runway to board the aircraft.

Above the noise of the people around them, Izel could hear the roar of engines. He turned to watch as the plane taxied down the runway, building up speed before finally breaking free of the ground. It climbed up through the dark rain clouds gathering to the north and disappeared.

He turned to his father: 'You okay, dad?'

'Just a couple of bruises,' he said rubbing his arm. 'Desperation makes people forget their manners,' he smiled dourly.

They waited patiently in line and were finally rewarded with a box each. Inside was water, rice, noodles, tinned sardines and biscuits. There was no negotiating, one box per person. Other family members would have to join the queue if they wanted more. Rogelio tried to ask about medical supplies. The soldier shook his head and pointed at the officer who had used his pistol to silence the crowd earlier. Izel returned to his waiting family with both boxes, as Rogelio went to investigate further.

Izel shared out the supplies. Water bottles were grabbed thankfully and plastic wrappers torn from dry biscuits. They hastily ripped off the lids of the tinned sardines and scooped the contents into their mouths, then licked the greasy oil off their fingers, savouring every morsel. Initial hunger pangs sated, Felipe, Adelaida and Elena joined the back of the queue to collect their rations. Izel had kept a share for his father. Rogelio returned empty handed from his quest for medical supplies.

'They are taking everything directly to the hospitals. They won't hand anything out here. I suppose I can understand. I hoped I would be able to get something to help your mother.'

He took the offered food and shovelled biscuits into his mouth, gulping at the fresh water to wash them down.

'Adelaida and her parents have joined the queue. When they get back you can take some food for mum and you back to the hospital. Who knows when supplies will reach there.'

Small fires started to burn around the airport car park. The smell of cooking rice drifted in the air.

'Well I guess firewood won't be in short supply,' said Izel looking around at the debris. 'Angelina, stay here with granddad.'

Izel collected up a bundle of firewood and found a discarded metal container, then set about making a fire to cook their rice.

A second Hercules thundered down the runway. Izel wondered how long it would take until they could be aboard and escaping from the chaos. He could see more people piling into the airport car park. Crying children at their mother's side, their clothes in tatters, streaked with mud. The injured with makeshift bandages trying to keep the blood in and infection out. He shook his head as he returned to the now boiling water and added rice. It was sitting cooling when Adelaida and the others returned with the second load of boxes. Izel handed one to his father. They walked together for a few moments before saying an emotional farewell, unaware of when they would be able to see or speak with one another again.

'Don't worry, son. I'll take care of your mother and I promise I'll visit the convent to see if there's news of Lika Faye. If she's here, she'll be safe with us until you return.'

'What about the farm, dad? We don't know what state it's in. We owe money for the extra land we rented. All the rice, it could still be edible,' he stopped. A thought occurred to him as he remembered the warehouse he had raided. 'If it's still there.' His shoulders dropped as the enormity of how much their lives had been altered hit him.

'Izel, we can't worry about that. Family is what is important now. Make sure your wife and child are safe.'

Izel looked at his father with tears in his eyes. They hugged once more. He watched as the older man started his trek back to the hospital, fighting his way through the tide of people arriving. His heart felt like lead as he turned towards the airport. He was unhappy to be leaving his parents and devastated he couldn't look for his daughter.

'They'll be okay, Izel,' Adelaida took his hand when he reached them. 'You'll see. Now your mother has been treated, she'll get well. We'll be back, once we have some money together and Tacloban is ready to be rebuilt.'

He smiled thinly at his wife, unable to mention the sorrow he felt at leaving because of Lika Faye. He pulled away from Adelaida and picked up Angelina. He held her tightly to him, trying to assuage his feelings of guilt, torn between his remaining family and his conviction that his other daughter lived.

***

It took two days of waiting, queuing, bargaining, pushing and pleading before Izel and his family crept to the edge of the tarmac. The first Hercules of Thursday morning rumbled to a standstill. Soldiers hastily unloaded her cargo before a whistle blew notifying the police to stand aside. The next group of evacuees raced toward the tailgate.

Izel carried Angelina, pushing Adelaida and his in-laws in front of him so he could be sure they would all reach the plane. As they reached the tailgate Izel stopped. People poured past him, knocking into his shoulders in their desperation to get on board. He watched his wife and in-laws scramble up the ramp and into the plane.

Adelaida turned round as she found a place against a wall inside the fuselage. A look of surprise slowly spread across her face as she realised Izel was no longer behind her. He watched as she scanned the people around her frantically looking for him. Finally she saw him and opened her mouth to scream at him to get aboard. His moment of deliberation passed. He rushed forward and thrust Angelina at his wife.

'I'm sorry. I can't…' He pushed his way back to the tarmac and the rest of his words were swallowed up by the noise of the huge propellers bursting into life. He shook his head and backed further away from the plane. He could see Adelaida's outstretched arm and a look of desperation on her face. He couldn't hear her words but he knew she was begging him to go with them. The anguish was too much for him to bear. He turned, resolute in his decision and strode back to the airport building. The whining of the engines intensified as the huge plane started its taxi to the end of the runway. Izel didn't look back. He marched into the crowd of waiting people, elbowing his way through them. He stopped only once as he thought he heard a familiar voice above the rumble of the plane. Looking around he saw no one he knew, only a sea of desperate faces. One set of eyes caught his. A thin woman, her hair in a ponytail stared at him briefly, before turning away.

Izel forced his way out of the airport and into the car park. He covered his eyes with his hands and let out a tormented howl.

CHAPTER TEN

Arriving at the remains of the terminal building, Rosela, pushing her case in front of her to part the hordes of people, forced her way into the throng. She ignored the angry protestations of those she disturbed. Lika Faye followed in her wake, grasping the woman's shirt. Rosela stopped and looked around her, then turned to Lika Faye.

'This way, stay close to me, I'll never find you again in this crowd.'

'Where are we going?'

'To catch a flight. We have priority seats thanks to this.' She patted her chest.

Lika Faye frowned at her, she had no idea what the woman was talking about.

'Don't worry, you'll see in a minute.'

After scouring the mass of faces once more, Lika Faye watched Rosela wave her free hand at someone she couldn't see and they set off once more. Rosela stopped in front of a policeman. He was hopping from one foot to the other.

'Alfredo,' said Rosela smiling thinly at the man in front of them.

'Where've you been?' he said irritably when they reached him. 'I should be holding the line on the tarmac. If they realise I'm missing I'll be in big trouble.'

'Oh stop complaining,' said Rosela. 'I'm paying you well. Here.'

Lika Faye watched as Rosela reached into her bra and pulled out a wad of peso notes. 'Here's the other half. Now get us on that plane.'

'Us?'

Lika Faye could feel the policeman's eyes on her and bit her lip.

'You didn't say anything about a child.'

'What difference does it make to you?' Rosela snarled at him.

Lika Faye looked from one to the other. The policeman stood his ground, hands on hips.

'It's going to cost you more, Rosela, for two of you.'

Rosela hesitated a moment and shook her head. 'Ah the Filipino police force, there to serve the people,' she said sarcastically. 'More like serve themselves! I have two thousand more. Take it or leave it.'

'Five! Or you don't get past me and on a plane today.'

They haggled for several minutes, finally settling on four thousand. Lika Faye watched in silence as Rosela turned her back to the policeman, reached into her bra once again, counted out the agreed amount and handed it to him.

The policeman looked furtively around him as he put the money in his pocket then told them to follow him closely. 'The next plane is still unloading,' he explained. 'Once it has emptied, you'll hear a whistle. It's the signal for the police to let the next load of people through. You will need to run to the tailgate and climb aboard. Okay?'

Rosela nodded and Lika Faye felt bony fingers in her shoulder as she was pushed to follow the policeman. He slipped the two of them in front of him at the head of the waiting crowd. A couple of people grumbled as they forced their way in, but a steely glance from Rosela shut them up.

'Be ready to run to the plane when you hear the whistle, okay?' Rosela bent down and whispered to Lika Faye.

She nodded, but inside her stomach was fluttering. Was this really the right thing to do? Why would her mum and dad have gone to Cebu? How would they find them there? Before she had a chance to think any further, the whistle sounded and the police stood aside. Lika Faye raced across the tarmac with Rosela and out to the plane. One of the first aboard, Rosela wrenched open one of the red webbing fold-down seats behind the flight deck and indicated Lika Faye do the same.

It didn't take long for the Hercules to fill to capacity, people squeezing in to every available space. Lika Faye stared at the families surrounding her. Maybe her parents were on this plane. She looked around at the mothers trying to soothe their children, while clutching tightly the scarce belongings Yolanda hadn't stripped from them. She strained her head to search the faces for a familiar one.

'Do you think my mum and dad could be on this plane?' she asked Rosela.

'Oh I don't think so, dear. I'm sure someone told me they got out a few days ago.'

The tension inside the plane built as the tailgate was raised. Voices increased in pitch as nearly two hundred people waited in anticipation, finally leaving the horrors of the past six days.

The four engines throttled up, the plane shuddered and shook. The occupants fell silent as the vibrations increased and the aircraft started her slow rumble along the runway. Lika Faye grasped her chair tightly as they gathered speed, the engines screaming. The nose lifted off the ground, Lika Faye stared down the body of the plane at terrified children screaming at their parents and clutching at their legs. She had never flown before, but she was going to be brave, she wasn't going to cry out.

The aircraft suddenly banked, people gasped and stumbled against one another. Lika Faye trembled. Her heart thudded so hard she thought her chest would explode, but she stayed quiet. She gripped the seat until her knuckles turned white. She glanced sideways at Rosela. The woman sat impassively with her case on her lap, detached from her surroundings. Despite the hot, clammy air inside the plane, an icy chill ran up Lika Faye's spine.

Thirty-five minutes later, the pitch of the droning engines lowered as the Hercules started her descent into Cebu. They landed with a thump and a squeal of tyres. Spontaneous clapping broke out and people started crying, hugging and laughing.

'We made it.'

'Thank the Lord, we're safe now.'

The plane filled with shouts of jubilation.

Once the tailgate lowered, Lika Faye watched as people streamed out. Rosela waited until it was half empty before standing. Lika Faye did the same; the fold-down chairs snapped back against the wall.

They walked into the sunlight, blinking in the sudden brightness. Lika Faye nearly tripped over as a passenger in front of her knelt and kissed the tarmac. She regained her footing and followed the case bobbling behind Rosela out through the terminal building.

'Get in.' Rosela pointed to a motor-taxi sidecar as she barked instructions at the driver. The motorbike was gunned into life and the woman squeezed in beside her. Scenes of Cebu flashed past Lika Faye's eyes as they juddered through the streets

'Are we going to see my mum and dad now?' she called to Rosela above the noise of the engine.

Rosela ignored the question and turned her head away.

Fifteen minutes later they pulled up outside the gates of a large white house surrounded with high concrete walls.

'Out!' Rosela commanded. 'And bring my case.'

Lika Faye scrambled out of the sidecar and the woman paid the driver. Rosela pushed her towards the metal gates and prodded at the intercom several times.

'Yeah. Who is it?' A tinny, disembodied voice drawled in English.

'Phil, it's me. Open up,' Rosela replied.

'Rosela? 'Bout bloody time.'

There was a buzz, then a click as the lock retracted and the gate slowly slid open. Lika Faye stared up at the house as she followed in Rosela's footsteps across the driveway and up five semi-circular marble stairs, bumping the case behind her. The front door was ajar. Rosela pushed it open and stepped inside.

'Christ, Rosela, what took you so fucking long? I said you could go for a couple of days.' A man's voice boomed.

'I'm sorry, Phil, the typhoon…' she stammered.

'It was here too y'know! Get your scrawny arse in the kitchen and bring me another tinny.'

Rosela seized Lika Faye's arm and marched with her into the vast kitchen.

'Where are we? Who's that man?' she asked

Opening the fridge door, Rosela picked up a can of beer. 'Shut up and come with me.'

Lika Faye opened her mouth to say something and closed it when she saw the expression on the woman's face. Something wasn't right. She looked nervously around her. She needed to get out of here. She turned to make a run for the front door, but Rosela was too quick and grabbed her by the hair.

Lika Faye yelped in pain, her eyes opened wide.

'Let me go.' She kicked and punched at Rosela as fear consumed her.

Rosela banged the beer on the kitchen counter and Lika Faye felt a sharp pain on her cheek as Rosela struck her. She gasped and stared at the woman in shock.

'You're in my house now, you do as I say,' Rosela hissed at her.

She picked up the can and strode into the lounge dragging a stunned Lika Faye with her.

The man called Phil, his back to the doorway, was sprawled on an L-shaped beige sofa which dominated the huge room. In front of him an enormous flat screen television hung on the wall. He was engrossed in a sporting game Lika Faye didn't recognise. It looked a bit like football but the players were throwing an odd shaped ball. It wasn't until Rosela stood in front of him offering the beer that he turned his attention to them. He snatched the can, then did a double take as he realised she wasn't alone. Rosela let go of Lika Faye and pushed her towards him.

'Well, well, well, what have we here?' He sat up, pulled the ring on the can, took a long gulp of beer and grinned. 'You're a pretty little thing, aren't you?'

Lika Faye stared open mouthed at the man in front of her. He was dressed in a grubby vest straining across his vast belly, which overhung a pair of grey underpants. Grey stubble covered a fleshy face and his double chin wobbled as he spoke. Broken veins crisscrossed his bulbous nose and ran up towards his bloodshot eyes. He ran a liver-spotted hand through his thinning sandy hair and hauled his flabby body off the sofa. Lika Faye's eyes followed him as he moved towards Rosela, grasped her chin in his free hand and planted a kiss on her lips.

'Nice work, she'll be perfect,' he said.

'I thought you'd like her,' Rosela slowly exhaled, a smile playing on her lips.

Lika Faye trembled. She couldn't understand all the conversation, but she knew they were talking about her and it terrified her. Unable to control her fear, she was horrified to feel a hot wet trickle run down her thigh and she started to cry.

'Oh for fuck's sake, Rosela, isn't she house trained!' Phil yelled. 'Get her out of here and clean up that mess.' He pointed to the small puddle on the tiles. He flopped back down on the sofa, sloshing beer over his vest and returned his attention to the television.

Lika Faye felt her hair being wrenched from her head as she was dragged from the room.

'How dare you make me look a fool, you little bitch.'

In the kitchen Rosela threw a towel at her. 'Clean yourself up. Put your shorts in the washing machine over there and wait here. If you think I'm mopping up after you, think again.'

Lika Faye stood in the middle of the room. Hot, silent tears coursed down her cheeks and dripped onto the floor. What had happened? They were supposed to be looking for her family. Why was she here with that horrible man? Why was Rosela behaving like this? She felt scared. This wasn't supposed to be happening.

When Rosela returned she flung a pair of shorts to the floor.

'Put them on. Grab a mop and bucket from the cupboard over there and clear up your mess.' She pointed to the far end of the kitchen. 'Now!' Her screech made Lika Faye flinch.

When Lika Faye had finished, Rosela was sitting in the kitchen drinking tea.

'Come here, child.'

Lika Faye slowly approached the woman. She felt her ear being gripped tightly between a thumb and index finger: 'If you ever show me up like that again, I'll find every surviving member of your family and I'll kill them,' she hissed. 'Now put everything away and follow me.'

Lika Faye trembled as she followed Rosela. She couldn't understand what had happened. This morning she had believed they were going to be looking for her mum and dad. Now this woman she had trusted had completely changed.

'Rosela, did I do something wrong? I thought we were coming to Cebu to look for my mum and dad.' Her voice was barely a whisper in case she angered the woman further.

Rosela stopped, turned and bent down. Her face was so close to Lika Faye she could see where an old scar had cut one of Rosela's eyebrows in half, snaked up her temple and disappeared into her hair.

'Let's get a couple of things straight, shall we? Firstly, from now on, you call me Miss Rosela, is that clear?'

Lika Faye bit her bottom lip as she stared at the woman; the expression in Rosela's eyes made her look away.

'Yes,' she mumbled.

Rosela grabbed her chin and turned her face towards her. 'Yes what?'

'Yes, Miss Rosela?'

'Right! And as for your family, I have no idea if they are alive or dead. Here is your 'family' now.'

Her sinister smile sent a cold shiver through Lika Faye's very being. Surely her parents couldn't be dead. Why had Rosela been lying to her all this time? Before she could ask any more questions,

Rosela gripped her arm and dragged her to a bedroom and hurled her inside.

'Don't get used to this, it's just for today,' Rosela sneered.

'What am I doing here, Miss Rosela?' Lika Faye whispered.

'You'll find out soon enough. Best get some sleep while you can. Tomorrow you start working for your living.'

Lika Faye looked around the smartly decorated bedroom. A large double bed dominated the room, covered in a white sheet and multi-coloured scatter cushions. A metal scraping at the window made her jump and she watched a shutter slowly descend cutting out the daylight.

Rosela turned and with the shutter remote in her hand, walked out. The door closed plunging Lika Faye into darkness and she heard a key rasp in the lock. She shuffled towards the bed until she felt the soft mattress against her thigh. She climbed up and sank into the softness.

Where was she and why was she here? What had happened to the woman she had met in Tacloban? She had been friendly and helpful. Now she had turned mean and scary. And who was that horrible fat man? Lika Faye was scared, even more scared than when she had woken up alone after the typhoon. What were they going to do with her? She curled up into a ball. Every strange sound from the house made her heart beat faster thinking they were coming for her.

She must have fallen asleep because the next thing she knew, Rosela was unlocking the door. She sat up, wide-eyed, her heart thumping, wondering what was going to happen to her now.

'Let's go!' Rosela beckoned her out of the room.

Lika Faye slid off the bed and silently did as she was told. Downstairs Rosela took a large bunch of keys out of her pocket and unlocked a padlock on a metal door in the kitchen. She slid back two hefty bolts, at the top and bottom, and wrenched it open. She reached inside and pulled a light switch. A solitary low wattage bulb lit the stairs. Pushing the girl in front of her they descended into the gloom.

At the bottom was a second doorway and on the wall beside it a bank of light switches. Rosela flicked them all on before jabbing at a keypad six times. A bolt clicked and the door swung inwards, banging against a wall on the left. Lika Faye felt a prod in her shoulder and shuffled into the basement. To her right, bare bulbs hung down from the ceiling and in the dim pools of light she could make out mattresses. She watched as they started to come to life. Disturbed by the sudden brightness, several girls rubbed their eyes and sat up.

'Jenny, Rebecca, you're on kitchen duty, upstairs with me now. Lourdes, you can do the toilets.'

'Yes, Miss Rosela,' their voices called in unison from the shadows.

'Phoebe, get your arse over here,' Rosela called out.

A young girl, slightly taller than Lika Faye scrambled off her bed and ran over to them.

'Yes, Miss Rosela.'

She was dressed in shorts and a vest, her feet bare. She stood solemnly to attention in front of the woman. Her eyes were cast downward, as she waited for instructions.

'Teach her what we do here, her name's Faye.'

Lika Faye frowned and looked up: 'Miss Rosela, my name is Lika Fa...'

The crack to the back of her head cut her short.

'Not anymore! It's too much of a mouthful, get used to it!' She turned on her heel, closely followed by two older girls and the door slammed shut.

Lika Faye rubbed the back of her head, tears in her eyes. She looked at the taller girl waiting for some explanation of what had happened.

'Miss Rosela and Mr Phil will call you what they want. We belong to them now. You'll get used to it. So, it's Lika Faye, yeah? My name is Phoebe. I'm twelve. Come.' She took Lika Faye's hand

and pulled her towards the mattresses.

'There's a spare one next to mine, you can sleep there. How old are you? Where are you from' Phoebe giggled and put her hand to her mouth as the questions poured out of her.

'I'm eleven.'

'Oh, we're practically the same age.' She lowered her voice so Lika Faye had to lean closer to hear. 'The older girls, they don't like to talk to us younger ones. You saw Jenny and Rebecca go with Miss Rosela – I've nicknamed her Ratface.' She sniggered at her own joke. 'Then there's Lourdes and Marianne, over there.' She pointed out two girls lying in their beds and lighting up cigarettes. 'Their customers bring them cigarettes as gifts. They think it makes them look grown up, horrible smelly things.' She said the last three words louder.

'Shut up, Phoebe, you're just a silly little girl,' one of them said unkindly.

'That's Marianne, best to keep out of her way. Then there's Bella and Monique,' she pointed to two younger girls lying together on one mattress. 'They're sisters, they keep to themselves mostly. You and me, we can be friends.'

Lika Faye tried to follow what Phoebe was telling her, but none of it made sense. Who were these girls? What were they doing here?

'I...I don't understand. What is this place?' she whispered to Phoebe. 'What are we all doing here?' Her tears started again.

'Shhhh, it's okay, we're all a bit scared when we first arrive.' Phoebe tried to console her

'Why are we here? What do they want with me? I want to go home. Where are my mum and dad?'

The girl Phoebe had said was Marianne laughed. 'This is your home now, your mummy and daddy ain't never gonna find you here.'

Lika Faye stared at the older girl for a couple of moments then covered her face with her hands. It had to be a bad dream, this couldn't be happening. But when she took her hands away, she was still in the dingy basement. She started to sob uncontrollably.

'Oh, shut up, Marianne. Now look what you've done. Lika Faye, shhh. It'll be okay, I'll help you, shhh.' Phoebe hugged Lika Faye to her. 'Come on, Jenny and Rebecca will be back soon with rice, I bet you're hungry.'

Lika Faye wiped at her tears and nodded. Phoebe smiled at her. Lika Faye looked around her. Ten mattresses in total filled the floor, five on each side, with a small gap between each one. There was space down the middle dividing the older girls from the younger ones. There were no sheets or pillows. All the girls were dressed in shorts and vests.

Blue-tinged cigarette smoked swirled and snaked upwards towards the light bulbs. The air was heavy and reeked of sweat and urine. She sat down on her mattress, facing the way she'd come in. Behind the older girls' mattresses on her right, a black curtain ran the width of the room. She turned to her left, a plywood wall had been erected with a door at one end and a large padlock glinted halfway up.

Phoebe sat beside her as one of the older girls walked past carrying two buckets; water splattered onto the mattresses.

'Be careful, Lourdes,' moaned Marianne. 'Especially when you come back.'

Lourdes disappeared through a curtain behind Lika Faye. She reappeared moments later with two different buckets, the smell of urine got stronger as she got closer.

'That's the bathroom,' said Phoebe holding her nose until Lourdes had passed them. 'There's four buckets, two with clean water and two for the toilet. Don't get them mixed up. Bella did once and we didn't have any clean water left in the morning. Marianne attacked her, her legs were covered in bruises and she bit her ear!'

Lika Faye nodded uncertainly at her new friend. The sound of the basement door made her look up. The girls Phoebe had called Jenny and Rebecca entered carrying trays filled with plastic bowls and beakers. One of the trays was put on the floor at the base of her mattress. Phoebe reached over, picked up a beaker and a bowl and handed them to Lika Faye, before taking her own. Suddenly starving, she shovelled the rice into her mouth. The room was silent apart from the slurping of water and licking of fingers. When everyone had finished, Phoebe picked up the empty containers and put them beside the basement door.

'What happens now?' asked Lika Faye.

'We wait. It's pretty boring usually, but now you're here we can chat. Where are you from?'

'What are we waiting for?' Lika Faye ignored Phoebe's question. She wanted to know what they were doing in this horrible basement.

''Til we're told it's time for work, of course,' Phoebe retorted.

'Work? What kind of work?'

'Oh, Lika Faye, you'll find out soon, I don't want to think about it now. Can't we just chat for a while?'

Lika Faye nodded, although really she wanted to find out what work they would be doing.

The rest of the day passed slowly by until Rosela appeared at the door. She clapped her hands.

'Time to get yourselves ready,' she said and disappeared.

The older girls returned to their own mattresses and from beneath them pulled out cheap make-up. With the absence of mirrors they helped each other apply eye shadow, khol pencil, blusher and lipstick. The heavy and exaggerated make-up gave them the appearance of dolls, Lika Faye thought as she watched them.

Finally she turned to Phoebe. 'What's behind the black curtain?' she asked.

'It's where they work. The men will start to come soon.'

'What men?'

Phoebe rolled her eyes. 'You know, men who pay to have…sex,' she lowered her voice as she said the last word.

Lika Faye blushed. She was confused, she'd heard about where babies came from, but this was something different, men paying for sex. Her heart thudded as she asked her next question, terrified what the answer might be: 'And behind that door?' She nodded towards the plywood wall.

'It's where we work,' Phoebe said quietly and bit her bottom lip.

CHAPTER ELEVEN

Relief aid had reached Tanauan. Izel and Rogelio took their tickets and waited in the queue to collect their food parcels, then in a second one to receive some clothes and shoes. Izel was still wearing the mismatched pair he had found on the day of the typhoon. They returned to their temporary refuge at Our Lady of Assumption Catholic church, along with all the others who had lost their homes.

Using foraged materials, Izel and Rogelio had created their own space within the church over the five days since they'd left the airport. In one corner they kept a metal container to cook rice and a small stock of firewood, to keep it dry. Thanks to the relief aid, they now had a small collection of mismatched and ill-fitting clothes.

'I thought I would take a look at the house today, see if there is anything worth salvaging,' Izel said.

'I was going to take some food to your mother,' Rogelio looked apologetically to his son.

'It's okay, dad, I wasn't expecting you to come with me. We should go out to the farm soon though and see what's happening there, maybe tomorrow? How much longer do they expect to keep mum in hospital?'

'Another couple of days, as long as she's healing okay. They seem pleased with her progress so far. Tomorrow will be good, Izel. I'll let her know not to expect me until later. How will we get there?'

'Brian will lend me his motorbike. Petrol could be a problem though, I know he only has a few litres and we'll need to replace it.' Izel sighed. The queues outside the gas stations were as bad as those for food. Petrol prices had skyrocketed, plus they had no access to money.

'I'm not sure when the banks are going to reopen. I hope he can wait until they do.'

Izel was praying the farm might provide some hope. If some of the pigs had survived and rice still remained, he would be able to sell them or use them to trade for other items.

They ate the dry goods from the food parcels. The box was from a Non-profit organisation in Turkey. Izel thought it odd the items inside were Filipino sardines, rice, noodles and salted crackers, but the thought swiftly left his mind. It was food.

He accompanied his father as far as the Pan-Philippine highway before they set off in separate directions.

'Give mum my love.' Rogelio nodded and headed off to the hospital. Izel sighed, wondering what he would find when he reached his home. His heart raced as he got closer. The memories of the typhoon were brought sharply back to him. The images of Lika Faye and Ellijah still fresh in his mind as they were wrenched from him. His eyes prickled.

He stood at his gate. It was dangling from one hinge, a coconut tree trunk lying across it. The shock of the damage to his home left him breathless. It was a wonder any of them had survived he thought. Concrete walls had crumbled under impact. Exposed rebar twisted and rusting snaked out like tendrils. Piles of rubble spewed across the path and throughout the house. He clambered inside what had once been their kitchen and stood in front of the sink unit. The white tiles were chipped and cracked. It stood defiant but incongruous without any surrounding walls. He climbed up the steps they had last used ten days earlier. Only a few of the wooden floorboards had survived. Those remaining were splintered and rotting.

In the bathroom, a handful of white tiles still clung to the remains of the walls. The fractured toilet bowl stood resolute and alone. He trod carefully over the damaged floor towards the back of the house. Mangled and corroding bed frames dangled down into the garden. Their old television, exposing its innards, rested in one corner. Jagged glass like a rabid dog's bared teeth warned him away.

He sat on the edge of the remains of the back wall staring down into the garden. His shoulders slumped as he looked around him. His eye was caught by something glinting in the sunlight. He carefully lowered himself down and pulled wooden planks out the way. It was a medal. Attached to a red, white and blue ribbon, it was covered in mud. He picked it up and brushed it clean with his tee-shirt. It was one of Lika Faye's. She'd had half a dozen hanging from her bed, presented by the school for achievement. Izel remember her pride as she had brought each one home. One had been for maths, another for running, one for English. He couldn't recall what the others had been for. He rotated it in his hand as he thought of happier times and then put it in his pocket.

He spent several hours rummaging around in the debris of what had once been their home. He didn't find much of use, but he did find some mementoes. He gathered them together – two of Ellijah's toy trucks; a favourite doll of Angelina's now minus one arm; a blue and white china cup with the handle missing; a matching sugar bowl miraculously unscathed and a figurine of a cherub, one of the many his mother had collected. He put them all carefully in his backpack. As he walked back towards the gate, glass crunched under his foot. He lifted his leg and looked at the ground. It was a picture frame facing downwards. He picked it up, shaking off the broken glass before turning it over. His heart lurched, his eldest daughter smiled up at him. Her school photograph taken last term. There was some water damage, but only on the edges. He pulled it free of the frame and kissed her cheek.

'Where are you, Lika Faye? I promise I'll find you, my darling, whatever it takes.' He added it to the items in the bag and trudged back to the church.

***

The next day at sunrise, Izel picked up his brother-in-law's motorbike and set off towards the farm with his father. They rode in silence as Izel picked his way carefully along the Pan-Philippine

Highway. Although the army had been through with moving equipment, it had only been cleared one vehicle wide. He had to weave his way through oncoming traffic or wait behind other vehicles as they let approaching trucks pass.

A few jeepneys were on the road again, the bright colours of their paint work in sharp contrast to the surroundings. They lumbered past, belching fumes and sounding their horns. Passengers hung from every handhold and were crammed to bursting point inside, while still others perched precariously on the roof. They were prepared to suffer the discomfort to reach their destination and hopefully find food.

The hills around Tacloban, once lusciously green were now a dirty brown. Sorry stumps of surviving trees stripped of their fronds slumped forlornly, propping each other up among others which had been wrenched from the ground and unceremoniously dumped. The livelihoods of the farmers, reliant on the coconut palms were now in tatters along with the trees.

As they left the outskirts and drove into the rural areas, the number of buildings diminished, although the devastation had continued. The settlements of wooden shacks which had lined the highway hadn't been spared Yolanda's might. Sheets of corrugated iron and timber littered the ground, in most cases only struts indicated where homes had once stood. Villagers had collected together debris to form shelters for their families and salvaged coconuts to feed them. They too were hungry and thirsty, travelling into the city to try and find food and water.

Izel slowed the motorbike and turned inland towards their farm. He tensed as they drew closer. He stopped the bike and both men dismounted, removed their helmets and surveyed the scene in front of them.

The storage barns had collapsed. Rice grains from split bags spilled onto the ground like millions of tiny white beads. Sacks were scattered across the fields and abandoned where the storm surges had dragged them. The water hadn't been as high here as they were further from the coast. However, seawater had still seeped its way into much of their stock, ruining the rice. Many of the sacks which had survived the salty water, hadn't escaped the rain.

They made their way to the pig pens. Two weeks ago, two of their four sows had been suckling their young. With no food or drinking water the milk had started to dry up and only the strongest piglets had survived. The metal railings of the pig sty had endured the bashing from the typhoon and had kept the animals imprisoned. Izel opened the gate, the animals shuffled out to drink from rainwater puddles and snuffle for any morsels they could find.

Izel sighed as he tried to weigh up their options. He pulled back the tarpaulins they had secured before the typhoon, it seemed such a long time ago now.

'What do you think, dad? Could we salvage some of the rice?'

'We'll need to sort which is rain damage and which has been subjected to salt water. Maybe twenty percent will still be edible. We won't be able to manage this alone, son, we'll need to get the workers back.'

'Yes I think you're right.' Izel tugged at the hairs on his chin. 'We won't be able to pay them with money, but I'm sure they'll take rice. Some of those piglets won't survive. We can slaughter them and share out the meat as well. It's not as if we could store it.'

Leaving his father to start sorting through the damage, Izel kicked the motorbike into life. He rode back the way they'd come to try and find as many workers as he could muster. He couldn't offer them water, but he felt sure they would be happy to work for food.

When he returned an hour later, his father had started to lay out tarpaulins for them to spread the wet rice. Workers started to appear. They worked side by side for five hours sorting and spreading. Izel slaughtered the weaker piglets and butchered them. He handed out meat and rice to the men at three o'clock when they'd finished for the day and arranged for them all to return the next day. He wrapped up his share of pork and rice, plus some for his brother-in-law's family and they set off back towards Tacloban, exhausted. They were just outside Tanauan when he suddenly brought the bike to a skidding halt. His father's head knocked into the back of his helmet.

'What the...'

Izel stared at a young girl in a pink and white polka dot vest and shorts. He jumped off the bike and ripped the helmet from his head. The motorbike crashed to the ground. He barely heard Rogelio's angry shouts behind him.

'Lika Faye, Lika Faye, it's me, daddy,' he yelled as he grabbed the girl in front of him. She spun round and he dropped her arm as he realised it wasn't his daughter. He knew it was the same outfit he had seen Lika Faye wearing on the morning of the typhoon. The child in front of him started to scream for her mother. Within seconds she appeared and picked up her daughter, demanding to know what Izel was doing.

'Where did she get these clothes?'

Surprised by the question the woman stammered: 'Erm, they... erm it was...' She recovered and went on: 'not that it's any of your business, but they were handed to us the other day. The woman said her daughter wouldn't need them anymore.'

Izel's heart pounded harder as she said the words 'her daughter'; it was his daughter. He was sure.

'They were my daughter's clothes. Lika Faye's clothes. What did the girl look like?' He cursed he hadn't brought the photograph from the house with him.

The woman's voice softened, 'I'm sorry I didn't see her clearly, she was in front of the woman and had a cloth over a face. The smell was so bad.' Her face clouded, 'It wasn't her mother?'

Izel shook his head. It didn't make sense, who was this woman? If she had found Lika Faye why hadn't they come to the convent in search of them?

'And the woman, did you know who she was? What did she look

like?'

'I didn't pay her any attention. I only saw her for a moment and her face was covered too. I'm sure your daughter will turn up.' She gave him a feeble smile and turned away leading her daughter by the hand.

'What was that all about, Izel?' his father asked as he approached the bike. Izel recounted the exchange, expressing his bewilderment at Lika Faye not coming to the evacuation centre. He thumped his helmet on his thigh in frustration.

'And this woman was sure it was Lika Faye she saw?'

'Well, no. She didn't exactly see her, but it's her clothes, dad. I would put my life on it.'

'Son, I know how much you want to believe she's still alive, we all do. But there's no proof it was Lika Faye and those clothes, well, are you even sure it was what she was wearing that morning? Everything happened so quickly, can you trust your memory? And it could just be coincidence, other kids would have had the same vest and shorts.'

'I'm telling you, dad, it was her, I know it.'

He wrenched his helmet back on and mounted the bike. Rogelio shook his head and climbed up behind him.

After dropping his father at the hospital, Izel took the motorbike back to Brian. He handed him a share of the rice and pork and filled them in on the state of the farm.

'I heard today that the Smart mobile network is working again, Izel,' Brian informed him.

'It'll be a while before I'll be using it. My phone was lost along with everything else. And I don't have the money to buy a new one,' he replied glumly.

'We need to find somewhere to recharge ours before we can use it, the battery's dead. If we get to speak to Adelaida later, can we give her a message from you?'

Izel thought for a moment. Should he ask if Adelaida could

remember what Lika Faye had been wearing on the morning of the typhoon? No. She was already angry with him for not going to Cebu and she had made her mind up about their missing daughter.

'Tell her I'm sorry and give my love to Angelina,' he said. 'Say we were at the farm today and we may save some of the rice.'

Brian walked out into the street with him and handed Izel a couple of hundred pesos.

'I know it's not much, Izel. It's all I can spare. At least you can use the jeepney to get to and from the farm. I need my bike, I'm sorry.'

Izel took the money. This was no time for pride.

'Thanks, Brian. I'll pay you back when we sell the rice, and thanks for your bike today.' He smiled and headed off in the direction of the hospital. As he walked through downtown Tacloban, amid the chaos, people were rebuilding their lives. Izel noticed the sound of generators as they spluttered and throbbed. Hand-written notes on bits of cardboard were taped to windows and offered mobile phone recharging services at ten pesos a device but it was another sign which caught Izel's eye. "Copying service, two pesos a sheet". A thought occurred to him. Tomorrow after working at the farm he would bring Lika Faye's photograph and get it copied. He would be able to post them up, maybe someone would recognise her and know where she was.

***

Each morning for the next week Izel and Rogelio made the journey out to the farm to salvage as much of their crops as possible. Painstakingly they dried and re-packaged the rice. Each afternoon they set up outside the church and sold kilo bags to those who could afford it. Izel hated taking money from people who had so little left, but he had to find a way to survive. To ease his conscience he always filled the bags with more than a kilo.

He had copies made of Lika Faye's school photograph and added it to the picture board of missing people at the government offices. He put it up in police stations, shop windows, the hospitals. Every couple of days he returned to see if anyone had left a message with Lika Faye's whereabouts. As he approached the police station in Tanauan, he noticed a policeman staring at the photograph. His heart raced, did he know something? Had he seen her? The man turned suddenly as Izel called out to him.

'It's my daughter, she's missing. Have you seen her?'

The policeman turned back to the photograph, a puzzled look on his face, he turned back to Izel, opened his mouth to say something, then apparently thought better of it. Shuffling his feet and staring downwards he shook his head.

'I thought maybe I'd seen her sir, but I'm sorry no, I was wrong.' He quickly turned on his heel and headed into the police station.

Izel let out a heavy sigh and kicked at the wall. Anger and frustration raged inside him. Someone, somewhere must have seen her, he was not going to give up.

CHAPTER TWELVE

Lika Faye looked up from her mattress as the basement door lock clicked. She swallowed nervously as she watched the horrible man from the previous day waddle in. The four older girls sighed. Wearing cheap, short, low cut dresses they hobbled on ridiculous heels to the entrance. Phil stepped to one side as a man followed him in. Marianne snaked her arm around the man's neck, flirting and seductive, claiming him for herself. When he nodded and smiled his toothless smile, she led him away giggling to one of the small, functional cubicles.

Lika Faye opened her mouth to ask Phoebe what was happening. She stopped abruptly when she saw the warning look on her new friend's face. When all four of the older girls had been claimed by a man and had taken them behind the black curtain, Phil closed the door and turned his attention to the younger girls.

'What are you waiting for? Time for work!'

He pulled a key chain out of his pocket and unlocked the padlock. The girls filed in, each of them going to a laptop and switching it on. Lika Faye hesitated in the doorway, trembling and uncertain of what was expected of her.

'Come along, girl, time is money.' Phil pushed her roughly. 'Sit with Phoebe, she'll show you what we do here, until I set up your own computer.'

Lika Faye frowned and looked around her, unsure of what to make of the room. A worktop ran the length of one wall, on it sat half a dozen laptops. Bella, Monique and Phoebe each sat at one, already tapping the keys. At the other end of the room was a rail, with an array of clothes hanging from it. On the shelves beside it she could see make-up and some other objects she didn't recognise.

Phoebe hissed at her, beckoning her to come and sit down.

'Don't make him angry,' she whispered. 'He'll make us work longer if he's angry, or sometimes if we make him really mad, he'll get Ratface to make us eat hot peppers.' She stuck out her tongue and shook her head at the memory. 'They burn your mouth for hours and then it burns when they come out the other end too. So we must talk quietly all the time and when we have a customer we must tell him so he can get ready.'

'Get ready for what? What are you doing, Phoebe?'

'Okay, so we have to find men online. They're all from far away. I have a lot of American boyfriends.' She smiled proudly. 'Maybe one day one will like me so much he'll want to marry me and will pay Mr Phil my debt so I can go and be with him.'

'What debt? I don't understand.'

'I'll explain about that later, now you must learn quickly to keep Mr Phil happy. Look.'

The two girls hunched together over the laptop as Phoebe started to type:

BigboyTx: asl?

12 f Cebu: 12, f, Philippines.

12 f Cebu: u?

BigboyTx: 59, m, Texas, usa

12 f Cebu: ok

BigboyTx: What are u wearing, dear?

12 f Cebu: What u like

BigboyTx: U do show?

12 f Cebu: Yes

BigboyTx: How much?

12 f Cebu: 15 mins $50

BigboyTx: ur expensive, what u do for so much money, dear?

12 f Cebu: What u want

12 f Cebu: u transfer money?

BigboyTx: I wanna see u first.

12 f Cebu: sorry, sir, I only do show for money

BigboyTx: kk, give me transfer details, u better be good, I'm horny.

'What are you talking about Phoebe? What do you mean show? Who is he?'

'Shhh. I told you already.' Phoebe looked over her shoulder. 'Mr Phil will be angry if he catches us talking. Stay here.'

Lika Faye watched as Phoebe left her laptop and went to get Phil. While he organised the money transfer with the customer, Phoebe led Lika Faye to the end of the room with the clothes rack.

'Mr Phil, he taught us how we should act,' she struck a pose, index finger on her chin, eyes skyward, hand on hip, chest out. 'And how to make the customer happy,' she explained to Lika Faye. 'Sometimes they only want us to dance naked. I don't mind that so much, other times they want us to put things inside us,' she pointed to the objects on the shelf, 'or to touch ourselves. That's pretty gross.' She pulled a face. 'See the computer there? That's where we see them and they can see us.'

Lika Faye felt sick. She couldn't believe what she was hearing. Tears welled up in her eyes. What was she doing in this nightmare? She was going to have to perform for men on a screen. It was crazy.

'Hey, Lika Faye.' Phoebe crossed the room to her, a frown on her face. 'It's not so bad. The first time is a bit, well, weird. I was so embarrassed, but after that it's okay. I mean, at least they're not actually touching us,' she whispered.

Phil shoved past the two girls. He picked out some clothes and a feather boa from the clothes rack and threw them at Phoebe then went to set up the webcam. By the time Phoebe had changed, a skinny, balding man had appeared on the computer screen.

'Hello, dear, you look nice, can you dance for me?'

Phoebe started to prance around in the oversized platform shoes and a flowery dress Phil had picked out for her. She swirled the feather boa over her head, then enticingly over her small prepubescent body.

Lika Faye watched open-mouthed. A feeling of terror crept through her. She turned away. She couldn't understand that Bella and Monique continued to stare at their computer screens and tap at the keys, as if nothing was happening. Behind her, Lika Faye could hear the man from the screen directing Phoebe's performance, intermingled with grunts and moans.

After what seemed like a lifetime, it went silent. Over her shoulder she watched as a naked Phoebe put on her shorts and vest. She put away the props and returned to her laptop, dragging Lika Faye with her.

'You probably won't have to do that today. Mr Phil will need to set up your accounts and teach you to pose like me first. But tomorrow, you'll have to get some customers or you'll make Mr Phil very angry and then we will all suffer.'

'What are you whispering about?' said Phil as he banged their heads together.

Startled, the girls turned to the fat Australian. An oily film of sweat had formed on his skin. He was shirtless, only wearing a pair of navy shorts; over the waistband his grey belly hung and wobbled as he shuffled across the room.

'Get back to work,' he cuffed Phoebe across the ear and scratched at his crotch.

'You,' he prodded Lika Faye's shoulder. 'Come with me.'

Lika Faye looked at Phoebe in terror, but she was already staring at her computer screen and typing. Dragging her feet, Lika Faye followed Phil and stood beside him as he sat in front of a laptop. She tried to follow what he was saying about chat rooms and dating sites and her username, but it made no sense to her. He spoke too quickly and his accent was strange. She knew a little about computers, but this was all new to her. She started to feel faint and reached for the back of Phil's chair to steady herself.

'Faye...are you listening?'

She opened her eyes to see Phil's angry face staring at her.

'I'm...I'm sorry... I don't understand,' she sobbed.

'Oh for fuck's sake! Get a chair and we'll go through it again.'

She sat at the laptop following Phil's instructions, using the name he had registered for her: 11_f_leyte.

'Okay, I've had enough, go and sit with Phoebe and watch what she does. You better learn fast, I'll be expecting you to start earning me money tomorrow night.'

Lika Faye stood up and nodded to him: 'Ahh, ye...yes Mr Phil.'

He licked his lips and grinned at her before grabbing her chin tightly in one hand.

'Such a pretty little face. I think you're going to bring in a lot of money and who knows maybe I'll get some pleasure from you too, when the time is right.'

Neither of them had heard Rosela enter the room.

'She's a bit young for you, Phil, isn't she?' Rosela put a possessive hand on his shoulder.

Lika Faye hurried to sit with Phoebe but could feel Rosela's dark eyes burning into her back.

'What?' Phil said crossly. 'Why aren't you upstairs letting the punters in and collecting their money?'

'I was only bringing you a cold beer, Phil.' She smiled at him as she handed him the can. 'Just looking after my man.'

Lika Faye shuddered at the look Rosela gave her as she uttered the words.

Phil snatched the can from her. 'Thanks,' he mumbled gruffly. 'Now get back upstairs. How many are waiting?'

'Six, all the girls are busy at the moment.'

'Well get back to work then. And don't go telling me who's too young for me, okay?'

Lika Faye could hear Rosela's footsteps as she marched across the room. She stopped at the door and gave Lika Faye a chilling stare.

That evening Lika Faye watched as the other three girls called Phil at various times to arrange fund transfers when they had a customer ready to pay. With a dead look in their eyes they took up position in front of the webcam and another customer gave them instructions on what acts they wanted the young girls to perform. Phil called Lika Faye over each time to watch the performances. He laughed at her as she wriggled uncomfortably in her seat and tried to turn away in disgust.

'Get used to it, pretty girl. It'll be you up there tomorrow night. Better watch and learn.' He belched, the smell of stale beer washed over Lika Faye making her feel sick. He crumpled up a beer can and threw it, missing the bucket. It lay with half a dozen others, littering the floor.

Lika Faye's eyes were gritty and she felt exhausted when Phil yawned loudly and decided to call it a night. He switched off the computers, ushered the girls out of the room and clicked the padlock back on the door. He lumbered past the mattresses, punched the code on the door and disappeared up the stairs.

A single bulb lit the cold rice and water waiting at the bottom of the stairs for them. The older girls were already sleeping. Lika Faye sat on Phoebe's bed, as they scooped the rice into their mouths with their fingers and drank thirstily of the water. After eating they lay side-by-side, whispering in the darkness and listening to the murmurings of the others as they dreamed.

'How long have you been here?' Lika Faye asked.

'I don't know. It was August when I got here. I remember because it was just after my twelfth birthday. What month is it now?'

'Erm, November. Where are you from, did they take you too?'

'I'm from here in Cebu. My dad sold me to Mr Phil. My mum died about a year ago. My dad used to come here to see the older girls, still does sometimes. But he's a drunk and he needed money for booze so he asked Mr Phil if he wanted me.'

'Your own dad?' Lika Faye thought of her father, he would never do such a thing. She was sure he would be looking for her in Tacloban or Cebu. She had no idea where he was but he would never abandon her like Phoebe's dad. She sighed. He'd never find her here though.

'So why are you here then, if your dad didn't sell you?' Phoebe said indignantly.

'Miss Rosela. She found me after the typhoon.' Lika Faye told her story until neither of them could keep their eyes open any longer and drifted off to sleep.

***

Phoebe was right. The first time Lika Faye had to perform for a customer, she was filled with shame and disgust as she took off her clothes and did his bidding. She was so embarrassed to be undressed in front of the camera, Phil and the other girls. As the evening progressed, she was told to touch herself, dance, even smoke a cigarette naked. She had coughed as she had tried to copy what she had seen Marianne do. She felt light-headed and sick, the taste was disgusting. But after the first night, it didn't seem so bad. She became numb, like the other girls. She began to resign herself to the fact that this was her life for now.

Phoebe had told her each of the girls had a debt to pay off. In her case, it was the amount Phil had paid to her father. Each day she was there, the amount grew as interest was added.

'Then there's the cost of food and a bed. Ratface adds more if we have to see a doctor or need medicine. But we earn fifty pesos a week and once our debts are paid off, we'll be free,' she said with a flourish.

Marianne scoffed at Phoebe as she listened to the explanation. 'You don't believe that old witch do you, Phoebe? You really are stupid!'

'Well, Marianne, it's what she told me. Just because she doesn't speak to you, there's no need to be rude,' Phoebe replied haughtily.

'Oh, Phoebe, she tells us all that. If you ask her how much you've paid off or how long you have to keep working, she always tells you there's a long, long time to go. We'll only leave here when we're too old to work,' said Rebecca gently.

'Shut up, shut up! I don't believe you, I'm not listening,' Phoebe had covered her ears and started to hum.

The older girls shook their heads and carried on smoking their cigarettes and playing cards. One of Marianne's customers had smuggled the pack in last week, it had given them something to do when they weren't working and the lights were on.

The daily monotony was broken from time-to-time when Rosela ordered a couple of the girls upstairs to do chores: laundry, cooking and cleaning. They were watched closely by her, receiving the whip of a stick to the back of their legs if she felt they were being lazy, which she did frequently. At least it was an opportunity to get out of the dark, dank basement for a couple of hours and see some sunlight. Lika Faye had mixed feelings whenever her name was announced. The chance to get some fresh air was diminished by the amount of beatings she got at the hand of Rosela. Far more than the other girl she was teamed with. She tried to work harder, to please the woman, to reduce the number of bruises she returned to the basement with, but nothing she did was ever enough.

'Why does she hate me so much?' Lika Faye said to no one specific after one particularly brutal beating.

'She doesn't like the way Phil talks about you,' said Lourdes. 'I heard them arguing last week, when Jenny and I were doing the laundry. He must have noticed the bruises on your legs and was having a go at her. She was screaming at him how he goes on about Faye this and Faye that. In the end he hit her to shut her up. Did we get it when she came back into the kitchen.'

'But I don't do anything...it's not my fault,' snivelled Lika Faye.

'Yeah, like it's going to make a difference to Rosela,' jeered Marianne.

'What can I do?'

'Nothing, kid, get used to it is my advice. It ain't ever gonna change until Phil takes a shine to another girl, then it's her turn. Rosela is just a jealous, bitter, fucking bitch,' said Marianne as she lit another cigarette.

'I heard from one of the older girls, before they threw her out, Rosela was like us once.' All eyes turned to Jenny. The eldest of all the girls in the basement, she rarely spoke. When she did, everyone listened, including the usually disinterested Marianne.

Jenny looked from one to the other before continuing. 'Yeah, so she was like one of Phil's first girls. Not sure how she made it upstairs, but she was one of his favourites. It was always her he called on when he wanted some jiggy jiggy! Made sure all her customers used condoms. He found out one of them hadn't once and nearly beat him to death. Well that's what I was told anyway.'

The basement was silent as the girls considered this piece of news and waited for more, seven pairs of eyes staring at Jenny.

'What?' she looked back. 'That's all I know.'

CHAPTER THIRTEEN

A month after typhoon Yolanda had ripped Tacloban apart, Izel, Rogelio and Lorna were summoned to a meeting outside Our Lady of Assumption Catholic church. The priest and a handful of relief aid representatives addressed the twenty-eight families gathered in front of them.

'Hi to you all, my name is Mary. We are pleased to announce you have all been allocated temporary accommodation in the Assumption Academy tent city here in Tanauan,' the representative informed them. 'We know this will not replace your homes, but at least you will have a bit more privacy than sharing the church with a hundred other people,' the exhausted relief worker continued. 'If you would like to follow me, my colleagues and I will assign you your tents.'

One hundred and thirty-eight people, collected their paltry belongings and made their way across the square to their new homes.

'The water in this bladder is for cooking and washing.' Mary pointed to a huge container with several NGO banners beside it, specifying who had donated towards its installation.

'It will save having to walk to the stand pipe at the other side of town all the time,' said one of the women.

The throng nodded and murmured their approval.

'There is a plaque on each tent. It has the family name and number of people residing in it. If things change you need to let your Evacuation Centre Manager know so we can update our records. Her name and telephone number are on the banner at the entrance to the city,' said Mary. 'Or if anyone is sick or leaves, we will need to have that information, so please let her know.'

They walked past the Emergency Response Haiyan banner, it detailed how many women, men and children would reside in the tents.

'Look,' said Lorna. 'It says we have eight latrines, oh but no bathing facilities or kitchen counters.'

For the past month they had been using saucepans over open fires fuelled by scavenged wood. With no electricity and no other facilities it looked as if that method would continue for some time.

'Drinking water and food will still be handed out at your usual distribution centres. Are there any questions?' Mary's expression showed she hoped not.

'How long will we be here?' one of the women, cradling a baby, asked.

Mary sighed wearily. 'I'm sorry I can't answer that. You will have to talk to your Barangay Captain to find out what provisions are being made for people who lost houses within the new exclusion areas.'

Some other questions were asked and answered to Mary's best ability before the relief workers consulted their clipboards and called out family names to give them their tent number and show its location on the map. When they'd finished, they climbed into their 4x4, leaving the families to settle into their new homes.

Lorna, Rogelio and Izel followed the map to their new home.

'It says five people in the name of Sombilon, Izel,' said his mother as they checked the plastic identification tag.

'Well, yes, I registered Adelaida and Angelina when they came round taking names.'

'Are they coming back then?' Lorna asked her face lighting up.

Izel looked away. 'Erm...nothing has been agreed yet.'

'Oh, Izel, I'm sure they'll be home soon,' Lorna patted Izel's hand and laughed dryly looking round the empty canvas tent. The air was hot and stale. Sweat beads gathered on her forehead. 'Home! I suppose it's an improvement on the church.'

She busied herself taking a bag at a time and arranging their scarce belongings into piles. Rogelio watched as she struggled with her surviving arm and moved to help.

'I can manage,' she said a little sharply, then smiled up at him. 'Sorry, darling. I need to get used to this, you've got to let me do things on my own.'

He nodded and went to stand with Izel at the entrance of the tent. 'I think she finds it easier to adjust than I do. Has Adelaida said anything about coming back from Cebu?'

'Nothing certain, although I'll call her today and let her know we've moved out of the church. She knows about the farm and the other work we've been doing and that we do have a little money now.'

Izel and Rogelio, along with their farm workers had managed to salvage nearly fifty percent of the rice stock. It was no longer top quality, so they had had to sell it cheaply. A buyer in the town of Ormoc had taken nearly forty percent of it, enabling them to settle their loans and purchase a couple of mobile phones. A Buddhist organisation, the Tzu Chi Foundation had recently set up a 'Cash for Work' programme around Tacloban. They organised work parties of local people to start the clean-up process, paying participants. Once their work at the farm had finished, Izel and Rogelio had signed up, earning five hundred pesos a day.

'Now we've got somewhere to call our own, perhaps she could run her Sari Sari shop from here,' Izel pointed to the space at the entrance of their tent. 'We can at least afford to get some stock now. I'll call her later. I don't have any credit on my phone at the moment.'

'No time like the present, son. Why don't you go and do that now. Then we can help your mother with dinner. We don't want to leave it too long or we'll be cooking by candlelight,' Rogelio smiled at Izel, who nodded and set off to buy credit.

As he walked across the square he passed the plaza, where a few weeks earlier he had laid the body of Ellijah. Grass was already growing over the mass grave which the army had dug and filled with over seven hundred bodies. Soon there would be no evidence of what lay beneath.

Izel paused to watch some young boys flying their kites. He

smiled as he remembered Ellijah doing the same at home. His son had chuckled at the simple pleasure of tying string to the corners of a plastic bag and getting it airborne, then it swooping up and down as he ran round the garden pulling it behind him. The memory brought tears to Izel's eyes and made him yearn even more for the return of his wife and Angelina. As if to remind him of the day he had lost his son and his eldest daughter had been wrenched from his grasp, the scar on his left arm started to itch.

He sighed and as he did each time he walked past the plaza, said a little prayer for Ellijah.

He started off again, now in a hurry to call Adelaida. He realised living in a refugee tent wasn't the most glamorous of homecomings, but they should be together. They should start re-building their lives as a family.

He turned a corner, his mind on what he would say and almost collided with someone. It was Maria, the woman who thought she had seen Lika Faye on the day of the typhoon.

'Hi, Maria. I'm sorry, I nearly knocked you over there. How are you?'

'Izel. I'm okay, I'm living with my daughter in Palo, visiting a friend here.'

'Felipe?'

'He didn't make it. We found his body three days after Yolanda.'

'I'm so sorry.'

She nodded and smiled at Izel. 'It was a terrible time. Did you find Lika Faye and Ellijah?'

'Ellijah's body. No sign of Lika Faye, I'm so sorry if I scared you that day…'

'No, no, we were all desperate, no harm done. I wish I could have offered you more help. It has haunted me, not being sure if it was her or not. It did look like her, but without my glasses, I couldn't be sure. You've had no news at all?'

'Nothing certain, but I'm still hopeful.'

Maria patted his shoulder. 'Good luck.'

'Thanks Maria, take care.' He watched the woman continue on her way.

'Don't think I've forgotten you either, Lika Faye. I know you're out there. I will find you,' he muttered aloud, taking the meeting of Maria as an omen.

He desperately wanted his wife and Angelina to return to Tacloban, although he knew he would have to keep the searching for Lika Faye hidden from them. Things had got better with Adelaida now, but he knew she was still angry with him for not going to Cebu. He didn't want to risk upsetting her again by mentioning his beliefs about his eldest daughter. He would have to be careful. He had continued to put up her posters and had now added his mobile number to them. He had distributed about thirty around downtown Tacloban and Tanauan. He had received a couple of calls, but they had come to nothing so far. Although disappointed, he wasn't about to give up.

After purchasing credit for his phone, he called his wife. He listened as she told him all her news from Cebu before broaching the subject of their return.

'We were allocated a UNHCR tent today. It's in Tanauan. We have our own space now, Adelaida, please come home.'

His pleading worked and Adelaida agreed to return in time for Christmas.

The time passed slowly, but finally the day of their return dawned and he took a jeepney out to San Jose and met them at the airport. Angelina ran at him the moment she saw him. He picked her up and swung her around, relishing the sound of her giggles.

'Oh I've missed you, sweetheart, how you've grown in six weeks.' He kissed the top of her head as he set her down and went to help Adelaida with her luggage.

'Gifts from Auntie Imelda,' she explained as Izel raised his eyebrows at the bags surrounding her. 'She thought we might need clothes and food. We've been hearing how expensive things are here. There're also toys for Angelina and some bits and pieces for the... house.'

'That's very generous. Things are better than they were, but any help is welcome. You mum and dad have decided to stay with them?'

Adelaida nodded, biting her lip. 'They tried to convince me we should stay, should get you to come to Cebu. So many painful memories here, Izel.' Her eyes brimmed with tears.

Izel pulled Adelaida to him and put his arms around this wife and child.

'Thank you for coming home, I've missed you both so much,' he whispered into her hair.

They loaded the bags onto a jeepney heading to Tanauan. A lot had changed since Adelaida and Angelina had boarded the plane out of Tacloban.

'Is that what we'll be living in now?' Angelina pointed to a tented city as they left the airport. 'Mummy said we would be living in a tent.'

Izel smiled thinly and nodded. 'Yes, that's right, sweetie.' He turned to Adelaida 'I know it's not ideal, but we need to start somewhere. You can open your Sari Sari shop again. Mum and I bought some things to get you started,' he said.

'Mummy, look at the trees,' Angelina said pointing out the window. 'They look so sad, all broken.'

They stared out at the logoed tarpaulins and recycled corrugated iron sheets, being used as fencing, additional shelter or kitchens. Debris still littered the roadsides, but people seemed oblivious to it, rebuilding their homes around it. They arrived at the Assumption Academy tent city mid-afternoon. Hot, stale air billowed out at them as they opened the zip and entered their new home. Adelaida looked around at the blue canvas interior. Light shone in through the back where the canvas had been rolled and tied up. Izel brushed past her.

'There's some storage space here at the back,' he said. 'Mum and dad have been sleeping there,' he pointed to a mattress on the floor and raced on. 'These curtains can be let down in the middle here to make two rooms.

'Dad and I have managed to patch up some chests of drawers so you can put things away. Look Angelina, this is your bed.' He pointed to a corner. On top of the small mattress was the one-armed doll he had rescued from their home.

Angelina's face lit up. 'Fifi,' she squealed with joy and clutched the toy to her chest.

Adelaida sat heavily on their bed and screwed up her eyes. Izel's shoulders sagged and his chin dropped to his chest. The excitement he had felt at seeing them left him and he was filled with sadness.

'I'm sorry, maybe you should have stayed in Cebu. I was being selfish.'

Adelaida looked up him. 'No, we should all be together,' she said softly. 'Tacloban is our home. It's just a shock, Izel. Don't worry, we'll make it work.'

'I saw Maria,' he looked at the floor. 'You know, who thought she saw Lika Faye.'

He glanced up at Adelaida, a frown creased her forehead.

'She, er, she's living with her daughter in Palo now. Felipe didn't make it, but she seemed okay,' he rushed on. 'She said she was sorry she couldn't confirm it was Lika Faye. But that doesn't mean it wasn't, I mean…'

Adelaida stood and looked him in the eye. 'No more, Izel. No more nonsense about Lika Faye being alive,' she spoke so quietly he had to lean towards her to hear her. 'To move on, we have to accept she's one of the many that just weren't found. It's too painful to keep searching, to build up our hopes and then have them shattered again. Angelina still has nightmares. I don't want anything else upsetting her.'

Izel looked at the floor and nodded.

They were silent for a few moments. He shouldn't have brought the subject up so soon, Izel thought, he was such an idiot.

'Where are your parents?' Adelaida asked finally.

'Dad's in one of the Work for Cash parties, mum will be outside somewhere, probably gossiping.' He smiled, glad for the change of topic. 'She's recovered well from her operation and is constantly thanking God she survived. As you can tell,' he mopped at the droplets of sweat which had formed on his forehead, 'it's too hot to stay inside the tent during the day.'

***

Within two days Adelaida's Sari Sari shop was set up and doing brisk business. She welcomed back old neighbours who were also housed in the tented city as well as gaining new customers. Angelina very quickly settled into her new home and raced around with the other children.

When Christmas day arrived, the five of them dressed in the new clothes brought from Cebu to attend Mass. They remembered those who had lost their lives to Yolanda and thanked God for saving those who survived. The first festive season without two of their children was an emotional time for them all and despite exchanging small gifts they didn't feel like celebrating the birth of Christ with quite the same enthusiasm as previous years.

The mayor of Tacloban was keen to return children to education as soon as possible. News spread through the tented city that temporary classrooms had been erected at Tanauan school and it reopened on Monday sixth of January.

'Come on Angelina.' Izel waited impatiently outside the tent. 'You don't want to be late on your first day back.'

'Do I have to go? I don't have a uniform,' she whined from inside.

'I don't think you'll be the only one. Get a move on.'

Finally she emerged, her bottom lip stuck out in defiance. Izel ignored it and took her hand.

They walked through the battered school gates and could hear the shouting and screeching of children before they saw them. Long white canvas tents stretched out across the grass. Inside desks and chairs were lined up, ready for school to begin, in stark contrast to the outside. Chaos reigned as teachers battled to be heard above the babble of excited children running in and out of the damaged and roofless classrooms

'Look, daddy, it's Kimberly and Sheila Mae,' Angelina tugged at Izel's hand as she called to her friends.

Slowly the volume decreased as teachers restored order, lined up children into their classes and marched them into appropriate temporary classrooms. Izel watched as his daughter chatted animatedly to the other girls in her line. All reservations about returning to school had evaporated, his presence completely forgotten. He turned and wandered through what was left of the school. In some of the smashed buildings, homeless families had created makeshift shelters. Tarpaulins hung from ropes secured to the remaining walls providing limited protection from the rain.

Izel bent to pick up a text book lying open in a puddle. Muddy water dripped from the torn pages of fractions. He threw it among the smashed chalk boards on a classroom floor and stepped over broken desks and chairs strewn across the pathway. He entered one of the courtyards, which had remained almost intact to find a man with two huge cooking pots heating water on gas burners.

'Hi there,' he said. 'What you making there?'

'Hi,' the man looked up at Izel from his chopping. 'Lugaw for the kids lunch. I'm just waiting for the water to boil for rice, then I've got a few veggies to add and some ginger, of course.' His round, friendly face lit up as he smiled. 'Do you want to give me a hand?'

'Sure. My name's Izel, my daughter goes to school here.'

'Nice to meet you, I'm Raul. I'm a chef from Manila. I came

down after Yolanda to see if I could help. My cousins live here.'

As they chopped and stirred the cooking gruel, Raul told Izel how he had wanted to help after the typhoon. He had arrived mid-December with cooking pots and gas burners and as much food as he could carry. He had spent the past three weeks going out to the tented cities and feeding the children, apart from a trip home at Christmas to be with his family. Once he knew the schools were due to reopen he had met with Principals and agreed to provide lunches for the younger kids.

'I'm here for two days this week, then I move on to a school in Palo. I've taken some time off from the hotel restaurant where I work. I wanted to help and cooking is what I know.'

Raul's ambitious plan was to help out as many of the areas affected by the typhoon as possible. He was setting up soup kitchens in schools to ensure the younger children got at least one hot meal a day.

'If you're visiting all these schools,' said Izel. 'I wonder if I could ask you for some help?'

'Well, if I can, I will. What is it?'

Izel explained how he had lost his son and daughter on the morning Yolanda hit. How he was convinced that while Ellijah had perished, Lika Faye was still out there somewhere. Raul looked at him doubtfully.

'Man, if I can do something to help you find her, I will, but are you sure? I mean, what if your wife is right, you could keep looking and looking and never find her, won't you be stuck in a crazy loop?'

'Do you have children, Raul?'

'Two, boy and girl, they're a little bit older than yours: fifteen and thirteen.'

'And if something happened to one of them?'

The man nodded thoughtfully: 'Well, yeah, I guess, if you put it like that. What do you want me to do?'

Izel took out one of the posters of Lika Faye. He always carried a handful with him in case he saw opportunities.

'All I'm asking is if you're travelling round all these schools, maybe if you see her…my number's on the back.'

Raul slapped his new friend on the back. 'I promise I'll keep my eyes open for her, Lika Faye, is it?'

He took the poster and made some notes on the back, folded it and put it in his pocket.

'Put my number in your phone, Izel, just in case you find her, you can let me know.'

They continued to chat and cook until the Lugaw was ready, then switched off the burners to wait for lunchtime. Suddenly at noon, the squealing and shouting of children freed from a morning of lessons grew louder until more than a hundred of them erupted into the courtyard. They carried bowls, plates, even the drinks bottles handed out by relief aid agencies. Flustered teachers battled to be heard above the cacophony of shrill youngsters jostling for a place near the front. Raul grabbed a chair, mounted it and boomed at them.

'Hi kids, you ready for some Lugaw?'

'Yes!' they called back.

'I can't hear you. Put some effort into it!' Raul cupped his hands round his ears, a questioning look on his face. 'Try again. Are you kids ready for some Lugaw?'

This time a hundred plus kids screeched back at him: 'Yeeeessss'

'Okay then, listen to your teachers and line up and we can start dishing it out. There's plenty for all of you.'

There was some pushing and shoving as some of the more surly boys tried to edge their way nearer the front. Vigilant teachers seized hold of their elbows and guided them to the back of the queue. One at a time they approached the huge, hot cooking pots and waited while Raul or Izel ladled some into their container, then ran off into their little groups to devour the sticky rice meal.

After the last in the queue had been served, Raul and Izel mopping their brows with their tee-shirt sleeves, turned to each other, grinned and high-fived. A little hand pulled at Izel's shorts, he turned to see a small, shoeless boy looking sheepishly up at him, his emptied bowl offered upwards.

'Is there any more?' he asked.

As they looked around, a few children, mainly boys, were standing nearby, a look of uncertain hopefulness on their faces. The men stooped back to their pots and beckoned them over.

'First come, first served for second helpings,' called out Raul. The kids swarmed in; hot, free food was a luxury they couldn't afford to ignore.

Once the pots had been scraped clean, they took them to Raul's small red van and loaded everything in.

'I enjoyed today.' Izel felt the happiest he had been since the loss of his children. 'Helping out those kids, it's an amazing thing you're doing, Raul.'

'You know, some of the school principals I've been speaking to have said parents will be more inclined to send their kids to class if they hear they'll be fed there. Education is so important for these children to get on in life. If my doing this helps just one child, it's worth it. I'm not a religious man, Izel, but I was sent here for a reason, this has changed my life.' His usually smiling face had become solemn as he spoke, then a grin quickly reappeared. 'Anytime you fancy helping out, my friend, I'll be happy for the company.'

CHAPTER FOURTEEN

After the cold and rain of England, the heat and humidity of Tacloban were draining on Helen. However, the initial shock for her had been the state of the city and surrounding areas. Debris was piled high everywhere. Running water and electricity still hadn't returned and living conditions were desperate. She had never experienced such tragedy or adversity before. Nothing she had seen on television or read about on the internet had properly prepared her for the sheer extent of the damage. Despite the sadness it evoked, she marvelled at the resilience and positivity of the Filipino people. Although she was in Tacloban to help them, she felt they were helping her come to terms with her situation.

She and the WDR team spent their first couple of weeks taking up two rooms in a hotel with Hank's organisation. It was one of the larger NGOs supplying medical staff and equipment to the region. Hank had assured them they were welcome to stay until the end of December. A new team of doctors and nurses were arriving then and they would need the accommodation for them.

Ian, Ruth and Neil, used the experience they had gained in previous disaster areas to network with local NGO's. They started to formulate plans of how WDR could best put their funding and manpower to use. Helen tagged along to the meetings feeling completely out of her depth. After a couple of days she voiced her concerns to her roommate, as they shared a rare bottle of warm white wine they had managed to find.

'I feel I'm not contributing anything here. I don't know what I'm doing,' she said to Ruth.

'We all feel like that the first time,' she assured Helen. 'Don't beat yourself up. You'll pick it up. We're not expecting you to do anything but observe for now. Once we find some accommodation, that's when you'll start getting more involved.'

'Doesn't the sheer enormity of it get to you though? I mean where do we begin, can we actually make a difference? I'm so overwhelmed by the immensity of the damage. Or is it that once you've seen it before you don't feel that way?'

'Don't get me wrong. Every time you arrive in a disaster zone, you are hit by the destruction, how these people have been affected by it. But if we can help just a handful of them get back on their feet, we're doing our job. It's not only that. In these situations, the fact we are here is a sign people care. It helps with morale.'

As the days passed Helen started to feel more confident and got more involved with the meetings. She started to ask questions about finding suitable accommodation. She knew WDR would be looking to house up to twenty-five volunteers. They needed to find an appropriate building with affordable rent.

After Yolanda a lot of families had left Tacloban to go and live with relatives in unaffected areas. Many were people who had lost everything. However, some more well-to-do families had also abandoned homes which had been relatively untouched by the typhoon. Helen's task was to find owners who would be prepared to rent out their house for up to a year, the length of time WDR were anticipating being deployed in the Philippines. It took her several days of being consistently and frustratingly disappointed with viewings until she finally found something she thought could work. She burst into the room she shared with Ruth, a triumphant smile on her face.

'Where are Neil and Ian? I think I've found us a home.'

Helen showed them the photos she had taken with her Smart phone. She explained how she thought the big four-bedroomed house in the V&G area of the city could be what they were looking for. It was out of downtown Tacloban, but on a main jeepney route. They could be in the centre of the city within fifteen minutes. It was also within easy access of the Pan-Philippine Highway, enabling them to get to the badly affected coastal areas.

'It needs some work. The roof has been damaged, nothing

majorly structural. It leaks, but is fixable. There's a generator with the house, although it will need to be checked out. It's pretty old. And there are a couple of outhouses, which could potentially provide a bit more accommodation if we put in some time on them. I need to negotiate a better monthly rental, but I think it could be functional. We can all take a look tomorrow and if you guys agree, we could move in on the first of January.'

They took a jeepney to the house the next day. Corrugated iron sheets which had been ripped from the roof lay in the garden, twisted and rusting. Others hung precariously from the rafters. Inside, it needed a good clean. There was some water damage, apart from that it was habitable. Helen led the way inside to the entrance hall.

'Over there,' she pointed to her right. 'Are two bedrooms with en-suite bathrooms.'

They followed her to the back of the house to an open plan lounge and dining room.

'The kitchen is a good size. Look, lots of cupboards, enough for each volunteer to have their own shelf. Obviously none of the white goods are working. We could set up a couple of gas burners on the counter here.'

They walked back through the lounge to the left side of the house.

'These two bigger bedrooms could house about ten people in each if we can get some bunk beds made up. They'll have to share the bathroom, but there is a separate toilet. We'll have to bring in water from the hose outside. It's the only water supply at the moment.'

The predominant paintwork throughout was pale green. It reminded Helen of olive tree leaves. It came halfway up the walls and was then replaced with wallpaper, flocked pale green willow leaves on a slightly darker green background. Only the bathroom and kitchen were spared. Fortunately the house contained a lot of windows which gave the eyes a break from the décor.

'We'll need to give the curtains a wash,' she pointed at the beige material which had largely succumbed to grey mould due to the dampness from the leaking roof. After being shut up, a mouldy odour pervaded throughout, causing the visitors to wrinkle their nose in distaste.

'I know, I know. It needs some work and they're asking too much for the rent. But do you see the potential?' Helen asked expectantly after the other three had wandered around.

'I've stayed in worse!' said Ian. 'And I can see how we could make it work. It's a good size and there's plenty of space in the garden. If you can get them down on the rent, we'll take it. What do you guys think?' He looked at Ruth and Neil.

They nodded their agreement.

'We've got a week until we need to be out of the hotel,' said Ruth. 'It will give us time to clean it up a bit and start buying the things we need to make it functional for now. How long do we have before we start getting the first volunteer intake, Ian?'

'A month. I thought the beginning of February would give us enough time to find somewhere to live and identify some projects we can start working on,' said Ian. 'I've got about six people ready to book flights once I give them the go ahead. We can expect a steady trickle of others after that.'

Their enthusiasm grew as they spent the next couple of hours discussing volunteers and how they could adapt the house. It looked like they had found their base. Helen was thrilled. She felt she was starting to contribute and was now part of the team. After two months of despair and hopelessness, she allowed herself to feel some optimism.

With some negotiation, WDR managed to agree a rental amount they could afford and the owner was prepared to accept. They found a nearby builder's merchants. It had recently re-opened its doors with a limited stock of materials and they started the process of making the house liveable. They swept and mopped and washed the curtains in buckets in the garden.

'Look,' said Ian and nodded at the gate. Half a dozen young

children watched with curiosity.

'Come on in,' Ian beckoned at them.

They giggled and chatted excitedly to one another. Eventually the eldest boy took a few tentative steps into the garden.

'Whass your name?' he asked Ian.

Now braver, the others followed behind. Before long they were helping, although much of that appeared to comprise water fights and laughter more than actual work.

Slowly their base took shape. Neil painted the letters WDR on the gate. Their neighbours, intrigued by what the foreigners were doing, called round with offers of help and welcomed them to the area. They even managed to locate an engineer who fixed the generator.

'With the price of diesel, we'll only be able to afford to use it every couple of days for an hour or two,' said Ian. 'But it will mean we can re-charge mobile phones and laptops. Don't get ideas of lights or a working fridge.'

'I'll start a search for candles, we might need a few,' laughed Helen.

'And buckets. We're going to need buckets of every size to transport water,' suggested Neil.

'I was thinking I'd get some scoops too. We can use them to pour water over us for showering.'

Finally after a week, they had cleared two bedrooms and the living area and had moved in.

'Ta-dah,' Helen and Ruth emerged onto the front terrace with plates of food. 'Our first meal in our new home.'

They clinked bottles of warm beer in celebration and tucked into their rice and chicken dinner.

Helen had her work cut out for her. She found carpenters to make bunk beds. She cleared the other two bedrooms: random children turning up to assist from time-to-time. She located suppliers of water and food. Her time was filled with readying the house, meeting people and organising deliveries. It was only when she collapsed into bed she had time to think of Charlie. Then the tears would start, until exhausted, she would fall into a deep sleep.

One evening after dinner, the four of them were sitting in candlelight on the terrace. Ian had been to an NGO meeting and was telling them about some of the workshops which were being offered by the various organisations.

'Back in the UK I was working with an organisation involved in human trafficking, I'd be interested in going to the workshop about it here,' said Helen.

Ian consulted his list: 'That one's being held on Friday. I'll call them tomorrow and if they still have places, I'll book you on it. Anyone else?'

On Friday morning Helen waited near the market for the next jeepney to arrive. At that time of day they were filled to bursting. Young men hung off the bars at the back, others sat on the roof. Finally one stopped and the passengers inside squashed even tighter together to make enough space for Helen to clamber in and sit down. A few of the women nodded and smiled at her. The young man next to her started a conversation asking where she was from.

'Para!' shouted one of the passengers clinking a coin on the metal rail which ran the length of the vehicle, the sign she had reached her destination. The jeepney braked and as the stout middle aged woman went to get off, she patted Helen on the arm. With a toothless smile she thanked her for coming to Tacloban to help them. Helen nodded and smiled back. Her eyes prickled and she was suddenly filled with emotion for these people who had lost so much and yet were so determined to rebuild their lives. She shook her head and wiped angrily at the tears, seeing the concerned looks from the people sitting opposite her.

When they reached downtown Tacloban, Helen called out and tapped on the metal rail. She was outside Stephanie's Place, one of the few eating places which had reopened. After a five minute walk she found the building where the talk was being held. She introduced herself to the other attendees waiting by the tea urn. The phut, phut phutting of the ubiquitous generator seeped in through the open doors and windows while they named the organisations they represented. Finally a man, looking hot and harassed, bustled in. His arms were full of papers and folders. A black laptop bag emblazoned with his NGO's logo was slung over his shoulder.

'Sorry. Sorry I'm late,' he apologised to the waiting group, waving them into one of the seminar rooms. 'I'll be with you in just a moment. I need to connect up my laptop,' he said as he inserted connectors and switched on his computer. The logo from his bag, Ménage des Enfants, filled the screen behind him.

Helen looked to the screen then back to their presenter. He was tall and slim with a mop of unruly, curly blond hair. There was a faint trace of stubble on his chin and he had a slight accent when he spoke. Dutch, thought Helen.

'Okay, let's get started,' he announced. 'My name is Pieter Van de Berg and I'm from Holland.'

Helen smiled to herself and looked down. She had got the accent right. When she looked back up, he was staring straight at her. Her cheeks flushed pink, as if she had been a naughty schoolgirl.

'I work for Ménage des Enfants. We are predominantly concerned with trafficked children, although we aren't limited to that. We work with any trafficked individuals: men, women and children.'

His presentation covered the increase in the numbers caught up in trafficking and how vulnerable people in disaster areas are unwittingly recruited into the slave trade.

'Particularly rife in the Philippines is something called webcam child sex tourism. With so much poverty here, some of it is done voluntarily by young children to earn money, however, there are others who are being held against their will. They are forced to perform for people around the world. It's becoming increasingly popular because the person paying can direct the child to do what he, or it can be a she, wants them to do. It's considered safe as it's difficult to trace who these people are. It is live, so not stored on computers like other types of pornography.'

Pieter went on to explain how predators would have come to Tacloban to find children or adults.

'They may have been told there were jobs for them in Manila or Cebu. Or in the case of vulnerable children, they could have been befriended by a recruiter and unwittingly found themselves trapped. Once there they're held against their will and made to work to pay off a fictitious debt. In some cases members of their family are threatened to make them work.'

After a coffee break, they were split into pairs and given tasks to work on. As there were eleven in the group, Pieter paired up with Helen. Her heart skipped a beat as he sat beside her. Now he was closer she could see his eyes were green, flecked with amber and his cheeky smile brought dimples to his cheeks.

When the workshop finished at lunchtime, Helen lingered behind. She wanted to talk to him some more about the webcam sex tourism trade. It was something she'd never come across before. It had disturbed her to hear such heinous people existed and they would take advantage of a disaster to recruit. Although a small part of her also admitted she just wanted to talk to him about anything.

They stood discussing the workshop for twenty minutes. Pieter looked at his watch.

'Sorry, I didn't mean to keep you,' Helen said.

'Actually, I was wondering if you would you like to grab some lunch? We could go to Stephanie's,' he said.

Two hours later, their lunch long finished, they were still sitting and talking in the humid, airless restaurant. The generator-driven fans were unable to create much of a breeze.

Pieter caught sight of the clock on the wall.

'Oh shit, I didn't realise the time. I'm so sorry, Helen, I must go. I've a meeting in ten minutes.'

'Yes, yes of course. Sorry to make you late.'

'Not at all. I'd like to continue our talk. Maybe we could arrange to meet again? If you want to, of course.'

They exchanged mobile numbers, Pieter promising he would call her to arrange something after the weekend. He stood and grabbed his things. Then he bent and kissed her on the cheek, before turning and walking out of Stephanie's. Helen felt the heat rise in her face. She put her palm to the spot he had kissed her and watched him confidently striding out of the restaurant. She chuckled to herself. It had been a very long time since a man had made her blush and Pieter had caused her to do it twice today.

Stephanie's was one of the few places with an internet connection. Helen decided to take the opportunity to Skype with Sarah; she had been sending texts and brief emails using 3G on her Smart phone, but hadn't had the chance to talk since arriving. She checked the time. It would be early morning in England.

'Sarah?' she asked of the tinny voice which answered. 'It's Helen.'

'Oh wow, Helen. How are you? It's so good to hear your voice. How's it going out there?'

They managed a ten minute conversation before the line became too distorted to understand one another properly.

'I hope you can still hear me, Sarah. Please give my love to everyone. I'll call again when I can.' Helen ended the call, left the restaurant and headed back to the house, a big smile on her face.

CHAPTER FIFTEEN

Time for Lika Faye passed in a haze, as it had done for all of them in the basement. With no means of marking the passing of days, she soon lost count of how long it had been since she arrived in the den.

Phil had been right. She had proved very popular with clients and had built up a lot of regulars. She was the biggest earner for webcam sex. She had also become his favourite. He didn't speak to her as harshly as he did to the others. When Rosela was out running errands, he would appear at the door, call her name and take her upstairs. He taught her how she should dance, stand, walk and undress to please her customers. Afterwards he would put on the television and let her watch cartoons. When he heard the scraping and groaning of the gate to the driveway, he would return her downstairs.

'No point in making Miss Rosela more mad at you, is there?' he said the first time he had brought her upstairs. 'This is our little secret. When you are up here with me and it's just the two of us, you can call me Uncle Phil,' he had grinned, a lewd look on his face.

Sometimes he would send her to the kitchen to get him beer or bring him his lunch. Lika Faye could see him gazing at her while she watched television. To her surprise and relief he only touched her when he was correcting the new poses he taught her. Even so, she found the time she spent upstairs with him unnerving. None of the older girls believed her when she told them he hadn't made any attempt to fondle her or have sex with her.

'Why else would he take you upstairs?' Marianne had said spitefully one day after she had returned to the basement.

'Ignore her,' Phoebe had pulled Lika Faye away from the older girl. 'She's only jealous, she would like to be Phil's favourite.' She stuck her tongue out at the older girl. She narrowly managed to sidestep a slap to the face as Marianne lashed out at her.

'Stupid little bitch,' she muttered and went back to her mattress for another smoke.

One day Lika Faye was summoned by Phil while Bella and Monique were already upstairs cleaning. Knowing Rosela closely scrutinised the girls while they worked, she started to tremble. She had come to accept the beatings she suffered at the hands of the jealous and embittered woman, but she knew if Rosela found out about the time she spent alone with Phil it would make matters worse. Lika Faye was filled with dread, her heart beat furiously as they got closer to the top of the stairs.

She crept soundlessly beside Phil, following him into the lounge. Her eyes darted from left to right scouring the house for Rosela. She expected to hear her rasping voice screaming abuse any second. She barely heard Phil's words as he explained how one of her clients wanted her to dance in the next webcam session. Her heart pounded in her ears.

'Faye! Did you hear me?'

She looked at him, then looked at the floor.

'Sorry, Mr Phil.'

'What on earth's the matter, girl. Haven't I told you it's Uncle Phil when we are alone!'

'But, Miss Rosela…' Lika Faye stammered.

'Oh don't worry about her. She's out. I sent her to get me more beer and to go to the bank. She'll be gone at least an hour.'

The hammering in Lika Faye's chest calmed.

'But Bella and Monique…' she looked up again at the fat Australian.

'Stupid woman thinks she's the only one who knows how to do things around here. How does she think I managed before she was up here,' he muttered. 'They're upstairs cleaning.'

Relieved she wasn't going to evoke further wrath, Lika Faye turned her attention to Phil. She listened to his instructions and practised the dance routine he explained. Once he was satisfied, he turned off the music and switched on the television. He pressed buttons on the remote control until he found the cartoon channel. It wasn't long before he grew bored and ordered her to get him a beer from the kitchen.

'Make sure it's one from the back, dear, and put it in a tinny cooler.'

Lika Faye crossed the hallway into the kitchen. She was about to open the fridge door when she caught sight of the two young girls. Monique was standing on a chair in a corner reaching for a tin. Lika Faye looked over her shoulder before whispering to them: 'What are you doing? If Phil finds you here, he'll be so angry.'

'It's where Rosela keeps her money. We saw her hide some there one day when she thought we weren't looking. We're running away,' Bella whispered.

'Bella, ssshhh.' Monique gave her younger sister a warning look as she climbed down with a fistful of pesos.

'She can help us,' Bella pleaded with Monique, her eyes wide.

'Wh…what…how?' Lika Faye frowned, looking from one sister to the other.

'Faye, where's my beer?' Phil's disembodied voice boomed from the lounge.

Lika Faye stared at the two girls.

'Sorry, Uncle Phil, I need the bathroom.'

'Well get a move on, I'm thirsty.'

'Yes, Uncle Phil.'

'What are you going to do?' She hissed at them.

'We saw Rosela type in the gate code last time when we were hanging out the laundry. She was letting in the water delivery boy. But the gate is so noisy, Phil will hear it. We won't have time to get far enough away before he realises it isn't Rosela coming back. We were about to give up trying to run away today, then we heard you. Can you distract him so he doesn't hear it?'

'Where will you go? You can't stay here, they'll find you and punish you.'

'We have an auntie in Tacloban. With this money, we'll be able to take the ferry and the bus,' Monique said.

Lika Faye longed to go with them. Hearing the word Tacloban made her even more homesick. She wondered if all three of them could make it. She saw the begging faces on the sisters in front of her. Maybe if she helped them, they would be able to bring help and set the rest of them free. She thought for a moment, then nodded.

'Okay, I have an idea. When you hear the music turned up really loud, run, run as fast as you can and bring help for us. Promise me you'll look for my mum and dad and tell them where I am,' she whispered.

The girls nodded solemnly and hugged her.

'Faye!' Phil's voice came from just outside the kitchen door. 'What are you doing? Did I hear voices? What's that chair doing there?'

As soon as she heard his voice, Monique quickly ducked down behind a kitchen cupboard, pulling her sister with her. Lika Faye glanced at them, then up at Phil.

'I erm, I was singing to myself, Uncle Phil and trying the dance. That's, that's why the chair's there. I'm so sorry. I wanted to get it right for you. I think maybe I need some more practice.' She looked at him imploringly, hoping he was buying it. She was sure her heart was going to give her away it was beating against her chest so hard.

He smiled down at her. 'Good girl, Faye, I'll grab my beer and we can try again if you want to.'

She backed across the kitchen towards the fridge. If he got to it, he would see the sisters.

'I'll do it, Uncle Phil,' she blurted. 'You get the song ready and I'll get your cooler too.'

Phil frowned at her and stepped closer. 'Is everything alright? You seem a little nervous, dear.'

Lika Faye licked her lips. 'Yes,' she glanced at the frightened faces of the sisters a metre away from her. Monique's hand was clamped tightly over Bella's mouth, as the younger girl, her eyes wide, could barely contain her fear. Lika Faye moved towards Phil, determined to block him from advancing any further. She dropped to her knees at his feet, hanging her head, desperate to buy a bit of time.

'What's the matter? Get up, girl.'

'I thought you might be angry I was taking so long. I was only practising. I just wanted to get it right.' She looked up at him, through her eyelashes, using one of the coy poses he had taught her to use for her customers.

'Okay, okay, come along on your feet.'

She jumped up and headed back to the fridge. She wrenched the door open and reached for a beer. Phil turned and shuffled towards the kitchen door. Lika Faye blinked and exhaled. She started to nod at the girls, then recovered quickly as she saw Phil turn back.

'Hurry up then,' he said.

She closed the fridge door. Her heart was still thudding wildly. She crouched down and took a cooler from the freezer. Making sure Phil was out of sight, she looked behind her.

'Get to the gate and when you can hear the music, go!'

She slammed the freezer door closed and strode out of the kitchen with more confidence than she felt.

No sooner had she handed Phil his beer, he lumbered off the sofa and started towards the door. Lika Faye's mouth hung open as she stared after him.

'Uncle Phil?' she said uncertainly.

'I'm going for a piss, watch your cartoons, dear. We'll try your dance again when I get back.'

Lika Faye slumped into a chair. There was nothing she could do. She feared for Monique and Bella when he caught them trying to escape. Her heart sank.

She heard Phil's voice, then Monique's. She couldn't hear what was being said above the television. She strained her ears but all she heard was the toilet door slam.

She sat frozen in the chair. If they didn't escape, they wouldn't be able to tell anyone she was being held captive here. She would never get out of this place. She looked up at Phil as he walked in.

'Lazy bitches,' he mumbled as he flopped back onto the sofa, his grey belly wobbling as he pulled himself into a comfortable position. 'They'll slack off if they're not watched.'

Lika Faye nodded, not trusting herself to speak. There was still hope.

'Right, I think we have time to run through this again a couple of times. Then those two should be finished. 'Bout bloody time too.'

Lika Faye spotted the remote control for the music on the coffee table. Before Phil had a chance to roll over to reach it, she snatched it up.

'I'll do it, I know how.'

He settled back down as Lika Faye punched at some buttons. She hoped it was not all in vain as the music blared out. The sudden rush of noise made Phil start before he covered his ears. Lika Faye could see his mouth moving but the volume drowned out his voice. She pretended to panic. She hopped from one foot to the other, then threw the remote away from her. It skidded across the floor and under a chair. Phil was desperately trying to haul his obese, flabby frame from the sofa, roaring angrily at the girl. Trying to appear she was helping, she ran over to the chair. She dropped to her knees pretending to fish it out from underneath. Phil finally got to his feet and lumbered over to her. He grabbed her shoulders and pulled her out of the way. He shoved the chair backwards and seized the offending item. The room went silent apart from Phil's laboured breathing.

'What...the....fuck....are ....you....trying....to....do....to....me!' He managed between breaths.

Lika Faye stayed in a heap on the floor. She strained for sounds of the gate. Despair overwhelmed her. Monique and Bella escaping had given her some hope she might get out of this hellhole. She was sure they hadn't had enough time to get out. Tears slid down her cheeks. Then she heard it. A clunk. It was barely audible above Phil's panting and swearing. She looked at Phil to see if he'd noticed it but he was too busy complaining.

'I'm so sorry, Uncle Phil.' She tried to look contrite, while inside she felt a bubble of hope rising through her body.

'I think we've done enough for today,' he managed finally, hauling himself up and straightening the chair. 'You'll have to practice on your own downstairs.'

He followed her down the stairs to the basement and locked her in.

It wasn't long before Rosela appeared in the basement doorway, agitated. The sudden brightness as the lights were switched on in the dark basement caused the girls to blink and shield their eyes, as they looked up at her from their mattresses.

'Bella? Monique?' the woman shrieked.

She was met with silence. The girls looked at one another, frowning. Rosela turned on her heel and slammed the door behind her.

Lika Faye smiled to herself. They had done it, they'd escaped. The appearance of Rosela confirmed the girls weren't upstairs. Now she only had to wait for them to tell someone and she would be saved.

CHAPTER SIXTEEN

Izel could feel the mood in Tacloban City was slowly changing. In the time since Yolanda had ripped through the Philippines people's attitudes had started to change from victim to survivor. Banners began to appear in shop windows, hanging from apartment balconies, tied to fence railings or strung between coconut trees: Tindog Tacloban – Rise Up Tacloban.

Day by day more shops were reopening, their stocks may have been depleted but they were ready again to do business. Robinsons Mall, where Adelaida had bought stock for her Sari Sari shop, had partially reopened. Electricity had still not been restored and the nights had an eerie darkness lit by flickering candles; occasional light spilled out onto pavements from a bar running a generator, but during daylight hours the city was regenerating.

'Adelaida, Adelaida?' Izel had been out looking for work.

'Did you find something?' Adelaida appeared from inside the tent.

'No, but I've just heard Gawad Kalinga are coming to Tacloban.'

Known throughout the Philippines as a movement to end poverty by providing housing to those in need, they were already building in Ormoc city.

'The rumours are they will build here in Tauauan. We might get one of the houses. They're saying we need to help with the building work, but in a few months we could have a real home again.'

People had started rebuilding as more materials began to find their way to the city. Coco wood suppliers had sprang up and felled trees were turned into planks and posts. Izel had watched in frustration as other people's destroyed houses became habitable again. Their own home was now in a build exclusion zone as it was too close to the sea. With the huge loss in income they had suffered on the ruined rice and lost pigs, he had no money to buy materials and no land. The Sari Sari shop was making a small profit and Izel was determined to find other work. However, they would need the money to buy seeds and pigs to get the farm working again. This latest news gave him some hope he may be able to provide his family with a home again and they would be able to move out of the tented city.

'I'm off to help Raul, he's at the school down the road.'

He kept in touch with Raul and when he had time, helped him with the school feedings. He enjoyed the man's company and admired what he was doing. Izel was ever hopeful a sighting of Lika Faye might happen.

When he returned to their tent later in the afternoon he found Adelaida in a foul mood. Her face was thunderous as she slammed tins and bottles down on the Sari Sari table, sighing angrily and grunting. He couldn't imagine what had changed in the few hours since he had left her. Normally an even-tempered woman, it was unusual for her to behave in this way.

'What's the matter? Has someone upset you?' Izel was concerned about her obvious fury.

'You could say that.' She stared at him, her eyes icy.

'What is it?' he touched her arm. She pulled away from him as if he had slapped her. 'What?'

'You tell me, Izel. What could I be angry about?'

He shook his head, racking his brain for something he could have done to affect such rage in his wife. He looked at her blankly, waiting for an explanation. Adelaida disappeared into the tent, returning a few moments later. She threw a piece of paper at him. He knew before he picked it up it was a poster of Lika Faye. His heart sank.

'What did we agree, Izel?' Her voice was low, barely above a whisper. 'You promised. You promised me no more. And then I find this in a shop window.' Tears started to roll down her cheeks. 'You don't think I don't miss her too? That I don't dream about her and Ellijah or hear or see something that reminds me of them, every single day. But we have to accept what happened to them.' She slumped to the floor, her body shaking from the sobs which wracked her.

Izel slid to the floor beside her. He took his wife's hand in his and stroked her hair gently.

'I'm sorry, my love. I don't mean to upset you.'

They sat in silence for a long time, both deep in their thoughts of their two lost children. Adelaida's sobbing slowly subsided and she wiped at her tears with her tee-shirt.

'You and Lika Faye always had a close bond, stronger than the other two. I know losing her has hit you hard, Izel.'

'I had her in my hand, her and Ellijah both. They slipped away from me. I'm their father and I should have been able to protect them.'

'It wasn't your fault, you did everything you could. You can't keep blaming yourself and you will never move on if you refuse to let her go. We still have a family, Izel. You have to make the most of what we have now.'

'But I can still feel her, Adelaida. I don't believe she's dead. I'm sorry. I know how you feel about this, but I know she's out there. I can't give up on her.'

Adelaida sighed heavily and they sat again in silence. Finally she got to her feet and looked down at her husband.

'I guess it's not my place to tell you what you feel, Izel. If this is what you need to do, I can't stop you. But please, I beg of you, no mention of this to Angelina. She's starting to return to normal, she's laughing and playing again. I don't want your quest to set her back. Okay?'

Izel stood, hugged his wife tightly to him and whispered in her ear: 'Thank you.'

He felt relief they had reached an understanding. He wouldn't have to keep his searching a secret from her any longer. He also respected her views and would keep his activities to himself.

'I was going to help Raul out again tomorrow morning. He's still at the school here. Do you mind?'

She smiled, stroked his cheek and shook her head.

***

As the two men prepared the Lugaw the next morning, they chatted comfortably and exchanged news.

'How long do you think you'll keep going with the school feeds, Raul?' Izel asked.

'As long as I can. As long as I still have money to do it, I guess. I didn't come with a set plan, it's just evolved. Actually, I have an organisation coming to speak to me today. They are interested in doing a joint project with me, apparently. We'll see.'

At midday the mad rush started as hungry children swarmed from their classrooms. They carried an array of containers in every shape and colour, eagerly awaiting their steaming ladle of rice and vegetables. An orderly queue formed. The youngsters squatted on their haunches excitedly chattering and laughing, patiently anticipating their turn to approach the cooking pots.

They were about a third of the way through the snaking line, when three foreigners wearing tee-shirts emblazoned with World Disaster Response Team logos approached them across the school yard. The two men stopped short of the queuing children to finish their conversation, while the woman approached him.

'Raul?' she asked Izel.

He smiled at her and indicated with his head while pouring hot Lugaw into a bowl. 'No, ma'am, he's over there.'

'Thank you. Great job you guys are doing here,' she said looking at the rows of expectant kids. 'You look like you've got your hands full.'

She walked over to the other pot.

'Hi. I'm Helen from WDR,' she looked down at her tee-shirt and smiled. 'But I guess you've probably worked that out! Have you got another ladle? I'll give you a hand.'

Raul pointed to his little red van parked behind him.

'In there, and could you bring me some of the spare bowls and spoons please. Some of these kids have forgotten their containers. They're on the passenger seat.'

Helen returned, handed the bowls and spoons to Raul and squatted beside him, ladle at the ready.

'Who's next?' she smiled at the little boy in front of her and carefully spooned the hot sticky food onto his plate.

'Salamad,' he said shyly and ran off to join his friends.

'That's a pretty girl in the photograph taped to your windscreen,' she said to Raul. 'Your daughter?'

'Err, no, actually that's Izel's daughter,' he said quietly nodding at the other man. 'She's still missing. I see a lot of kids and I said I'd keep an eye out for her when I'm visiting the schools.'

'On no, poor man. It must be terrible not knowing.'

They continued in silence until the queue diminished and second helpings had been dished out.

'Thanks for your help,' Raul said wiping his hand on his shorts and holding it out to Helen. 'Now we can be properly introduced. Raul!' he smiled broadly.

'Helen,' she said shaking his hand. 'A pleasure to meet you. We're hoping we can work together, let me introduce you to my colleagues.'

They wandered over to Raul's van, where Neil and Ian were waiting. While the three men talked about a possible joint project, Izel loaded the pots and burners into the van and collected the loaned dishes and spoons. When he had finished he stood patiently behind his friend.

Raul turned, grabbing Izel by the shoulders, and pulled him into the group.

'This is Izel. He comes and helps me when he has time. He's

from Tauauan,' he introduced him. 'He lost his home in the typhoon and is living in one of the tented cities.'

Izel smiled and shook their hands. 'Sirs, ma'am, I don't want to be rude,' he turned to Raul. 'I hope you don't mind,' then looked back at the WDR team. 'If you have any work? I'm looking for job, I can be driver, interpreter, anything.' He looked at them hopefully.

'Let me take your number, Izel. We could be looking for someone quite soon,' said Ian.

The two men swapped mobile numbers. Izel clapped Raul on the back. They exchanged a few words in Filipino, then saying his goodbyes, Izel left.

They watched him as he walked out of the school. Ian turned to Raul.

'What do you know about him?'

'He's a good man, hard worker. He used to have a rice and pig farm, lost most of it, his home, his son and daughter. Yolanda was tough on him, like so many people here.'

'Hmmm, well we might have something for him. I'll give him a call in the next couple of days when I've had a chance to sort out my budgeting.

'Raul, do you have time at the moment? Can we talk back at the house? I think we should discuss further how we could work together.'

Neil and Helen rode in the back of the little red van with the empty cooking pots. Ian and Raul sat in the front. Ian explained WDR's philosophy and the type of projects they liked to get involved with. By the time they reached the house, the outline of a joint venture was in the making.

Raul moved into the WDR house. Previously he had relied on friends of his cousins to find a bed for him, now he had a more permanent base. He also had a kitchen to prepare the pots of Lugaw. The World Disaster Response team learned how to make the rice dish and funded the ingredients. They also benefitted from Raul's chef's skills for their dinner.

Both parties had agreed the feeding programme should continue under Raul's supervision. WDR's involvement was to provide support through funding and volunteers to help with delivery and serving the food at the schools. They also discussed ways of developing it into a more sustainable project for the future. When Raul's van wasn't being used for feedings, it gave WDR a form of transport to get to meetings. They were still waiting for the arrival of the small passenger truck they had ordered. It had been promised at the beginning of January, it was now two weeks overdue.

***

A week after the meeting at the school, Izel received a phone call from Ian asking him to come to the house. He had a job proposition for him. Twenty minutes early for the meeting, Izel paced up and down the street outside the house, practising his English aloud and wringing his hands. Occasionally he stopped to tug at the sparse dark hairs on his chin. He finally got the courage to push open the gates and walk in. Ian was sitting on the terrace looking though a report and jumped up when he saw the slight Filipino approaching. Smiling, he shook Izel's hand, directed him to a chair and asked what he would like to drink.

'Thank you, sir, some, erm, water please.' Izel cleared his throat and sat on the edge of the seat.

'Call me Ian, I'll be right back.'

He returned with a glass and handed it to him. Izel took a sip and put it on the table, his shaking hand causing water to slosh over the edge.

'I'm so sorry, sir...erm, Ian.' He tried to wipe the offending drops off the table. He cursed inwardly, he was already making a mess of things.

'Izel, it's okay.' Ian touched the other man's arm. 'Take a breath, it's not a problem.'

Izel took a couple of steadying breaths and smiled timidly at his interviewer. 'I never done this before and I need job so bad.' The words tumbled out in a rush.

Ian sat back in his chair and smiled gently. 'Let me explain what we are looking for and we can go from there, okay?'

Izel giggled nervously and nodded.

Ian outlined the work they needed to employ someone to do. They were looking for a driver of their truck when it arrived. It would be needed to ferry volunteers to and from the projects as well as pick up and deliver supplies. They also needed someone who could work as a translator when required. As it would be a couple more weeks before the volunteers arrived, they would be looking for that person to help get the house ready until then. Izel listened carefully, bobbing his head. He concentrated on Ian's words, a solemn look on his face.

'What do you think? Are you the man for the job?'

'Oh yes please, sir…' Izel started.

'Ian.'

Izel giggled again, a high pitched nervous laugh. 'Sorry, Ian. I can do all those things. If you give me chance I will be best worker.'

They discussed salary, a trial period and for Izel to come back on Monday to start. Shaking hands, Ian said: 'Welcome to the World Disaster Response team, Izel.'

'Thank you, thank you so much, you won't be sorry.'

Izel almost danced out of the garden and into the street. He pulled out his mobile phone and rang his wife with the news, barely containing his excitement.

'I have a job, a proper job,' he sang down the line at her. 'I'll tell you the details when I get home, but I start on Monday. Our luck is changing, Adelaida.'

CHAPTER SEVENTEEN

It was a little after six o'clock in the evening. It was already dark as Helen walked towards the light spilling out of the restaurant and washing onto the pavement. She was shown to a table for two in Guiseppe's, downtown Tacloban. It was an Italian restaurant and one of the few open for business so soon after Yolanda. It was obviously popular with the relief workers. Only one table hosted Filipinos, the rest were speaking a myriad of foreign languages and clearly enjoying a change from rice and sardines.

Helen looked around and spotted a chalk board behind a cold counter housing white wine and desserts, it advertised the pizza and pasta dishes on offer. Menus weren't available and she could hear waiters reeling off the selection in English to other tables. Amid the chaos and devastation outside, Guiseppe's felt like an oasis. A large private generator ensured light and refrigeration and a modicum of air-conditioning. It offered temporary relief from the heat and humidity outside and gave Helen the chance to cool down after her hot journey in the crowded jeepney. Black square tables and chairs filled the big rectangular room. There was a staircase at one end leading to a second level. Loud chatter reverberated off the brick walls and chairs scrapped on the tiled floor as people came and went. It hadn't survived Yolanda unscathed. They only accepted cash, Helen heard a waiter explaining to a customer. The credit card machine had 'drowned' and as yet hadn't been replaced.

The owner, clearly a businessman, had worked hard to refurbish and reopen as quickly as possible. The rumour was it had taken him only two weeks to welcome back his first customers after the typhoon. It had paid off. A favourite for all the foreign workers, it was filled to capacity during open hours and today was no exception.

The aroma of wood oven pizzas washed over Helen. She closed her eyes and inhaled deeply. She wasn't sure what she craved most, the food or the thought of cold white wine. She had set off early from the house. She could never be sure how long she would have to wait for a jeepney. For once one had arrived immediately as she walked onto the road near the house. Now she found herself at the restaurant with twenty minutes to wait for Pieter. She couldn't resist the temptation of the chilled wine. She hoped her dining companion was happy with her choice. Then she smiled to herself. If not, she would have to drink it all. The idea was not an unpleasant one.

She caught the eye of a passing waiter.

'I'd like a bottle of the Sauvignon Blanc please.'

'Yes, ma'am.'

He dipped behind the counter and emerged with a bottle. Returning to her table he peeled the plastic covering from the top, inserted the corkscrew and drew a satisfying pop from the neck as he pulled out the cork. He poured a dribble into Helen's wine glass. She rolled the cold liquid around in her mouth savouring the cool temperature as much as the flavour. She swallowed, closing her eyes as it drained down her throat.

'That's fine,' she said. 'Actually it's a lot more than fine. It's delicious.'

Once again she was reminded of how much she had taken for granted before coming to the Philippines. A cold bottle of inexpensive white wine would not normally have been on her luxury list, now it was nectar. The waiter filled her glass and left her to enjoy it. Droplets of condensation streaked down the bottle in front of her. She was momentarily reminded of the rain she had watched on the window pane at home that fateful morning. She shook her head to ward off the memory. This was not the time or place. She was not going to let it spoil her evening. As she sipped gratefully from her glass, she thought back to Pieter's invitation.

He had called, as promised, after the weekend. He'd told her how much he had enjoyed their talk and would like to meet up again. How did she feel about dinner at Guiseppe's? Helen hadn't eaten there yet. She had walked passed it numerous times, thinking how much she would appreciate some Italian cuisine for a change. She'd liked the tall, confident Dutchman. He had a good sense of humour and she had felt very relaxed in his company. He was also extremely good looking. The decision hadn't been a difficult one.

What to wear had been more challenging. She had discussed it with Ruth, who had assured her anyone working in relief aid would only have a functional wardrobe. He wouldn't be expecting her to turn up in anything glamorous. She had settled on a calf length navy blue cotton skirt with a small white flower pattern and a sleeveless cerulean blue shirt tied in a knot at her waist. Her choice of shoes had been between flat sandals, trainers or a pair of Timberland steel-toed work boots. The sandals won. She had applied a line of black Kohl pencil under her eyes and some waterproof mascara; the only make-up she had brought with her and the first time she'd worn any since arriving in Tacloban.

As she sipped the wine, she sat back in her chair listening to the chatter filling the room and watching the other customers in the restaurant. There was a sense of camaraderie among the relief agencies. Many were clearly identifiable by the logos on their tee-shirts. People called greetings to fellow NGO workers as they walked past or members from one table would cross the restaurant to have a discussion with another organisation. The disaster of the typhoon had brought them all together in a common cause. It was the closest to a sense of normality Helen had felt since arriving. A restaurant, the smell of the food, the hubbub of conversation all had a soporific effect on her. Although the two glasses of wine she had greedily consumed could have also contributed. She was feeling very mellow by the time Pieter bustled in shaking her from her reverie. He apologised for being late. He waved back at the greetings from other customers who recognised the popular aid worker and bent to kiss Helen's cheek. He pulled out his chair and sat opposite her. His boyish smile lit up his face and his eyes crinkled and sparkled mischievously.

'Welcome to Guiseppe's. Don't say I don't take you to the best restaurant in town,' he laughed as he dramatically waved his arm around, nearly hitting a plate-laden waiter.

'Ooops sorry,' he said to the waiter. He smiled broadly at Helen. 'That was close. We were nearly wearing someone's order. Ahhh, I see you've ordered some wine already, excellent.' And he poured himself some. 'Cheers!' he held up his glass.

Helen picked up hers and they chinked them together.

'So, lovely Helen, what have you been up to since I last saw you?'

They spent the evening talking and laughing and getting slightly drunk. The first bottle was quickly followed by a second before their food had arrived. Pieter had recommended pizza and Helen hadn't needed much persuasion. The flavours of cheese, Parma ham and salami caused a riot in her mouth. She had only eaten rice, chicken, sardines and a scarce selection of vegetables they had managed to locate for the past month. Pieter laughed when she asked for quiet when the pizza arrived and she took a bite.

'Oh my God,' she said, eyes closed, leaning back in her chair. She slowly chewed the first mouthful. 'I hadn't realised how much I'd missed western food, it tastes amazing.'

The restaurant was starting to quieten as customers finished their meals, paid their bills and made their way back to their accommodation.

Pieter went to pour Helen another glass of wine. The bottle was empty.

'Another one?' he winked at her.

Helen sat forward, smiling. 'Are you trying to get me drunk, Mr Van de Berg?'

He leaned in, elbows on the table, chin in his palms. 'Are you feeling a little, what do you English say, tiddly, Ms Gable?'

'Not at all,' she said defiantly. 'Another bottle sounds like a great idea to me.'

Pieter held the bottle up and nodded his head to a waiter, who materialised a minute later, wine and corkscrew in hand. It was nearly ten o'clock by the time they asked for the bill. There were only a couple of bored waiters left leaning on a counter waiting to go home.

'Sorry to keep you so late,' Pieter said a little guiltily as he handed over pesos to pay the bill. 'Hopefully a large tip will cheer them up,' he whispered, winking at Helen.

'Please, let me pay half,' she said.

'I invited you to dinner, it's my treat,' he replied, waving her money away.

The streets were very dark and very empty when they emerged from the restaurant. Pieter pulled out a torch from his small backpack and slipped his arm into Helen's.

'Where to, ma'am? I have some Scotch whiskey in my room. The hotel is just around the corner. Or I can arrange for one of our drivers to take you home?'

In the darkness Helen couldn't see his expression. Her heart beat a little faster and she concentrated on the circle of light on the ground picked out by the torch.

'Erm…'

'No pressure,' he said. 'I would very much like for you to join me in a night cap, but understand if you would like to go home…' he left the thought hanging in the air.

They continued walking for a few moments.

'Don't suppose there's any ice?' Helen said and they both burst out laughing.

When they recovered, Pieter stopped and pulled Helen to him. He bent towards her and gently kissed her. She closed her eyes, parted her lips and abandoned herself to the moment. He drew her closer to him and they kissed passionately. Her hands caressed his neck and clutched his shirt. His hands gripped her shoulders.

When they moved apart he said, his voice low and husky:

'Definitely no ice.'

Helen took his hand in reply and they walked the rest of the way to his hotel in silence, following the pool of light from the torch. At reception Pieter asked for his room key. He led the way up two flights of stairs, turned left and walked along the corridor until he reached the right number. He unlocked the door and stood back to allow Helen to enter first.

'Straight or with water?' he spoke finally.

'Straight please.'

He poured two good measures of whiskey into a couple of tumblers. He handed her one, she raised her glass to him and knocked it back. Her heart was beating fast with excitement tinged with trepidation. A shiver of anticipation ran up her spine. Pieter gently took the glass from her hand and set it on a table behind him. His eyes locked on hers the whole time. He slid his arms around her waist and pulled her close to him until they stood nose to nose. He kissed her gently at first then with more urgency, Helen responded with matching fervour. They clawed at each other's clothing as they edged toward the bed until Helen was on her back, Pieter on top of her. Suddenly he tensed and jerked away from her. Helen opened her eyes and looked at him questioningly.

'Are you sure?' he said.

She put her hands on his face and smiled. As she pulled his face to her, she whispered: 'I'm sure.'

Their lovemaking was passionate and urgent, both of them abandoned to the desperate need of satisfaction. The emotion was too much for Helen and with the release of her orgasm tears started running down her cheeks. They were silent at first then as if a dam had burst, wretched sobs shook her body. Pieter sat up, a desolate look on his face.

'Helen? Helen? I'm so sorry, what is it?'

She shook her head and begged him with her eyes to give her a moment until she could find her voice.

'Is there anything I can do?' A frown wrinkled his forehead. He was biting his lip in alarm.

She pointed to the whiskey bottle. He got up and poured them both a large measure, sipping his as he handed one to the distraught woman on his bed. She sat up, modestly pulling the sheet over her. She sipped at the soothing liquor. Eventually she got her sobbing under control. Pieter sat patiently beside her, concern on his face.

She took a deep breath, hiccupped a couple times and told him about Charlie.

***

The rain had rattled against the window seconds before her radio alarm blared into life at seven o'clock. Katy Perry's Roar had filled the room, at odds with Helen's mood and the grey day outside. Hitting the snooze button and wrapping herself even more tightly in the duvet, Helen wondered how many more minutes she could savour the blissful, warm comfort of her bed. The harsh reality was none. She was due to meet with a new client and needed to run through her pitch again before dropping Charlie at school, then catching the train to Paddington. She reluctantly peeled back the duvet. She switched on the shower in her en-suite, cleaned her teeth until the water ran hot and then stepping into the prickling stream of water, washed the night's sleep from her body.

She and Charlie had argued again the previous night. It had been over such a silly thing, which seemed to be happening more and more. She had reminded him to take the rubbish bins out ready for the dustman in the morning. He had snapped back at her, complaining she was always picking on him and why couldn't she take them out for a change.

'Come on, Charlie, I've had a busy day and I'm about to start dinner. I'm not asking much,' she had tried reasoning with him.

'I've had a busy day,' he had mimicked back sarcastically.

'Hey, that's enough. Just take the sodding bins out for once without being so bloody insolent,' she had lost her calm and yelled at him.

He had given her a withering look, before going outside and doing as he'd been told. He had deliberately left the back door wide open, letting the heat out and a cold draught in. He knew it drove her mad. She'd pushed the door to, closed her eyes and counted to ten. She had thought about saying something as he marched back in, but bit her tongue.

'Okay if I go to my room now?' he had muttered as he'd stormed past her, not waiting for a reply. She had heard him stomp upstairs and slam his bedroom door.

They had eaten dinner in silence, but at least they had called a truce later that evening. He had kissed her on the cheek and apologised.

'Are you still going to Skype your dad tonight?' she'd asked him.

He'd used her computer in her study, calling to her once he'd finished for her to come and have a chat with David.

'Goodnight, mum,' he had called as he climbed the stairs.

'Is it me or is he getting more withdrawn each week and what's with the colour of his hair?' David had asked her.

'I know what you mean. I'm a bit worried in all honesty. I've tried talking to him, I wondered if he was being bullied at school, but he assured me he wasn't. His grades last term were a little down as you know, although not by much. I know hormones have an effect, but I just feel there's more to it. He's never kept anything from us in the past and has always spoken to one of us if something's bothering him. As for his hair, I came home last week and he'd dyed it, he said it was the in-thing, apparently. Did he tell you he's not going to the rugby club anymore?'

'No he didn't say anything about that. He loves his rugby, ever since he could catch a ball.'

'Exactly, something isn't right. I don't know what else to do apart from snoop around to see if I can find any tell-tale signs in his room or on his iPad, but I'd hate to do that'

'I can swing a business trip back to the UK and visit if you think it would help?'

'It might help to have a father/son chat if you think you can manage a trip back. I know he's a teenager, but I feel there's much more to it. Maybe you'll have better luck.'

'Okay, leave it with me, I'll email you when I've got some dates, I wanted to set up a meeting with the Sales Managers anyway.'

They had spent a couple of minutes catching up on his family, what the weather was like in San Francisco and David laughing at Helen's complaints about the English weather.

'Sorry, Helen, I have to go, I have a meeting in five minutes,' and he had finished their call.

She grabbed clean jogging bottoms, a rugby shirt and thick socks from the cupboard and threw them on. No point in risking creases in her business suit, she would put it on just before she left. She padded across the landing, down the stairs and into the kitchen. The weather was so miserable she needed to put the light on to make her coffee. With her elbows on the counter she rested her chin in one of her palms and traced a rivulet of water with her index finger as it snaked down the pane, joining together with others then dividing in its race to the bottom. God, she hated the UK weather. The endless grey of the Thames Valley winter; actually when she came to think of it, the spring, summer and autumn weren't much better! The percolator announced her coffee was ready with a last few chugs of steam. She sighed, poured it into her favourite mug, wrapped her hands around it savouring the warmth and went to her study.

Helen had an hour to go over the presentation for A-Excel. It would be a good contract if she could land it. Not yet ready to invest in an in-house marketing team, they were looking for a freelancer to work with them for the next six months on a part-time basis. With two other contracts currently running, this would fit in perfectly and be a good earner.

An hour and two more cups of coffee later, Helen had put the finishing touches to her proposal, printed it off and saved the presentation to the Cloud. She shook her head and smiled as she thought of how far technology had advanced over the past twenty years. She could in fact have given the presentation without leaving her home, but felt the personal touch was more important. It was always easier to deal with people once you made a face to face connection. This contract could potentially go on longer than the half year they had discussed, so today's meeting could be very beneficial. Pleased with her morning so far, it was time to make sure Charlie was up. She doubted it since she had heard no movement from the floor above.

'Charlie, Charlie?' She called up the stairs. 'Are you moving yet, it's just after eight, I'm putting some toast in for you now.'

She listened for some sort of acknowledgement. None came.

'You have five minutes, then I'm coming up.'

Helen turned on the small kitchen television and plopped two slices of wholemeal bread into the toaster. She put butter and Marmite on the table with a glass of orange juice. If he wanted cereal as well, he could help himself, it was so difficult to know these days.

The rain was still falling. A dreary drizzle looked like it had set in, another miserable day. Charlie still hadn't materialised. She didn't seem to be able to connect with her son anymore and she was getting increasingly concerned. He had always been a calm, easy-going boy, now he seemed jumpy and tense every time she asked him something. They had always worked together as a team in the past, now every conversation was a minefield. The fact David had remarked on it meant it wasn't just her being over-sensitive. Charlie had become so withdrawn, not wanting to go out or bring friends home. And quitting rugby, he loved all sport, but he had been fanatical about rugby. She shook her head, frustrated he no longer confided in her. She hated the dramatic change that had occurred in the past few months.

She inhaled deeply then made her way to the stairs. She noted on the hall clock it was ten past eight. Charlie would have to get a move on if they were to make school on time. At his door she knocked and called his name…nothing, not even a grunt. Surely his alarm would have woken him by now, even if her calls hadn't roused him. She knocked louder.

'Charlie, I'm coming in.'

Still nothing. She put her hand on the doorknob and turned it, pushing against the door. It was locked. Since when had he started doing that? She knocked again. Her pulse rate quickened slightly, a frown on her face.

'Charlie, Charlie, open this door. Come on, it's ten past eight. We'll be late for school.'

She crouched down to look through the keyhole. He'd left the key in. Damn, what was he playing at? A cold shiver ran up her spine and her hands had gone clammy. She wiped them on her jogging bottoms, thinking what to do. All three bedrooms used the same key, not that she had ever had cause to lock any of the doors in the past. Helen tried to visualise where there might be another key. Panic started to bubble up from her stomach. Something was very wrong, she could feel it. She needed to get into Charlie's room. Now. In the spare room she checked the door, nothing, then a thought occurred to her and she wrenched open the drawer of the dressing table. A key scraped on the bottom with the force.

She rammed it into the Charlie's keyhole, the intensity pushing out the internal key. She turned it and yanked the door open, her heart pounding.

'Char…' Whooshing crowded her head and thumping filled her ears as she registered the scene before her. A chair was overturned in the middle of the room. Above it was the lifeless body of her beautiful boy, a noose around his neck, tied off in the beams.

With trembling hands she righted the chair under his feet. She shouldered the weight of his body to take the strain off the rope. It was hopeless. His hand was ice cold and rigor mortis had already claimed him. Her world crashed in around her.

She dropped to her knees, grasping at her hair. A scream echoed round the room. She retched and was silent. She didn't know what to do. She couldn't get the body down on her own. She crawled to lean against Charlie's bed, her head thumping, heart pounding, acid in her throat. Incomprehension filled her every pore. She closed her eyes, bit her lip and rocked. When she reopened her eyes the scene hadn't changed. It wasn't a nightmare, this was real.

She stood up. A wave of nausea overcame her and she reached out to steady herself on his bedside cupboard. Gazing down she saw the envelope addressed to her. Snatching it up she slumped onto Charlie's unmade bed and stared at it, scared of its contents. An icy hand clutched at her heart as she slipped the single A4 page out of the unsealed envelope. Her hands were shaking as she unfolded it.

'Dear mum,

I'm so sorry. I don't know what else to do anymore. I'm rubbish like they say and don't deserve to live. They've told me for weeks I had to end it all as a favour to the world, that I'm a waste of space. I couldn't do it, mum. I didn't want to leave you and dad, but yesterday they said if I didn't, they knew where I lived and that dad wasn't here and they would hurt you.'

The words swam before her, blending in together. She wiped her tears away on her shirt sleeve. It was a moment before she could gain enough courage to continue.

'They wouldn't stop saying horrible things about me and said they'd tell the whole school how disgusting I was. I don't know why they hated me so much. They said it was because I was a ginger, that's why I dyed my hair, but they didn't stop, they got worse. I was so afraid, I didn't know what else to do. I love you mum and dad, I'm sorry I wasn't a better son.

Charlie. xx'

Clutching the letter to her chest, Helen wailed, rocking back and forth. Who had been doing this to him? Who were 'they'? He'd told her everything was fine at school. Thoughts whirred around her head making her dizzy. A whistle and a vibrating buzz pierced the silence as Charlie's mobile on the table beside her announced a message. She seized it and opened the Smart phone, password protected, emergency calls only. She dialled 999.

'What's your emergency please?'

'My son...' a sob escaped her chest.

'Ma'am, I need to know your emergency. What service do you require?'

'Erm, erm, ambulance I think.'

'Can you tell me the problem please, ma'am?'

'It's my son,' the tears wouldn't stop and she could barely speak through them. 'My...son....he's dead.' The last word brought a strangled cry and she dropped the phone.

***

There was silence as Helen finished her story. Tears glistened in her eyes.

Pieter sat staring at her, his face full of sadness and sympathy.

'I'm so sorry, Helen. I can't begin to imagine the pain you must be going through,' he said eventually. 'I don't really know what to say...' He shook his head.

She pulled his hand to her mouth and kissed it.

They sat in silence for a few moments.

'Did you find out why he...I'm sorry, this must be so painful for you, if you'd rather not talk about it.' Pieter turned and smiled reassuringly at her.

'No, I'm sorry. It's pretty heavy stuff to throw at someone, especially someone you've only just met. I'd rather not talk about it anymore tonight, if you don't mind.'

She turned her face to his, their lips met and they kissed tenderly. This time their lovemaking was slow and caring. They took the time to explore each other's bodies, softly stroking and caressing. Their passion built like a slow burning fire, until it burst into flames and they came together in an explosion. They lay back, panting. Their fingers entwined. Each lost in their own thoughts. Emotionally and physically exhausted, Helen turned onto her side, facing away from Pieter. He snuggled up behind her and they both drifted off to sleep, legs interlaced. A crumpled sheet was partially drawn over them.

When Helen woke up her head was fuzzy from wine and whiskey. Her mouth was dry. Early morning sun streamed in through the open curtains. It took her a couple of moments to orientate herself. One of Pieter's arms was draped carelessly across her waist. She could feel his warm breath on the back of her neck. She smiled as she recalled their lovemaking the night before. Then she remembered with dread how she had told him all about Charlie. Maybe she should leave before he woke up, to save them both the embarrassment. As she attempted to slide noiselessly off the bed, Pieter's arm tightened around her. Carefully disentangling herself she padded to the toilet. She squeezed some toothpaste onto her finger and ran it along her teeth. When she returned to the bedroom Pieter was lying on his back, his hands behind his head, grinning.

'Hi, gorgeous,' he said sleepily. 'How are you feeling this morning?'

She hopped back into bed and kissed him on the lips.

'Hi, yourself. Not too bad considering all the wine, whiskey and emotion.' She grew serious. 'I'm so sorry to have dumped that all on you last night. Not the ideal revelation for a first date.'

He put his arm around her shoulders and they lay in silence for a long time looking up at the ceiling. Helen was beginning to think her outpouring had definitely brought an end to their relationship before it had had a chance to begin. She cursed herself for drinking too much, breaking down and telling this man she barely knew about her son. As she was formulating the words to make a hasty retreat, Pieter spoke.

'I was wondering,' he said, 'do you have any plans for the weekend?'

'No. I think I can safely say I'm free,' she replied a little shakily.

'I don't suppose you can Scuba dive, can you?'

A feeling of relief flooded through her, she hadn't scared him off, he wanted to see her again. She hesitated for a couple of moments before smiling. 'As a matter of fact, I have my advanced Padi certificate,' she said proudly.

'Perfect. I know a great place for diving. San Roque, have you heard of it? It's about a three hour drive south from here. I was thinking we could go for the weekend. If you like, that is?'

'Hmmm, I don't know, are your intentions honourable?' she teased.

'Most definitely not,' he laughed and kissed her forehead, catching sight of his watch and the time as he did.

'Shit! I'm sorry, I have to go. I have a meeting in twenty minutes. I blame you if I'm late,' he laughed as he leapt out of bed heading towards the bathroom. 'Don't feel you need to get up though, take your time,' he called over his shoulder.

Helen lay back on the bed listening to the shower. A smile played on her lips, thinking how lovely it would be to get away for the weekend.

Pieter emerged naked from the bathroom, towel drying his curls. He crossed the room and dragged clothes out of a chest of draws and quickly dressed.

'I'll see you at four o'clock on Friday at your house, okay?' He bent to Helen and gave her a lingering kiss. 'How I wish I could stay and make love to you again.' He shook his head, picked up his bag and strode out of the room, whistling, leaving Helen's head spinning.

After taking advantage of proper running water and having a hot shower, Helen caught a jeepney back to the house. When she arrived, Ian, Ruth and Neil were sitting on the terrace drinking coffee and discussing the day's agenda.

'Ah ha, dirty stop out,' teased Ian. 'Good night?'

Helen smiled sheepishly, blushing slightly at the three pairs of eyes fixed on her. 'Erm, yes, you could say that. Guiseppe's was great. I can't believe we haven't been there yet! By the time we finished it was dark and....'

'Spare us the details,' Ian put his hands up smiling. 'Just glad you had a good time.'

'You can tell me more later, once the boys are out of earshot. We wouldn't want to offend their delicate sensibilities,' jeered Ruth.

'Just because we don't like to gossip,' Neil chipped in digging Ruth in the ribs. The sparkle between them didn't escape Helen.

'I'll grab a coffee and some breakfast and you can get me up-to-date on what we're doing today,' said Helen over her shoulder as she entered the house.

'What, Prince Charming didn't treat you to breakfast, tsk, tsk,' Ian called after her.

Helen poked her head back through the front door and replied with the middle finger of her right hand. Peals of laughter followed her inside.

'Hi, Raul,' Helen said as she boiled water on one of the gas burners and buttered some bread.

'Morning, Helen,' he called, looking up briefly from his vegetable chopping.

'Which school are you at today?' she asked.

'One in Palo. Actually I think we're all going today. Izel will be here about ten thirty to drive us.'

'Great. I'll be back in a bit to help you. I need to find out from the guys what we're up to.'

Raul nodded, gave her a bright smile and returned to his vegetables.

They spent the rest of the week meeting with schools in and

around Tacloban to see which one they could adopt as a project for the fast approaching arrival of volunteers. They divided the list in two. Helen and Ian took one half, Ruth and Neil the other, comparing notes and gathering a short list.

True to his word, Pieter turned up at four o'clock on Friday in one of the Ménage des Enfants vehicles. It was a silver Range Rover Discovery. Only Ruth was home, Neil and Ian had gone to buy building materials with Izel. Helen's heart skipped a beat when the car pulled into the driveway. Butterflies had been fluttering in her stomach on and off all day in anticipation of seeing him again. Now it was as if they were battling to escape. She introduced Pieter to Ruth and went to grab her backpack. As Pieter took it to the car, Ruth gave her a look of approval.

'Very nice,' she said with a broad smile. 'You have fun, girl, see you on Sunday.'

'You have a good weekend too.'

'Yes, can't wait. A weekend with the boys, mending a leaking roof.'

'Haha, I have my suspicions you will be doing a little more than that,' Helen grinned cheekily at Ruth.

'Touché!'

The road out of Tacloban was slow. It was filled with jeepneys, tricycles, pedi cabs, diggers and JCBs jostling for space along the Pan-Philippine Highway. Pieter drove patiently in the stop-start traffic, as people got on and off the various modes of transport. Debris along the roadside had made it narrower and more difficult to overtake, it was a matter of waiting until the vehicle in front started moving again. They chatted easily, talking about their respective week's work, the traffic, the view. Pieter pointed out various places of interest: the actual spot where MacArthur had landed in 1944 in Palo and the Metropolitan Cathedral, which had lost its roof in the typhoon. Cries for help were still visible where Yolanda survivors had painted on the roofs of houses in November: 'We need food and water' and 'Help us', although in addition, more positive banners were being displayed as well. Along with the omnipresent 'Tindog Tacloban' slogans, 'Jobless, Roofless, homeless, but not helpless' and 'Thank you for those who helped us, we will never forget you' hung from houses, apartment, schools and fences. Despite all the chaos still evident, Tacloban was indeed rising up out of the turmoil.

Eventually they passed the Tolosa area. The road cleared and they were able to make some serious headway south. As the sun set to their right, Helen noticed they were no longer in the typhoon affected area. Here coconut trees stood tall, their fronds gently swaying in the breeze, houses were in one piece, no tarpaulins. The only corrugated iron was on roofs.

'So this is what Tacloban would have looked like before Yolanda,' she said. 'It's been difficult to imagine it without the chaos and debris.'

'It'll be the journey back when you notice it more,' said Pieter. 'But let's not think about that now. We're booked into a small dive resort in the village of San Roque. I reckon we'll get there about seven o'clock, perfect timing for dinner. Then I thought tomorrow we could go diving, did you bring your dive card?'

'Sounds perfect and yes I did,' she replied.

***

When Helen woke the next morning, Pieter was snoring lightly. She quickly threw on some shorts and a vest and silently let herself out of the bungalow Pieter had booked for them. She hadn't been able to get a true sense of the place last night in the dark. She wanted to explore a little. Their veranda looked out over the sea, which was gently lapping onto white sand only ten metres from her. Two young girls were knee deep in the water towing a third child on a bright orange rubber ring. She could hear their chatter and giggling as they waded past, waving at her. Helen smiled and waved back. It was so peaceful. She took the few steps to the beach and wandered past the main building of the resort where they had eaten dinner the night before. Two hundred metres further along, a fisherman was unloading nets from his tiny outrigger boat, while another sat on the beach mending his. She walked along the shore, ankle deep in the water. To her left multi-coloured items of drying clothing hung on ropes stretched between coconut trees. Children playing in the shade stopped to wave and call out to her as she passed. It was a far cry from the bustle and devastation of the city they had left behind.

When she got back to the bungalow Pieter was sitting on the veranda watching her.

'Good morning, beautiful isn't it?'

Helen bent and kissed him on the lips.

'Spectacular.'

He pulled her onto his lap. They kissed passionately. Pieter looked at his watch.

'C'mon, I think we have some time before they stop serving breakfast,' he said lustfully.

Helen grinned, jumped up from his lap and dragged him inside.

They spent the weekend Scuba diving, making love and talking, endlessly talking, in the restaurant, on the beach, on the dive boat, in the bungalow. They shared their lives, thoughts, ideas and hopes. They didn't even notice the other guests at the resort. Helen had never felt so in-tune with someone before. She felt she could tell him anything and he would understand.

After dinner on Saturday evening, they strolled along the beach, carrying a bottle of wine and a couple of glasses. They nestled down in the white sand a few hundred metres away from the resort. Pieter poured them both some wine and they sat in silence sipping it and listening to the water lapping against the shore.

'Helen, I know it must still be a very raw subject for you, but if you ever want to talk about Charlie…'

Helen sat silently sipping her wine for several moments. She had wanted to speak to Pieter about her son, but had been reluctant to spoil the mood of the weekend.

'It was all so sudden,' she continued to stare out into the darkness towards the sea. 'Why didn't I insist he tell me what was wrong?'

'You said in his note he had mentioned "they", did you ever find out who "they" were? Or why they hated him?'

'Cyberbully trolls!' she said bitterly. 'Cowards who persecuted Charlie because they had found out he was gay.' She shook her head. 'The police were still investigating it when I left. I get the occasional email update from them, but no one has been arrested or charged.' She drained her glass and held it up to Pieter. 'Any wine left?'

They lay in the sand, watching a half moon steal across the night sky. Pieter listened as Helen shared with him stories of Charlie. The first time she had been able to talk so freely about him since his death. The sky had started to turn a pale grey as dawn edged its way into the night when they finally sloped off to bed.

Sunday afternoon came around all too soon. After lunch they packed up the car and headed north to Tacloban. As they neared Helen's house they both fell silent, neither wanting the weekend to end. Pieter turned the car into the drive, turned off the engine and they sat there for a few moments.

'I had….'

'Thank you…'

They spoke together and laughed.

'You first,' said Pieter.

'Thank you for an amazing weekend. It was perfect, everything was perfect,' said Helen smiling at him.

'I had a great time too,' he reached up and stroked her face. 'I really like you Helen.'

'Me too,' she replied and they kissed tenderly.

'I'll call you tomorrow,'

She nodded and reluctantly got out of the car. She pulled her backpack from the back seat and blew him a kiss as he started up the engine and reversed out of the drive. He waved back smiling at her. Helen walked into the house as if she was on air, happiness bubbling inside her.

CHAPTER EIGHTEEN

If the girls thought Rosela had been mean-spirited before, she now stepped up a couple of notches. She had become even more vicious and spiteful since Monique and Bella had disappeared. Lika Faye had decided to keep her hand in the girls' escape a secret, even from Phoebe. She had told the others only that Phil had said they had been upstairs cleaning during the time she had been with him. There was plenty of speculation about what had actually happened. It was obvious from Rosela's behaviour they had managed to get away. Despite the harsher beatings they all received at her hands, a feeling of hopefulness seeped into the basement.

'Perhaps they'll go to the police and we'll be set free,' an excited Phoebe had said a few days after the escape.

'A lot of good that will do us, Phoebe,' said Marianne unkindly. 'Who do you think our clients are? More likely they will end up back here if they go there, all the police are corrupt.'

'Okay, well maybe they'll tell someone who can help us,' Phoebe continued, determined not to lose faith they would one day be freed.

'They won't get far without any money anyway. Bet you Phil has the old witch out looking for them,' Marianne countered.

Lika Faye struggled to keep quiet at times. She desperately wanted to tell Phoebe, but knew her friend wouldn't be able to resist telling the others. She kept her mouth shut and avoided getting drawn into any of the conversations.

'You don't have much to say about all this, Lika Faye,' Marianne turned on her one day. 'Are you sure you don't know something?'

She felt her cheeks burn and hoped Marianne couldn't tell in the dingy light.

'I told you, I didn't see them. I was with Phil the whole time. Don't you think I would have gone with them if I knew what they were planning?' She clenched her fists tightly behind her back, holding her breath. She hoped she wasn't going to be pushed any further on the subject. Marianne looked at the younger girl a few moments longer as if making a decision, then turned away. Lika Faye slowly let out her breath and checked no one else was watching her.

The more time passed without Monique and Bella returning had conflicting effects on the remaining girls. On the one hand, it meant they had been successful in getting away. On the other, no rescue had materialised. Since the escape Lika Faye hadn't been summoned upstairs by Phil. Although she was relieved not to be alone with the fat, sleazy Australian, she missed the opportunity to get away from the confines of the basement and see sunlight.

Angry he was losing income, Phil forced Lika Faye and Phoebe to work longer hours until Rosela found the missing girls or replaced them. Days passed in a fog of webcam sex, sleep and occasional stints upstairs to clean or cook. The preoccupation of the escape meant Rosela didn't single out Lika Faye. Now they all received the same beatings; judging by her black eye and bruises, she was passing on what was being dealt out to her.

***

One afternoon Rosela appeared with the girls' food and while they were eating she unlocked the padlock to the computer room, entered and shut the door behind her.

The girls sat quietly eating, looks of confusion and concern on their faces. Rosela rarely entered the webcam sex area, it was Phil's domain. They had only ever seen her there when she had come to talk to him.

'What do you think's happened to Phil?' whispered Phoebe.

Lika Faye shook her head. The older girls spoke in hushed voices as they crammed rice into their mouths.

'Maybe he's had a heart attack?'

'Or a stroke.'

'Is she going to run things on her own now?'

'Well she can't manage it all by herself,' said Marianne. 'She'll get that old hag, Miss Miriam, in to help, like Phil did when she was away.'

The other girls nodded and mumbled in agreement.

'He's probably just passed out drunk, it wouldn't be the first time. He's been stinking of booze worse than ever the last few nights and stumbling about, just like my old man used to, when he'd been on the sauce,' said Jenny.

'Looks like you have the pleasure of working with the old witch tonight,' Marianne jeered at the two younger girls. 'Good luck!'

Lika Faye and Phoebe looked at each other in dismay. Eight hours with Rosela, in the evil mood she had been in since the sisters had escaped, was not a night they relished.

'Do you think Monique and Bella were ever going to tell anyone we're still here?' asked Phoebe.

Lika Faye thought back to the day she had helped them. Hope had lifted her spirits then. The belief she could be close to being freed from captivity and the degrading life she was leading had seemed very real. As time had passed the optimism had deserted her. They had said they were going to Tacloban and had promised her they would look for her family and tell them where she was. Maybe they hadn't made it that far.

'I think we wouldn't be here anymore if they were,' she replied sadly.

They had just finished eating when the door to the computer room opened.

'Phoebe, Faye, get in here.'

The girls looked at each other with concern. It wasn't the usual time they worked.

'Now!' she screeched at them.

They scrambled to their feet and rushed over to the door.

'Yes, Miss Rosela,' they chorused.

'In!'

They filed past her and stood against the wall, waiting for further instructions.

'Where does Mr Phil keep his book with all his passwords?'

They both looked at her blankly. Was this some sort of trick, thought Lika Faye. She didn't feel she owed Phil any loyalty, but neither did she trust Rosela.

'Well?'

They both remained silent and shrugged their shoulders. Rosela stepped closer to them and before they had a chance to react, Lika Faye felt a searing pain in her temple as Rosela banged their heads together. Phoebe went to protest but Rosela got in first.

'Don't play dumb with me, you lazy little bitches. I don't have time to mess about. I know you've watched him when he's setting up the computers. Where is it?'

Rubbing her head with one hand, Phoebe pointed to Phil's computer.

'Under the keyboard,' she said.

Rosela marched over to the computer and pulled out the small book Phil used to keep passwords and set up instructions.

'Since you're both here now, you can get on with setting the laptops and cameras up ready for tonight's customers.'

The girls continued to stare at her, until she made a threatening move towards them.

'Yes, Miss Rosela,' said Lika Faye and made a dash towards her laptop with Phoebe close behind her.

Rosela worked her way through the notebook and logged into Phil's computer. She was silent for a while as she made sense of the system. By the time Lika Faye and Phoebe had finished, Rosela was engrossed in reading Phil's emails. The girls stood behind her as she mumbled aloud in English while reading one of the messages, following the words on the screen with a finger. She suddenly realised they were there and turned around.

'Finished?'

'Yes, Miss Rosela.'

'Get out then.'

They quietly left the computer room as Rosela turned back to her email.

'Could you make out what she was saying?' asked Lika Faye.

'No not really. She's probably checking up on Phil.'

They returned to their beds.

Rosela emerged from the room sometime later and snapped the padlock back into place. A big grin stretched across her face as she walked over to the mattresses, causing the girls to raise their eyebrows as they looked cautiously at each other.

'Mr Phil isn't available tonight,' she sneered. 'I'll be organising Phoebe and Faye. Miss Miriam will be looking after you older girls. Time for you to get ready.'

She turned on her heel and disappeared up the stairs. Six pairs of eyes watched her leave.

'Well that's the happiest I've seen her since Monique and Bella got away,' said Jenny. 'I hate to think what she's got in mind, going by her grin. I'd say it won't be pleasant for one of us.' She looked sympathetically in the direction of the younger girls.

CHAPTER NINETEEN

The first wave of volunteers had arrived at the house. A couple in their late twenties, Sandra and Simon, had come from London. They reached Tacloban on Saturday having flown via Manila. Two Swedes, William and Lucas, backpacking in the Philippines after finishing university, arrived by bus having taken the ferry into Ormoc. And a young Australian girl, Bianca, from Melbourne landed Sunday morning.

Helen welcomed them to their new home. She walked them through the house, told them to choose a bunk bed and showed them where to fill buckets with water to use for flushing the toilet and for showering.

'We're going to build two shower cubicles – I use the term loosely as you will be scooping the water over yourself, no such luxury as shower heads – in the garden near the water hose,' she said. 'Not so far to carry the water and should help with queues for the bathroom, especially once the house starts filling up. Use the drinking water container for brushing your teeth and washing your face though.'

On Sunday afternoon, once they had had a chance to settle in, she gave them her orientation talk. She started by explaining how WDR worked, the rules of their new home, meal and work times and the projects they would be getting involved with.

'At the moment, the main one we are working on is the soup kitchen with Raul. I think you've all met him?' The four attentive volunteers nodded. 'We will start on Monday at a school in Palo. Rather than give you too much information at once, you can see the schedule on white boards over there.' She pointed to the lounge area which they had converted into the WDR office. 'They will be updated every week so you know what you're doing and where. There's only a handful of us at the moment, but more people will be arriving over the next couple of weeks. We're trying to keep it as straightforward as possible. Make the most of the space while you can,' she smiled. 'There will be ten of you to each of the bedrooms before long.

'We're all learning as we go along, so if you have any queries or suggestions, please feel free to come to me with them. This is supposed to be an enjoyable experience for you as volunteers, you are as important to us as the people we are here to help.'

Raul had dinner ready just before six o'clock so they could eat while it was still light. They served themselves from the food on the kitchen counter and squashed around one of the dining room tables, eager to find out more about their fellow WDR volunteers. After eating and clearing up they all gathered on the front terrace. They sat in candlelight, drinking beer and sharing stories. Helen watched and listened as the new arrivals laughed and joked and learned about each other. Finally she felt she was doing what WDR has brought her on board for. Feelings of satisfaction and achievement washed over her. She caught Ian looking at her, smiling and nodding his approval; she grinned back at him. By ten o'clock Helen was ready for bed. She yawned and stood up to bid the others goodnight.

'We'll start work at eight o'clock, preparing the Lugaw for the school. Breakfast is a free for all before that. You'll find eggs, fruit and bread in the kitchen, and tea, coffee, sugar and creamer – with no fridge keeping milk is a problem – in jars on the counters. Help yourselves. Sleep well, everyone.'

They all murmured their goodnights. They finished their beers, and torches in hand made their way to their beds in dribs and drabs. Ian and Neil were the last to leave. They blew out the candles and closed the front door before retiring for the night. Darkness and silence claimed the house for a few hours until the rain started. Gently at first, then with more vigour, playing its tune on the tin roof. It caused a few of the lighter sleepers among them to stir, before being soothed back to sleep.

Monday morning was grey and humid. It didn't dampen the

spirits of the new arrivals. They were keen to get involved in providing help to the victims of Yolanda. Raul explained how they made the Lugaw and the ingredients they were using.

'We've found if we leave the vegetables in larger chunks, the kids pick them out. If we make them tiny, they eat the whole lot. Happy chopping everyone.'

A lean-to area behind the kitchen had been turned into a food preparation space. Neil and Ian had built long wooden counters for the volunteers to use. Raul handed out vegetables and knives and the tedious task of fine chopping commenced. Rice was set to boil on the burners and Raul mixed up sachets of spices he had brought back from Manila, to add more flavour.

'Lugaw usually contains chicken as well, but since we have a tight budget we are sticking to vegetables and rice,' he explained to the willing volunteers. 'It's a hot meal, which many of these kids living in refugee tents, aren't getting very often.'

'Hey Raul, do you mind if we have some music on?' asked Bianca.

The others nodded hopefully and turned to the Filipino chef.

'My friends, music sounds like a great idea,' he grinned at them. 'No need to ask.'

Bianca went off to get her iPad and the preparation area resounded to the sounds of the latest pop music. The chopping volunteers added their voices to the songs, filling the house with joy and laughter.

'I don't know how long this will last. My battery is running a bit low. Do you know when we'll get a chance to re-charge, Raul?' Bianca shouted above the ruckus.

'I'll speak to Helen, but I expect the generator will be on tonight for a couple of hours. It's a noisy old thing and diesel is expensive since Yolanda. We usually crank her up every couple of days.'

By half past ten, the steaming pots of Lugaw were ready. Raul backed his little red van round the side of the house, close to the kitchen door ready for them to load it.

'William, Lucas, you guys ride with Raul,' said Helen. 'We're taking both vehicles today. The rest of you can jump in the WDR van.'

Izel was fussing round the recently delivered white Pasajero twelve-seater transport van currently sitting in the driveway of the house. A WDR logo had been stencilled on the front, the driver and passenger doors. He had rolled down the plastic sheet windows which served to keep rain out of the benches lining the back of the van. Using a spare tee-shirt he had carefully wiped all the raindrops from the seats and was now proudly polishing the wing mirrors.

Raul had left the volunteers to load up at the back of the house and appeared by Izel's side, laughing.

'You realise your pristine white van will be covered in mud before we reach the end of the road, my friend.' He slapped Izel's back playfully.

Izel grinned back at him, pride shining in his eyes. 'Then I shall have to clean her again when we get home.' They laughed together, both knowing how important this job had been for Izel. It was a chance for him to start earning a good wage and get his life back together. Thousands of others were still surviving on hand-outs and relief aid.

'What are you up to today?' Raul asked.

'I'll follow you to the school to drop off Miss Helen and the other volunteers. After that I'm taking Ian, Neil and Miss Ruth to meet with a couple of schools in Tanauan. We're going to get some supplies from the DIY shop this afternoon so we can start building the showers.'

'Okay. I won't be able to fit them all in my van to bring them back later. I guess Helen plans to use a jeepney to come home this afternoon.'

Helen appeared at the front door.

'We're loaded up, Raul. The Swedish boys and I will ride with you. The others are putting on sun screen and getting water, then they'll be out to Izel.'

They set off in convoy for the thirty minute drive travelling south to Palo. Raul lead the way. In Izel's truck, Bianca, Sandra and Simon were taking in their first real sights of Tacloban. They pointed to the colourful jeepneys and the pedi cabs draped with plastic sheeting to keep the passengers dry, the pedallers wearing colourful rain macs. They shook their heads as they passed destroyed houses and felled trees, sharing stories they had heard about the destruction and loss of life.

'I feel so sorry for these poor people," said Bianca, pointing to one of the tented cities. 'Nothing I saw on the TV at home prepared me for what it's like here.'

'We said the same thing when we arrived on Saturday,' said Sandra. 'We take for granted how lucky we are. It's impossible to imagine what it's like to have lost everything. Look at that there,' she pointed through the plastic sheeting as they passed a partially destroyed house. Leaning against one wall was a car. Its front wheels on the ground, the back tyres halfway up the wall.

'I have to get a picture of that next time we pass,' said Bianca.

'You'll see a few of those,' laughed Ruth. 'They floated there with the storm surge. The weight of the engine pulled the front of the car down and then got wedged when the water receded. If you want to see something even more bizarre you should go to the Anibong area. They still have six cargo ships aground and people are already re-building their homes around them.'

'Oh wow, I've got to see that,' said Simon.

'Get Izel to take you down there one Saturday. Probably better to go with him, it can be a bit dangerous,' said Ruth.

'Why? What do you mean, dangerous?' asked Simon, a frown creasing his forehead.

'Well, it's an area known for pickpocketing,' said Neil. 'You'd be better off going with a local, that's all. Don't let Ruth alarm you,' he smiled at her. 'We haven't had any problems while we've been here, to put your mind at rest. Mostly the locals are so pleased we're here to help them.'

The van stopped and Izel cut the engine. They climbed out of the back and looked around. The sing-song voices of children calling out words in unison floated to them from one of the UNICEF tents serving as a classroom. Three other tents lined up on the grass, muddy puddles surrounding them.

The new volunteers stood in silence, mouths open. The grass area where they were standing was surrounded by the remains of single storey yellow and green painted classrooms. Jagged sections of metal roof hung dangerously from the battered buildings. Corrugated sheets littered the ground. Exposed wooden eaves had started to rot and smashed desks huddled in classroom corners.

'Have a look around,' said Helen. 'You've got half an hour before the kids break for lunch. Raul and I will set up over there.' She pointed to a large concrete area. Once the school hall, the only indication of its previous use was the remaining wall with half a stage jutting from it.

The group of five, Smart phones at the ready to take pictures, set off to explore.

'Come and see this classroom,' called Sandra pointing out child-sized toilets, the porcelain smashed, walls around them no longer in existence.

'All these books ruined. Such a shame,' said William as a waterlogged text book disintegrated in his hand.

They continued to explore the school, moving out of earshot of the others. Helen spoke briefly with Ian, Ruth and Neil before they climbed back into the white van. The rain had stopped and the sun had come out. Izel was rolling up the plastic side sheets to give them some fresh air. The humidity was making it hot and sticky in the back.

Raul moved his van to the old school hall. He and Helen carefully lifted the hot pots from the back and set them on the concrete. They sat on the remains of the stage sipping water and watched the new volunteers wandering around. A small group of boys followed them, no doubt cutting classes, thought Helen.

'Wass your name?' they chanted at the group, giggling as they repeated the name back to whoever replied.

'Where you from? America?'

Helen smiled, shaking her head. The two stock questions asked by every child they met. She watched as Bianca patiently explained Melbourne and the Swedish boys attempted to educate them where Sweden was located.

The volunteers rejoined Helen and Raul at ten minutes to twelve. Filled with thoughts and comments about their surroundings, they chattered excitedly together, throwing questions out to anyone who would or could answer.

'Guys, the bell will go any second and we'll have children racing out of their classes,' said Helen. 'Sandra and Simon, we'll serve from this pot, Bianca and the boys help Raul over there. Serve out about two-thirds of a ladle into whatever container they hold out.'

'Some of them may have forgotten to bring something to school with them,' said Raul. 'We do have some bowls and spoons in the van. We give them out sparingly. Will you sort that, Helen?'

She nodded at him and the two groups prepared themselves for the onslaught of a couple of hundred ten-year-olds. As soon as the bell sounded, children streamed out of the humid tents. Shouts, screams and laughter filled the air as they flocked to the serving area.

Well-practised at these school servings, Raul was already on the stage booming at the rabble in front of him. He was making them laugh and organising them into orderly lines. The children squatted obediently, giggling along with the chef, containers at the ready for their turn. The new volunteers soon got the hang of filling the various bowls, cups and jars thrust at them as two kids at a time approached each scalding pot.

Helen returned to Raul's van to collect a few spoons and bowls from the front passenger seat. As she rounded the engine she saw a young girl staring in at the front window. Puzzled, Helen spoke softly: 'Hi there, do you need a bowl or spoon?'

The girl turned suddenly, her eyes wide. Helen could see fear in the child's face as she spotted her.

'Hey, what's the matter? No need to be afraid.' She approached slowly not wanting to scare the girl away.

'I know her.'

Helen frowned and shook her head. 'I'm sorry, sweetie, I don't understand.'

The girl turned back to the front windscreen and pointed. 'I know *her*,' she whispered.

Helen followed the girl's outstretched arm and saw the picture Raul had taped to the front window.

Helen's heart quickened. Thoughts raced around her head. The girl could have confused the picture with another girl, or they could have been at school together before the typhoon.

'Did you go to school with her?'

The girl shook her head.

'Where do you know her from?'

The girl swallowed hard. A look of terror flashed in her eyes. Helen moved to squat in front of the child.

'It's okay,' she said soothingly, stroking the girls arm gently.

'Cebu.' She said it so quietly Helen wasn't sure if she had heard correctly. It didn't make sense.

'When did you last see her?'

'A few weeks ago. She helped us.' Tears started flowing down the girl's cheeks.

Helen was completely confused and was becoming more convinced the likeness was a coincidence and the girl was mistaken. She tried one more question: 'Do you know her name?'

The girl nodded, sniffing and wiping her nose on the shoulder of her tee-shirt.

'Can you tell me?'

'Lika Faye.'

Helen gasped. She could feel her heartbeat throbbing in her temple as she tried to remain calm. She didn't want to frighten the girl away.

'And what's your name, can you tell me?' she knelt her knees sinking slightly into the wet ground. Before the girl could answer a shrill voice screamed out.

'Bella!' followed by a stream of Filipino. The girl jumped and her body stiffened as she looked round.

Helen couldn't understand a word, but she could tell from the tone Bella was being admonished by the older girl. Judging by their looks, they had to be sisters.

Bella looked from her sister, to Helen, then back again.

When the outburst stopped, Bella pointed again inside the truck and yelled back at her older sister.

Helen watched the exchange, unsure of what to do. She desperately wanted to get Raul, but was terrified if she walked away now she would never find the young girl again. She couldn't risk it. Not after it had been confirmed it was Lika Faye in the picture.

The older girl edged closer to Bella, her eyes never leaving Helen. She stole a furtive glance inside the van. She turned back to her sister hissing at her in Filipino and grabbing at her arm.

'Hi, my name is Helen, I'm a volunteer here,' Helen spoke to the older girl. 'What's your name?'

The girl turned, her eyes narrowing, breathing deeply.

'None of your fucking business,' she growled at Helen.

Helen jerked back as if the girl had struck her. The look of hatred and fear combined with the adult language had been completely unexpected. Before she could recover, Bella was being dragged away from her. Helen started to panic. For Izel's sake she had to speak to these girls.

'Bella, please,' she pleaded with the younger girl. 'I must speak to you.'

Bella looked from Helen to her sister and back again. She was clearly struggling to decide what to do. Suddenly she wrenched her arm back and screamed in English.

'No, Monique. She. Helped. Us.'

The girls stood looking at one another, their eyes locked. Defiance filled Bella's face through the tears still coursing down her cheeks. Then she turned on her heel and marched back to where Helen was still kneeling in the mud. Sobs racked her small body.

Helen gently wrapped her arms around the girl and stroked her hair. Bella buried her face into Helen's neck and whispered: 'Lika Faye helped us.'

Helen could hear Raul calling her before she saw him. Bella's body went rigid in her arms, but she stayed where she was.

'Helen, what are you…' his voice trailed off as he appeared round the van and saw the warning in Helen's eyes.

He slowly approached them and spoke gently in Filipino to the girl. She turned her head slightly so she could see him through one eye. Her small fists clutched tightly at Helen's tee-shirt. Helen stood up, pulling Bella with her.

'She knows Lika Faye,' Helen explained. 'She saw the photograph.' She nodded towards the van.

A frown creased Raul's forward. 'She's seen Lika Faye? Here?'

'No. She says she saw her a few weeks ago in Cebu.'

'Cebu?'

Helen nodded.

'Is she sure it's Lika Faye? I wouldn't want to call Izel…'

'It's her,' Bella turned to face Raul fully. 'She helped us, we were trying to get away from Phil and Rosela and she helped us…' the words tumbled out.

Raul and Helen looked at each other in confusion.

'Us?' was all Raul could find to say.

Helen nodded at Monique who was standing watching the events unfold. Her arms crossed, her eyes narrowed to slits. Her lips were pressed tightly together, a frown creased her forehead.

'Bella? Our friend is Lika Faye's daddy. He's been looking for her.' Helen stroked the girl's hair and tucked some behind her ear. 'Can you come with us and tell us some more?'

Bella nodded.

'Go and see if there's a room or office we can use, Raul.'

He nodded and walked off to find a teacher. Passing the volunteers, still busy serving, he smiled at them. 'Keep up the good work and if there's some left when they've all eaten, you can offer seconds.'

'Bella, I'm going to put you down.' The girl's fingers tightened their hold on Helen's shirt. 'It's okay, I'm not going anywhere.'

She gently lowered the girl to the ground and remained crouching, their eyes level. She couldn't begin to imagine what the sisters had been through, but something told her it wasn't good. Raul returned with the headmistress who said they could use her office. Helen stood, tenderly took hold of Bella's hand and they followed the teacher. Peering over her shoulder from time to time, Helen could see Monique trailing them.

Once inside, Helen sat Bella down and handed her a bottle of water.

'We're a bit confused, Bella,' Helen looked at Raul for support; he nodded. 'How did you meet Lika Faye in Cebu?'

'I, err, we, we were working for Phil and Rosela and so was she,' Helen frowned. 'Who are Phil and Rosela?'

'Rosela, she took us off the streets after mummy and daddy died,' Bella looked from Raul to Helen and then to Monique who was peering around the door.

Helen shook her head and screwed up her eyes, none of this made sense.

'I'm sorry, Bella, can you start at the beginning? What happened to your mummy and daddy?'

'They...they,' she started sobbing again, unable to continue.

'Oh for goodness sake!' Monique stomped in the room. 'I'll tell you.'

She explained how their parents had been killed in the earthquakes which had hit Cebu. The house had fallen on them while Bella and she had been playing outside. Homeless, with no money and unable to contact their aunt in Tacloban, they had decided to beg on the streets.

'We thought if we could get enough money for the ferry to Ormoc and then the bus, we would be able to find Auntie Susan. We had come with mum and dad a few times before, so we knew the way.'

Before they had managed to get enough for the fares, they had been approached by Rosela. Monique stopped her story as anger shone in her eyes. She crossed the room to Bella and sat beside her. She took her sisters hand, as if to find the words to carry on.

'It's okay, Monique. Take your time,' Helen spoke gently.

'She seemed very kind at first,' she said. 'Asked us why we were going to Tacloban and offered to help us. She said we could go with her and get some food and she would be able to give us enough money for the ferry.'

A feeling of dread clutched at Helen's stomach. She licked her lips and swallowed, afraid of what was going to come next.

'Raul? Helen?' Simon's voice called from outside.

'I'll go,' said Raul. 'Should I call Izel?'

'Yes, but tell him we need his help. He'll probably have an accident if you tell him the truth.'

He nodded and went off to organise the volunteers.

Helen dragged a chair over to sit in front of the girls.

'No one's going to hurt you now. No one is angry with you, we only want to find Lika Faye and get her back to her family,' said

Helen.

Monique nodded, took a deep breath, her eyes hard and continued. 'Rosela put us in the basement. There are other girls. Some older, they went with the men. We had to,' she faltered. 'We had to perform for men on cameras.'

'And...' Helen cleared her throat then smiled sympathetically at the sisters. 'And Lika Faye?'

'She came a few weeks later,' said Bella quietly. 'She was friends with Phoebe.'

'Phoebe?'

'She was there before us. Her dad sold her to Phil,' said Monique.

'Right.' Helen closed her eyes briefly and shook her head. 'You've done so well, girls, thank you for telling me. It can't be easy for you, I'm sure all you want to do is forget what happened.'

They both nodded.

'But if you can be really brave and help us, maybe we can find Lika Faye and get her back to her family too.'

The girls looked at each other and had a hushed conversation in Filipino. Helen heard Lika Faye's name mentioned several times. After a few moments, they stopped and turned to her.

'Okay,' said Monique. 'But can we go and have our lunch now?'

CHAPTER TWENTY

The excited squeal and hand clapping startled Lika Faye and Phoebe. They looked at Rosela in surprise, frowns on their faces.

'What are you looking at?' she snarled at them. 'Get back to work.'

The girls exchanged a glance, shrugged their shoulders and returned to their monitors. Lika Faye had an impatient client waiting for a show. She approached Rosela to arrange for the money transfer.

'What?' she shouted at the girl, turning suddenly, then looking quickly back to the computer and fumbling with a couple of keys to change the screen.

'He wants to transfer money,' Lika Faye said nodding in the direction of her computer.

'Oh, right, yes. Well get over there and get ready. I'll sort it out.'

Something was definitely up, thought Lika Faye. Rosela had been absorbed all evening, busily typing away and muttering to herself. A couple of times she had caught the woman staring at her. It had made her feel very uneasy.

As Lika Faye donned the clothes and make-up her client had requested, she watched Rosela. She had expected the woman to be more of a slave driver than Phil and had been dreading the evening with her in charge. Instead, she had barely bothered the girls and seemed almost irritated when they had approached her for money transfers. A shiver of fear ran up Lika Faye's spine. She didn't know what the woman was up to, but she knew it couldn't be good. She sighed heavily and turned her attention to the man on the screen in front of her. She faked a smile through her bright red painted lips and started to gyrate to the music the man had requested she dance to.

'C'mon, honey,' the nameless face leered at her. 'Start taking your dress off now…slowly, slowly.'

Lika Faye tried to shut out the grunts and groans which filled the room as she stripped for her client. Finally after one last loud, satisfied moan, the room went silent and the man's image faded from the screen. Lika Faye returned the clothes to the shelves, re-dressed in her shorts and tee-shirt and trudged back to her computer. Rosela didn't even look up as she passed behind her chair. She was typing two-fingered and Lika Faye could see the woman's tongue poking out of the side of her mouth in concentration. Her eyes darted to the screen. Rosela was chatting to someone online, she could see a message as it popped up on the screen.

'How long before Faye will be ready…'

She couldn't read anymore without Rosela becoming aware of her lingering. Her mouth went dry and a fizz of fear rose up from her belly. Why was she being punished in this way? She should be at home with her family after a day at school with her friends. Not living in a basement, performing for gross, old men. She slumped in her seat and a small sob escaped from her chest. Phoebe turned to look at her, a frown on her face. Lika Faye looked at her friend, shook her head and started back at work.

It was a slow night, despite there only being two of them. With so little money coming in, Phil would have been shouting and threatening them with no dinner. Rosela barely looked up.

'What do you think she's up to?' whispered Phoebe. 'I've never known her to leave us alone for so long.'

Lika Faye glanced at the woman to make sure she wasn't listening to them. 'I don't know.' She licked her lips and looked down before continuing. 'But, I saw my name on the screen. Whoever she's talking to, is talking about me. Why would she be doing that? It can't be good, right?' She looked at Phoebe, her eyes wide.

'What did it say?'

'"How long before Faye will be ready…"' I couldn't see anything else. Ready for what? I'm scared, Phoebe.'

Phoebe smiled. 'It's probably just a new client. I'm sure it can't be anything important. Anyway, Phil makes all the decisions. Ratface can't do anything without his say so.'

'But we usually find the men in the chatrooms. Phil doesn't find them for us. I just don't trust her, Phoebe.'

'Hey! What's going on over there?' They both snapped their heads round as Rosela yelled at them. 'Get back to work you lazy bitches.'

They turned back to their computers and started trawling the chat rooms for possible clients. It wasn't long before Lika Faye had a potential customer.

BigDK69: Hi. Asl?

11_f_leyte: hi. 11, f, cebu

BigDK69: What u doing in this chat room?

11_f_leyte: looking for friend

BigDK69: Are u really 11?

11_f_leyte: yes sir. u want be my friend?

BigDK69: Maybe

11_f_leyte: where u from?

BigDK69: Sweden. u know where that is?

11_f_leyte: no sir

BigDK69: Never mind

11_f_leyte: how old?

BigDK69: 63, but I like young girls like u. What do u do?

11_f_leyte: whatever u want

BigDK69: u have cam? Can I see u.

11_f_leyte: need money first sir

BigDK69: u have toys?

11_f_leyte: many toys sir, u tell what u want

BigDK69: how much for 15 mins

11_f_leyte: Special price for u sir, $50

BigDK69: Ur not cheap. Maybe I find other girl

11_f_leyte: not as good as me

BigDK69: u like big cock?

11_f_leyte: :)

BigDK69: U do strip show for me. Wear a pretty dress for me then use toys, put them inside u like my big cock

11_f_leyte: sure u pay now

BigDK69: yes, my cock getting hard and big. U like that?

11_f_leyte: yes sir

BigDK69: Hurry girl, get me transfer details

11_f_leyte: one sec sir

Lika Faye approached Rosela. The woman was so absorbed in her chat, she jumped when her name was called. 'What?' she said sharply.

'I have a customer, Miss Rosela.'

Rosela rose from her chair and marched to Lika Faye's computer to complete the transaction. She hadn't closed down her chat in the rush. Now Lika Faye had a chance to take a sideways glance at the screen.

Rosy: It will take a few days to get everything ready

Craig101: But you have done snuff videos before right?

Rosy: yes, yes, no worry.

Criag101: We're talking big bucks here. I want to know I'm getting my money's worth.

'Okay, Faye you can go and get ready.' Rosela looked up. 'What are you doing there?'

Lika Faye looked at the ground. 'Nothing, Miss Rosela. Waiting for you to transfer the money.'

Rosela strode over, lifting Lika Faye's chin with her hand. 'Best you go and perform for your client, before you feel my hand across your face then, eh?' she hissed at her.

Lika Faye backed away, bumping into Rosela's chair. She steadied herself and ran to the other end of the room. With trembling fingers she changed into a flowery dress and prepared for her latest performance. She found it difficult to concentrate on her client's demands at first. When he complained the second time, she put her thoughts aside. Finally the session ended and she went back to her computer. Her head was swimming with what she had read on Rosela's screen. She didn't understand all the words, but she was sure it wasn't good and that they referred to her.

Lika Faye committed the message to memory so she could repeat it to Phoebe later and ask her if she knew what they meant. Phoebe's words about Rosela being unable to do anything without Phil's permission gave little comfort.

Finally Rosela decided to call it a night and ushered the girls out of the webcam sex den and back to their mattresses. They picked up their bowls of rice and cups of water once the basement door was closed. Phoebe shovelled the paltry meal into her mouth, until she noticed Lika Faye hadn't started eating.

'Aren't you hungry?'

Lika Faye looked at her friend and shook her head.

'What is it?' Phoebe continued to eat ravenously, licking her fingers of the last grains of rice. 'If you don't want yours...'

Lika Faye handed over her bowl. 'Do you know what a "snuff" is?' she asked.

'A "snuff"?'

'Yes, it was in the chat Rosela was having online. I'm pretty sure it was about me, they were talking about making a "snuff video".'

'Never heard of it. Are you sure you read it right?'

'It was definitely what was on the screen.'

'Shut up you two, we're trying to sleep here,' yelled Marianne.

'Marianne might know, if you're brave enough to ask her,' whispered Phoebe.

Lika Faye looked over to the older girl's mattress.

'Erm, Marianne, could I ask you something?'

'Now? Are you for real?'

'Please?'

Marianne sat up. 'Stop your whining. What is it?'

'Do you know what a "snuff video" is?'

'Yeah, I've heard of it. I think it's when a video is made snuffing someone out, you know, killing them.'

Lika Faye and Phoebe gasped and looked at each other.

'Are you sure?' Lika Faye asked her voice trembling.

'Pretty much. I'm sure Jenny'll be able to tell you if you don't believe me,' she said sarcastically. 'Why do you want to know?'

'Lika Faye saw Ratface's conversation with someone about it. She thinks it's about her.'

Clearly intrigued, Marianne got up from her mattress and crossed to where the two younger girls were sitting. She flopped down beside them.

'What did you actually see?' She fixed Lika Faye with a stare.

Lika Faye looked at the ground and repeated word for word what she had committed to memory.

'Oh shit, kid, that really ain't good.'

'Marianne!' said Phoebe. 'Can't you see she's already scared?' Phoebe took Lika Faye's hand. 'Anyway, Ratface can't do anything without Phil's say so, can she, Marianne?' she looked pleadingly at the older girl.

'Yeah, yeah, that's right and you're his favourite. You probably got it all wrong, kid. Don't worry about it. Now get some sleep. I had a lot of customers tonight and I need to catch up on my beauty sleep,' she sneered and stood. She uncharacteristically bent down and stroked Lika Faye's head. 'It'll be fine, kid.' She quickly turned and went back to her own mattress.

'See. It'll be okay. You can sleep with me tonight if you like.' Phoebe smiled at her and the two girls lay down, hand in hand.

Lika Faye listened as Phoebe's breathing slowed. She lay looking up at the ceiling. She knew Rosela hated her. What if this was her way of getting rid of her? Would it be so bad though? She missed her family desperately but couldn't see how she was ever going to see them again. When she died, she would be with Jesus. She would see them all again in Heaven one day. Then a new fear gripped her. Would she be allowed into Heaven after the things she'd been doing in the den? She untangled her hand from Phoebe's and clutched her hands together on her chest in prayer. Her lips mouthed the words she offered up.

'Please God forgive me my sins. I didn't want to do the things they made me. Please let me into Heaven, so one day I can see mummy and daddy and grandma and granddad again. I miss them all so much.'

She repeated her prayer until eventually she fell into a fitful sleep, her hands still clasped together.

CHAPTER TWENTY-ONE

'Izel, I want you to remain calm, okay?' Helen stood outside the headmistress' office with Izel and Raul.

'Okay, Miss Helen.' He tugged at his chin hairs and a high-pitched giggle escaped from his confused face. 'What is it? Mr Neil said you need my help.'

'Let's sit over here,' Helen led him to a low wall a few metres away from the school building. 'Raul, could you get us a couple of bottles of water please? And perhaps you could check on…' she indicated the room they had come from to meet Izel.

He nodded and headed back to his little red van.

A frown crossed Izel's face and his heart started to beat a little faster. 'What's going on, Miss Helen?'

'I've been talking to a couple of young girls who go to school here.' She looked Izel in the eyes and took a deep breath. 'They've seen Lika Faye.'

Izel continued to look at Helen, he blinked a few times and his frown deepened, furrowing his forehead. His eyes narrowed and he nodded a couple of times while the words she said reached his brain. Suddenly his eyes widened and he jumped up with a squeal.

'What? Where? Where is she? I knew she was still alive.' He looked desperately around him. 'Lika Faye? Lika Faye?' he screamed.

Helen stood and put her hand on his arm. 'Izel. Izel. She's not here.'

He was staring at her and she could see the confusion in his face.

'But you said…Where is she then? You must take me to her now. Lika Faye! Lika Faye!' He pulled away from Helen and spun around calling out.

Helen closed her eyes briefly. She had known this wasn't going to be easy. She was dreading having to tell Izel where his daughter was and what she was doing.

'Izel! You have to calm down. Take a deep breath. Look at me, breath in….and out.' She took hold of his hands and tried to sooth the trembling man in front of her.

'But she is alive, Miss Helen?' he whispered after a few moments.

She nodded. 'She helped these two girls escape a couple of weeks ago…from Cebu.'

"Cebu? What she doing in Cebu?'

'I'm sorry, Izel, we don't know all the details. I can take you to meet the girls, but you must stay calm. Don't frighten them. Do you understand?'

'Yes, yes, let me speak with them, Miss Helen. I need to know my little girl is okay,' he clutched at his heart, whispering to himself. 'I knew you were alive.' He looked to the sky. 'Thank you, Lord.'

Helen let out a big sigh. She wasn't sure how grateful he would feel once he learned what had happened to his daughter over the past few months.

Raul returned and handed them both a bottle of water. He spoke gently to Izel in Filipino while the other man gulped down some water. He wiped his mouth and responded excitedly gesticulating to Raul's van.

'I told him it was the photo in the van, that one of the girls saw it,' he explained to Helen.

She nodded. 'Are they okay? Will they be okay to speak to him?'

'I've warned them he may be a little excited.' He smiled wryly.

'Ready, Izel?'

He nodded and they returned to the school building and the two young girls inside.

'Izel, this is Monique and Bella.' Helen introduced the girls.

Izel hurled the questions bubbling inside him at the girls. They shrunk back into their chairs and looked helplessly at each other, then Helen. She knelt down between them and took their hands.

'It's okay. He's a bit agitated. Give him a moment. He just wants to find out about his daughter.'

Raul gripped Izel by the shoulders and turned him away from the terrified girls. He was now speaking softly to the overwrought man. Izel nodded and hung his head, trying to compose himself. Raul grabbed some chairs, he handed one to Helen and the two men sat facing Monique and Bella.

Helen sat patiently between the girls as the four of them carried out a conversation in Filipino. The only words she understood were Lika Faye and Cebu. As the girls explained their story, Izel turned ashen and tears started to run down his cheeks dripping onto his tee-shirt. Finally he could take no more. He jumped up, knocking his chair backwards and headed out of the room. Helen and Raul looked at each other.

'I'll stay with the girls, you go after him,' Helen said. She smiled at Bella and then Monique. 'Well done, girls. I know that can't have been easy for you. Shall we find a Sari Sari store and get some Coke and sweets?'

The girls nodded and jumped up enthusiastically. At least they haven't lost all of the simple pleasures of childhood, Helen thought.

They left the office and wandered across the tented grass area and out of one of the school entrances. Sari Sari shops lined the street, but the girls had a favourite and ignored all the others until they reached it. Then they turned to Helen.

'Choose a drink and whatever sweets you want.'

They didn't need asking twice, jabbering away in Filipino at the store owner. Two cold Cokes were set on the counter. Droplets of condensation formed immediately and ran down the red and silver cans. They took it in turns deliberating over their sweets; finally satisfied, they walked away from the grill, giving Helen room to step up and pay. As the girls sucked on their straws and chattered together, Helen walked out of earshot and dialled Pieter's number.

'Hey, gorgeous,' his boyish voice sang in her ear. 'I was just thinking about you. Do you want to meet for dinner at Guiseppe's this evening?'

'Hi. I erm. I was actually ringing about something else. I was hoping you might be able to help me with something, or rather that Ménage des Enfants might be able to.'

'Sounds intriguing, what do you have in mind?'

'Do you remember the story I told you about Izel, WDR's driver?'

'He's the one with the missing daughter, right?'

'Yeah. Except we think we may have found out where she is. You won't believe this, Pieter. She's working in a webcam sex den in Cebu. She's only eleven years old.' Helen's voice cracked; the emotions she had managed to keep in check for the past few hours burst forth.

'Helen, Helen. Tell me where you are, I'll meet you there.'

She gave him the name of the school and ended the call. With her back to the girls, she dashed away her tears, blew her nose and took a few deep breaths. When she turned round Bella and Monique were engrossed in counting the number of sweets they had left. Helen smiled. Kids were so much better at adjusting.

'Have you got one for me?'

They both offered up their sticky palms. She laughed and picked one from each hand. They ambled back in through the school gates as several hundred children erupted from their classes and swarmed into the play area. Shouts and shrieks filled the air. Groups of boys kicked makeshift footballs or launched their homemade kites into the sky. Clusters of girls huddled together, deep in discussion, shouting angrily when disturbed by wayward footballs.

Bella and Monique ran to join their own little groups of friends. Faces turned to Helen briefly as they were asked why they had missed classes, but quickly returned to more important childish issues.

Helen looked around her and spotted Izel and Raul deep in conversation by the WDR truck. She thought it best to leave them to it and sat on a wall in the shade, waiting for Pieter to turn up. Sweat tricked down her back in the mid-afternoon humidity. She closed her eyes and leaned back against the wall. The words of the girls raced around in her mind. She rubbed at her temples. Poor Izel, she thought, how must he be feeling? On the one hand, it was great news, Lika Faye was alive, but the circumstances! She felt drained thinking about it and the heat was making her drowsy. She dropped her hands into her lap and the noise from the playground faded into the distance.

'Helen?'

She jumped, her eyes shot open. She wiped at the glob of dribble at the corner of her mouth with the back of her hand.

'Pieter. Sorry, I seemed to have drifted off.'

He bent and kissed her cheek then plopped down on the wall beside her.

'So, what's happened here today?'

Helen leaned forward and resting her chin in her hands, she told him what had transpired as they had started serving lunch. He listened without interrupting as she finished with Izel's reaction.

'How can people do this, Pieter? What is the matter with the world, that people will treat children like this?'

'There are some evil people about, Helen. It's an uphill battle and we do the best we can. Let's see if we can help Lika Faye be reunited with her family.'

'Where do we begin?'

'Well, I need to make some phone calls first, but I'd say we'll move very quickly once we have all the information. We'll need Bella and Monique's help to locate the house.'

'Okay, tell me when you're ready and I'll go and find them.'

Pieter had a team of people assembled at the school before the final bell rang. From Ménage des Enfants he had brought a Filipino child psychiatrist to talk to the girls and several logistics specialists. He had also managed to get a representative from the Visayas Hope

Organisation (VHO) to assist in developing a rescue plan. They were assembled in the headmistress' office discussing the meagre information they had received from Helen. It had been decided they wouldn't interrupt Bella and Monique's classes to save them any more embarrassing questions from their classmates. Helen and Raul waited outside the tents so they could subtly approach the girls after school finished.

'You've already built up a rapport with them, they trust you, it'll be best if you are the ones to explain what's happening next,' Martha, the psychiatrist had told them.

Izel stood listening to the discussions. He hopped from foot to foot and pulled at the hairs on his chin.

'What's happening?' He tugged at Pieter's tee-shirt. 'When are you going to Cebu to rescue my daughter?'

'We're working on it, Izel.' He smiled at the slight Filipino man. 'I know this is difficult for you and it's not what you want to hear, but you need to be patient. We have to get this right. We may only have one chance, we don't want it to go wrong, do we?'

Izel bobbed his head in agreement. 'I just want my little girl home. Can I come with you to Cebu?'

'I don't think it would be a good idea, Izel. I promise we'll bring her straight to you, but I think it would be best you stay here with your family.'

He nodded unconvincingly. He hadn't told Adelaida the news yet. He thought it best to speak to her in person, but he couldn't leave until he knew Ménage des Enfants' plan.

Finally the bell rang, releasing the children from their lessons. Bella emerged from the hot tent, blinking in the sunlight.

'Hi, Bella,' Helen called out to her.

Bella squinted and put up her hand to shade her eyes. She frowned. 'We told you everything before.'

'I know this isn't easy for you. You've been so brave, but I need you and Monique to come and explain where the house is. We need to find Lika Faye and the other girls. Please help us, Bella.'

The girl hung her head. 'My auntie will be expecting us,' she mumbled.

'We can go with you to her house if you like?' suggested Helen.

Bella's head shot up, a look of fear crossed her face. 'No!'

Helen looked at the young girl in front of her as realisation dawned on her. 'She doesn't know, does she? What happened to you and Monique in Cebu?'

Bella shook her head. 'Monique and me, we agreed. We wanted to forget…'

Helen crouched down in front of her. 'It's okay, Bella. I understand. We don't have to tell her.' She smiled reassuringly.

Monique and Raul materialised around the side of the tent, deep in conversation. They stopped as they reached Helen and Bella. Monique spoke quickly to her younger sister. They appeared to reach an agreement.

'Okay, let's get this over with. Then you leave us alone. Is that agreed?' said Monique.

Helen nodded and the four of them walked across the play area to the headmistress' office. As they walked in, the room fell silent and all faces turned to the sisters. Bella reached for Monique's hand, as Martha approached them. The rest of the group moved into the corridor to give them some space. The psychiatrist knew what information the group needed to be able to mount a rescue mission. She gently questioned the girls and tried to ascertain the psychological damage their time in the den had caused them. Outside, a plan was already being drawn up. Flights to Cebu were being booked and the rep from VHO was in contact with his people there to prepare a team to storm the address, once they had all the relevant details. Helen, Raul and Izel watched from the periphery as a strategy to free the girls was developed. Izel was visibly anxious despite Helen and Raul trying to convince him that the best people were involved.

'I asked Pieter, he won't let me go with them to Cebu. Could you speak to him, Miss Helen? I wouldn't get in the way.'

Helen looked to Raul for support. 'They know what they're doing, Izel. If they think it's best you stay here…'

'Don't worry, man. Look at them, they've already got a plan organised. They'll be back before you know it and you'll be reunited with Lika Faye. Why don't you go home and let Adelaida know what's happening. We can keep you updated on what's happening.' Raul nodded to Helen.

'Yes, Izel, Raul is right. Go and tell your family and we'll call you as soon as we hear anything, I promise.'

Izel tugged hard at his chin hairs. Finally he nodded. 'Okay. But you promise to call me the second you know anything?' He looked from one to other.

'We promise.'

After an hour, Martha appeared at the door. 'I don't think we can ask the girls to stay any longer, they need to get back to their auntie. Once they've gone, I'll fill you in with what I know.'

Helen smiled at the girls as they emerged. 'Thank you.'

Monique nodded at her and led Bella outside. Everyone poured back inside, notepads at the ready to listen to Martha's information.

'Luckily the girls are from Cebu, so at least have a rough idea of where the house is located. However, we don't have an address.'

There were groans from a couple of the team. 'This will make it a bit more complicated.'

Martha ignored them and continued. 'They have given a reasonable description of the house and the area and I've had them both draw what they remember of the inside and outside of the house. It's not ideal I know, but it's a start.'

She placed the drawings on a table and the team gathered round to look.

'Monique has agreed to look at photographs you send back from Cebu to confirm when you have found the right house.'

Pieter turned to Daniel from VHO. 'Do you have people on the ground in Cebu who can start canvassing the area?'

'I'll get on it now.' Daniel was already punching at his Smart phone.

'Okay, people. We need to be at the airport in an hour if we're to catch our flights. You have enough time to get back to your hotels, pack what you need and get out to San Jose. Let's go,' Pieter said.

'I'll call you when we arrive in Cebu and keep you up-to-date.' He kissed Helen before rushing out of the office and was gone before she had a chance to reply.

CHAPTER TWENTY-TWO

Izel left the headmistress' office in a state of agitation. He muttered to himself as he stumbled towards the WDR truck. He rummaged in his pockets for the keys and cursed when he couldn't find them. He was halfway back to the school building when he finally located them in a side pocket in his shorts. He ran back to the van and fumbled to get the key in the ignition, his hands were trembling so much. He finally got the truck fired up and sat back.

'Okay, Izel, calm down.' He wiped his hand over his face and took a few deep breaths. When he felt he was a little more in control, he slipped the truck into first gear and slowly let out the clutch. His mind was in turmoil. His daughter was alive, but in Cebu. She was having to perform…He braked suddenly, opened the door, leapt out and threw up. He put his hand against the side of the truck to steady himself. He was panting and sobbing. Finally he stood, exhaled deeply and climbed back into the truck.

'C'mon!' he yelled, beeping his horn at the jeepney in front of him as it stopped to let yet more passengers off. Seeing a gap in the oncoming traffic he overtook then slammed on his brakes, narrowly missing a pedicab as it veered across the road in front of him. He stalled the truck as he went to move off again and he leaned his head against the steering wheel for a moment. Sweat rivulets mixed with tears as he re-started the vehicle and moved off.

As he drove the thirty minutes to the Assumption Academy tent city, he thought about what he was going to say to Adelaida. Should he tell her everything? How could he explain to his wife what their daughter was having to do? He gripped the steering wheel until his knuckles turned white as rage engulfed him. How could they do this to his little girl?

He parked the truck and made his way to his tent. Adelaida was busy chatting to a couple of neighbours. She stopped midsentence when she saw his face.

'Izel? Are you alright? What's happened?'

'Where's Angelina,' he asked.

'Playing with friends? Should I go and get her?'

'No, no. Come inside, we need to talk.'

Adelaida said a hasty goodbye and followed him into their tent.

'What is it, Izel? You're scaring me.'

'Do you want to sit, Adelaida.' He pulled out a stool and indicated for her to take a seat. He paced the width of the tent, raking his hands through his hair.

'Izel! What is it?'

He stopped and looked at his wife. 'They've found Lika Faye.'

'What? Where?' Adelaida jumped up and put her hands to her cheeks, then her excitement faded. 'Oh no, she's dead, isn't she.'

'No, no, she's alive.'

'So where is she? Why isn't she with you?'

'She's in Cebu.'

'Cebu? What's she doing in Cebu? Is she with my auntie?' A puzzled frown crossed Adelaida's face as she tried to make sense of what she was hearing.

'Please sit, Adelaida.'

They sat together on their mattress. Izel took her hands in his and told her everything he knew.

Adelaida listened in silence as he explained how Monique and Bella had seen the photograph and confirmed it was Lika Faye. His voice softened as he tried to tell her as gently as possible what their daughter was doing in Cebu. Adelaida gasped and her hands flew to her mouth.

'Oh my, oh my.' She rocked back and forth. 'My poor baby. She's just a child, Izel. How can they do this to children?'

'This Ménage des Enfants organisation, they're planning to go to Cebu today and find her.'

Adelaida stopped rocking and stared at her husband. 'Who's going to Cebu? Can we go?'

'I begged them to let me go, but they said no. It's an organisation which works with trafficked people, especially children. They have some posters up by the church: Ménage des Enfants, you must have seen them. They said they would bring her straight to us once they get back here. Miss Helen promised she would call as soon as she knew anything.'

'Is she going? Why is she going if we can't?'

'I, err, no, she's not going, but she knows the man in charge.'

Adelaida nodded and looked at Izel with a small smile. 'You were right all along. You said she was still alive.'

'Yes,' he wiped a tear from her cheek. 'But I wish it was under better circumstances.' He shook his head, unable to continue.

They sat in silence with their own thoughts for several minutes. Adelaida seemed suddenly to come to a decision. She wiped her tears away and stood.

'Whatever has happened, she's still our little girl. Come on, Izel. No more moping. She will need a bed and some clothes. We need to get ready to welcome our Lika Faye home.'

Rogelio and Lorna returned home with Angelina to find a flurry of activity in the tent. Izel explained to his mother and father the day's events. Adelaida spared their younger daughter the details, only telling her that her sister had been found and was coming home.

'She can have her *Hello Kitty* bag back,' Angelina announced triumphantly and emptied her school things out of the grubby pink backpack.

'She'll like that, sweetie.' Izel said, stroking his daughter's hair.

That evening the adults ate their dinner of chicken and rice in silence, while Angelina chattered on excitedly about all the things she had to tell Lika Faye: how they were having classes in tents; she would have to show her where to get water from.

'Mummy, do you think I'll recognise her? It's been such a long time since I saw her. What happens if she gets here and we don't know it's her?'

'Ssshhh now, Angelina and eat your dinner. I'm sure you'll recognise her,' said Lorna.

Once Angelina had been put to bed, they sat outside the tent, candles flickering in the warm evening. Izel couldn't settle. He kept checking his phone.

'Maybe it's not working. Dad can you call my number?'

'Son, they'll call when they have any news. Come, sit, have some Tuba. I got some today from Ralph. It's good stuff and will help you sleep.'

'No thanks, dad. I want to keep a clear head in case she comes back tonight.'

'Izel, whatever happens in Cebu, they won't be back tonight. You know they can't land here in the dark yet. The control tower hasn't been rebuilt.' Rogelio held out a cup.

Izel accepted it and took a long draught of the palm wine. 'I think I'll just give Miss Helen a quick call anyway.' He wandered away from the tent, pulling his mobile phone out of his pocket.

'Hello, Miss Helen, it's Izel. Yes…yes, okay…I understand. I charged my phone. I will have it with me. Call me anytime, yes…yes, okay, thank you.'

The other three fell silent as he returned.

'No news. Maybe in the morning.' He filled his cup with more Tuba and the four of them chatted in hushed tones until bedtime.

'You go ahead,' Izel said to Adelaida. 'I'll be in soon.'

He gazed up at the star-filled sky willing the sun to rise and bring news of his daughter.

The beeping of his phone woke him. He rubbed his neck where the back of the chair had dug into him as he frantically opened the message. His heart thumped. The candles had all burned down and the light from the phone reflected in his face. It was from Ian telling him to take as many days off as he needed and they would arrange to pick up the truck in the morning. It was only eleven o'clock. He went to relieve himself in the latrines. He could hear snoring from some of the tents as he walked past, apart from that the tented city was quiet. When he got back, he lay fully clothed next to Adelaida, staring into the darkness. He hated the waiting, the not knowing. Finally sleep claimed him.

CHAPTER TWENTY-THREE

Lika Faye and Phoebe were in the kitchen. They had spent the last three hours cleaning the house and were making rice for the girls' dinner. Rosela was sitting at the kitchen table. She was poring over a trashy magazine. She looked up occasionally to shout abuse at the two girls.

'Get me another tinny.' Phil's voice roared from the lounge.

'You heard the man, Phoebe, take him a beer.'

Phoebe looked from Rosela to Lika Faye.

'What are you looking at her for? You heard me, take him a beer…now!'

Phoebe jumped as Rosela shrieked the last word at her and did as she was told.

Lika Faye continued to stir the rice, shrinking into herself, hoping Rosela would leave her alone. She was concentrating so hard on trying to be invisible she didn't hear the woman come up behind her.

'Not so smug these days are we, Missy?' Rosela hissed in her ear.

Lika Faye dropped the wooden spoon in fright and it clattered to the floor. She stood frozen looking into the rice pot. Her heart beat manically in her chest as she willed Rosela away. She felt hot breath on her ear.

'Pick it up then, you stupid little bitch,' Rosela spat at her.

Lika Faye slithered down to a crouching position and grabbed the spoon. She cowered, expecting a hail of blows or kicks from the woman. When none came she looked up to see an evil grin on Rosela's face. She stood slowly and returned to stirring the rice. Rosela turned and went back to her magazine.

The intercom from the gate buzzed. Lika Faye looked round to see Rosela frowning.

'Get that, Rosela,' Phil yelled as Phoebe walked back into the kitchen.

'I'm watching the girls,' she yelled back.

'And I'm watching TV, do as you're fucking told.'

'Lazy bastard,' Rosela said under her breath. Then to the girls: 'Stay in here and keep quiet.'

'Yes?' she spoke into the intercom.

'It's Sergeant Ramos. Let me in, quick now.'

'I'm sorry, Sergeant, the girls aren't working yet,' Rosela replied irritably.

'I'm not after a girl. Let me in, or do you want the whole street to know?'

Rosela buzzed him in and opened the front door.

'Who is it?' yelled Phil.

'Sergeant Ramos.'

'What's he want?'

'I don't know, Phil, he hasn't told me yet,' Rosela shrieked sarcastically.

Lika Faye and Phoebe exchanged glances. They knew the police used the services of the older girls, but why was one of them coming to the house outside of working hours?

'Do you think he could be from Monique and Bella?' whispered Phoebe, her eyes wide.

'I don't know. Sshh, maybe we can hear what he says.'

They took a couple of steps towards the half closed door, their curiosity overcoming the fear of being caught eavesdropping by Rosela. They could see Sergeant Ramos come through the front door and slam it behind him.

'Where's Mr Phil?' he said.

Rosela pointed into the lounge and followed him in, closing the door behind her.

'I wonder if they're in trouble,' said Phoebe. 'Let's hope so.'

Lika Faye looked at her friend and shook her head. 'He's probably just after more money from them. Remember Marianne told us they get paid to protect the house.'

They heard Phil's raised voice cursing at the policeman and the lounge door flew open. The girls nearly fell over one another as they headed back to the pot of steaming rice. They heard the front door open and bang closed. Rosela disappeared back into the lounge. They could hear Phil's voice, but couldn't make out what he was saying. After a few minutes Rosela appeared in the kitchen, her face pale.

'Leave that. Come with me, quickly.'

Lika Faye glanced out of the kitchen door as they passed it. Phil was shouting down the phone at someone, pacing up and down in the hallway. Rosela opened the door to the stairs and almost pushed the girls down them in her rush. At the bottom she fumbled with the light switches and the keypad and the three of them burst through into the basement.

'Get up all of you and come with me. Now!'

The older girls all looked up from their mattresses, blinking in the light.

Rosela kicked their beds as she walked past. 'Up! Now! Follow me.'

She strode to the door of the den and unlocked the padlock.

'Grab everything you can, all the laptops, quickly.'

'What's going on?' Marianne asked.

Rosela turned on her heel and slapped her across the face. 'Laptops, now!'

Marianne reeled back, gasping in surprise and put a hand to her cheek, but she did as she'd been told. Armed with what they could carry, Rosela marched them upstairs.

'What did he say?' she asked Phil as they emerged into the hallway.

'He's on his way. Costing a pretty penny, mind you,' Phil complained.

'How long have we got?'

'Sergeant Ramos' boss said they were still looking for the house, but they had started the process of a warrant. Once they have an address they can move whenever they want. Shit! That's more income lost.'

Rosela stepped closer to Phil. 'It's her I tell you, she's a jinx,' she nodded towards Lika Faye. 'Ever since she got here there's been trouble.'

'Oh shut up, Rosela. I don't have time for your ridiculous superstitions now.'

'But I have a great solution and we could get some of our money back if…'

'Not now,' he roared at her as the gate security system buzzed. 'That's Sam now. Let him in. Have you got everything from downstairs?'

Rosela nodded dumbly at him and opened the gate.

The girls stood in silence. The only sound was the beep, beeping of a truck reversing up to the front door. Phil shuffled out and exchanged a few words with the driver.

'Okay, let's go,' he yelled.

Rosela pushed the girls, still holding the equipment from the basement, out of the house. Five metres of empty truck yawned in front of them, the double doors flung open. To one side a thin man stood with Phil. The sun reflected off his smooth, bald head. Greying hair circled the back of his head and continued across his lip and down his chin. He squinted at the girls as they stumbled out of the front door.

'In, in, quickly, we haven't got all day.' Phil pushed the girls into the back. 'Are you sure that's everything?' he said as Rosela emerged into the daylight.

'Yes, Phil,' she replied sulkily and flounced down the steps to the passenger door.

Phil watched as Sam started to close the doors. 'You've got a padlock for them, right?'

'That's what you asked for,' the American voice drawled. 'You girls better put them things on the floor and sit down, unless you wanna end up being thrown about.' He winked at the six pairs of eyes looking out at them and slammed the second door into place and secured it.

Marianne was the first to speak. 'Better do as he says or we'll go flying.'

'I can't see anything,' cried Phoebe. 'What's happening?'

Marianne flicked on her lighter. 'Phoebe sit now or you'll be thrown all over us.'

Phoebe plonked down on the truck floor as the engine started.

'Shit,' said Marianne as the heat from the lighter burned her thumb and they were plunged again into darkness as the truck lurched forwards. A sliver of light seeped in from under the double doors at the back and a single door on the passenger's side. As their eyes adjusted, they could barely make out shapes in the gloom.

Lika Faye sat crossed legged. She had put the laptop she had been carrying down on her left against the side of the truck. On her right she was wedged against Jenny. Phoebe was in front of her. She reached out to touch her friend and could feel her shaking.

Finally Jenny broke the stunned silence which had filled the back of the truck. 'What happened upstairs, before you came down with Rosela?'

'We were cooking the rice and a policeman came to the door,' said Lika Faye to the shadow next to her.

'Must be a raid coming,' said Rebecca.

'Wh...where are they taking us?' said Phoebe shakily.

The vehicle turned suddenly, catching the girls unawares. Lika Faye hit her head on the metal side of the truck before she had a chance to steady herself. A sharp pain shot through her temple, but she bit her lip and stayed quiet. She sat in the darkness, her left hand on the side of the truck, her brain numb. She closed her eyes and tried to visualise the faces of her family. If she concentrated hard enough, she could shut out the fear of what was happening to her. Perspiration gathered on her forehead and dripped down her back.

The afternoon sun on the metal was making the air in the truck heat up.

'I feel sick,' Phoebe said.

'Don't throw up over me,' yelled Marianne and she flicked on her lighter as Phoebe vomited.

'Oh shit,' moaned Lourdes as the smell permeated the truck.

'I'm sorry,' said Phoebe woefully and hiccupped.

Finally the truck stopped and the engine was switched off. It shook slightly as first one and then another door opened and the occupants of the cab got out. The girls sat in silence straining to make out what the voices outside were saying as they drifted away.

'They're just leaving us here,' said Rebecca.

'They haven't even given us any water,' said Marianne in disgust.

'They're leaving us here to die.' Phoebe started to sob loudly.

'Phoebe, Phoebe! Think about it, Phil isn't going to spend money on a truck, get us to take all the laptops and then leave us to die. Calm down,' said Jenny. 'Let's move all the computers to one side, so we don't fall over them. Lika Faye, hand me what you brought out of the basement.'

They passed all the equipment over until it was stacked together to one side of the truck and waited. Eventually they could hear steps approaching. A bolt slid on the side door and it opened. Sam stood in the half gloom. The truck was parked under cover and Lika Faye could make out strip lights flickering in the ceiling.

'Here,' Sam handed her bottles of water and packets of dried biscuits. She passed them back to the others. Finally he handed her a torch and an empty bucket. 'That's for you to piss in. Don't mess up my truck and keep quiet.' He slammed the door and bolted it. They heard a scraping as he fixed a padlock to the side door and then one to the back.

'Looks like this is going to be our home for the time being, then,' said Jenny. 'Hand me the torch, Lika Faye and we can try and arrange some space for each of us.'

They reorganised all the equipment in one corner at the back of the truck. Using the plastic wrappers from the biscuits, they did their best to clear up Phoebe's vomit gagging as they scraped it into the bucket which they positioned in the other back corner. It left the area behind the cab for sitting and to lie down. They rationed out the biscuits and water. Jenny switched off the torch to save the batteries and they sat in silence drinking and eating.

Lika Faye and Phoebe sat side-by-side their backs against the back of the truck's cab.

'Has this ever happened before?' asked Lika Faye.

'Not since I've been with them. What about you, Jenny?'

'Nah. Too many of the police come to us. If they're asked to raid us, they say they have, but actually do nothing. This must be something else.'

'I told you, it's Monique and Bella,' said Phoebe excitedly.

'Even if it is, they're not going to find us parked here in a truck are they?' Marianne mocked. 'I hope we're not going to be here for long, I've only got a couple of cigarettes left. Do you think if I offer the driver a freebie he might get me a pack?'

Lika Faye hung her head in the darkness. She couldn't see how she was ever going to escape this vile life. She should have gone with Monique and Bella. At least she might have had a chance. Rosela was even more careful now about letting any of them out of her sight while they were upstairs. Phil no longer came for her when Rosela was out. She curled up into a ball and with her thumb in her mouth, drifted to sleep.

She assumed it was morning when Sam returned, there was no way of telling the time. As soon as they heard the scraping of a key in the padlock, Marianne pushed her way to the door. The bolt slid and the door was opened allowing the sallow, artificial light to creep in. Lika Faye watched Marianne adopt one of her suggestive poses.

'Hey, handsome. How're you today?'

'Hey, stand back there,' Sam obviously hadn't been expecting such a welcome.

Marianne wasn't going to be easily put off. She slid down to her knees so they were face-to-face. She took his chin in her hand. 'Maybe you like some jiggy-jiggy.'

He licked his lips. 'Phil told me to keep my hands off his girls.' He looked over his shoulder.

'Phil not here. I won't tell if you won't.' She leaned closer and kissed his cheek. 'What you want? I can do for cigarettes.' Marianne smiled at the weasel-faced man.

'Yeah, yeah, okay.' He fumbled in his pocket and handed her an open pack of Marlboro Lights.

She snatched them out of his hand and looked inside. Satisfied there were enough, she tucked the packet into the waistband of her shorts.

'Enough for a blow-job. You want more, you bring full packet next time.'

'Okay, blow-job now. Come on hurry up before Phil sends that bitch of his to check on me.' He helped her out of the truck, shut the door and slid the bolt home. After a few moments the occupants of the truck could hear him moaning. It got louder and then abruptly stopped. The door opened again and he lifted Marianne in. He quickly handed in more bottles of water, cans of Coke and food.

'Pass me out that bucket.' He emptied it into a gully and shoved it back through the door. He secured everything up again and they were left once again in darkness. The sound of Sam's whistling receded into the distance.

CHAPTER TWENTY-FOUR

As dawn arrived in Tanauan, the Assumption Academy tent city bustled with morning activity. There were shouts for people to hurry up in the latrines. Women chatted as they collected water for cooking and drinking. Babies cried for their breakfast and children raced around half dressed for school.

'Can't I stay at home today?' whined Angelina.

'I promise I'll come and get you if there's any news,' said Rogelio. 'Now get your bag, I'll take you to school today.'

Izel's eyes were gritty from lack of sleep and a little too much Tuba. Why was it taking so long? Why hadn't he heard anything? He checked his phone again, nothing. His mouth was dry and he grabbed a bottle of water from the Sari Sari store table.

His phone rang in his pocket and he nearly dropped it in his haste to answer it.

'Hello, Miss Helen? Oh hi, Mr Ian. I was hoping…oh right. I can bring the truck to the house if…oh okay. I'll see you in about half an hour. Yes, I'll be here.'

'What did he say?' asked Lorna.

'They're coming to pick up the truck. Miss Helen hasn't heard from Cebu yet. I can't bear this waiting, mum.'

Lorna raised her palm to stroke her son's face and smiled at him.

Ian and the two Swedish volunteers arrived, took the keys and drove the truck away. Still no call came from Helen. The morning crawled by.

Izel paced back and forth in front of the tent, constantly checking his phone for missed calls and for the time.

'Come and sit, have some lunch,' his mother called out to him at midday.

He shook his head. 'I'm not hungry. My stomach is churning as it is. Why haven't they called? What's happening?' He continued to pace, barely acknowledging neighbours as they called out to him.

It was after three o'clock when Helen and Pieter arrived at the Sombilons' tent. Pieter was red-eyed and unshaven. Helen looked solemn, her lips pursed tightly together. Adelaida saw them first and called out to the others. Izel failed to notice their serious expressions. His heart was beating quickly, he was about to see his eldest daughter again.

'Where is she?' he tried to peer behind them, 'Lika Faye?' He looked to Pieter, a frown started to crease his forehead. 'Where is she?' he whispered.

Pieter ran a hand through his curly blond hair. He briefly closed his eyes and took in a deep breath.

'I'm so sorry, Izel. We don't have her.'

'What do you mean? Where is she?' He shook his head. This couldn't be happening. They had gone to rescue his little girl, why wasn't she here?

'We found the house. Monique confirmed it when we sent through a photograph. VHO had arranged for the house to be stormed after dawn. Everything was in place. From what the girls had told us, they usually work all night. We thought we would be able to catch them by surprise if we went in after they had finished work and were sleeping,' Pieter said.

Four pairs of eyes bored into him. Pieter swallowed. 'At the agreed time, the VHO and members of the Cebu police force blew the keypad on the gate and took a ram to the front door. The girls' drawings were very accurate. One team went upstairs to arrest Phil and Rosela, the other into the basement to free the girls.'

'Oh sweet Lord, she's dead, isn't she?' shrieked Adelaida.

'No. Well, the truth is, we don't know.'

'What do you mean?' Izel gripped Pieter by the forearms and started shaking him. 'Where is my daughter?'

'We don't know, Izel. The house was empty.'

'It was the wrong house! Why aren't you still there trying to find the right one?' Izel screamed at him. All the waiting and frustration of the previous night and today and they had come back empty handed; it was more than he could bear.

'Izel, it was the right house. They had been tipped off. The basement was exactly as Monique had described it. The rows of mattresses, the cubicles the older girls used. The…' he searched for the right words. 'The place where the younger girls…worked. It was all there.'

Izel sank to his knees. This couldn't be happening. 'Nooooo!' His cry rang out through the tented city. 'You promised you were going to bring my daughter home.'

Rogelio, Lorna and Adelaida stood together in shocked silence. Adelaida was trembling as she clung onto her father-in-law.

'It's like losing her all over again,' she whispered.

Pieter's face was a mask of despair.

'I'm so sorry we couldn't bring you better news,' Pieter said, rubbing a hand over his stubble. 'We believe the local police were being paid by Phil and Rosela to tip them off if a raid was imminent. They left in a hurry. They even left a computer behind. We're having it analysed now.'

Izel looked up. 'Will it help you find where they've gone?'

'We don't know, Izel. The local police didn't want us to have it at all. But somehow VHO managed to get authorisation for us to bring it back. It's why we've taken so long to get back here.'

Izel turned to Helen accusingly.

'You said you would call when you had some news, Miss Helen. We've been waiting all day…'

Helen look at him, her face full of anguish. 'I know, I'm so sorry Izel, but I didn't think it was something I could tell you over the phone. We owed it to you to come in person.' She knelt down beside him and put a hand on his shoulder. 'Ménage des Enfants will do everything they can to try and trace them.'

'I thought…' Izel choked on his words. 'I thought my prayers were being answered. I never stopped believing she was still alive, but now this…it brings back all the pain of losing her the first time.' He felt as if his heart was breaking. Why was he having to endure such cruelty?

'What happens now?' asked Rogelio.

Pieter turned to the older man. 'We'll see what we can find on the computer first, sir and take it from there. We'll keep looking.'

Rogelio nodded at them. 'Come on, son.' He helped Izel to his feet. 'You'll let us know if you find anything?' He looked at Pieter.

'It may take a few days to examine the information on the computer. We have someone in Cebu keeping an eye on the house in case they decide to return. Once they think the danger of a raid has passed they may feel it's safe to go back. We'll keep you informed of any progress. I know this isn't the news you were hoping for.' Pieter looked apologetically at the family standing in front of him.

Izel gathered himself together. 'Miss Helen, could you tell Mr Ian I'll be back to work tomorrow morning.'

'You can take some time…'

'No. It's better I have something to do. I'll be at the house in the morning.' He turned and walked into the tent. He felt helpless and empty. Yesterday he believed he would be holding his daughter again now. Instead she was still with those evil people, the ones who…he shook his head free of the images haunting him. 'I'm so sorry, sweetheart. Daddy is so sorry. We'll keep looking, we won't give up.'

He sat on the mattress he shared with Adelaida and stared blankly at the bed they had prepared for Lika Faye's return. Things had changed so quickly. Yesterday they were filled with hope and excitement about getting their eldest daughter home. Now she was lost to them once again. Were they going to be able to find her? She could be anywhere now. He put his face in his hands and sighed heavily.

CHAPTER TWENTY-FIVE

'I feel so awful for Izel.' Helen and Pieter with Ruth and Neil were sitting drinking beer by candlelight on the terrace at the WDR house.

The volunteers had decided to go out for a few drinks and had headed off to one of the small bars up the road a couple of hours previously. Ian was inside organising rotas for the following week.

'He should have taken some time off. He was in a terrible state this morning,' said Ruth.

'We tried to convince him, but he insisted. I think he hoped it would take his mind off Lika Faye,' said Helen.

'Poor man. It must feel as if he's lost her twice now. I can't begin to imagine how dreadful it must be for his family,' said Neil.

'Don't make me feel worse,' Pieter put his hands up. 'I feel terrible we didn't bring her home.'

'No one's blaming you.' Helen put a hand up to his cheek.

'I'm blaming me. I was so sure we would succeed. How stupid am I? The power of corruption.'

'What happens now?' asked Neil.

'Sadly, we will only have a presence there for a couple of days. That's as long as the VHO guy can stay. We know we can't trust the local police to provide us with the facts once we've pulled out. There's only so much we can do as an NGO. Even if we locate them again, or in the event they return to the house, we'll need a warrant. And how do we keep it from the people being bribed to tip them off? This is the sort of thing we are up against in this type of pornography.'

'It must be soul destroying. How do you cope with it?' asked Ruth.

'It makes it all worthwhile when we manage to free some kids and get them home to their families. It's not so good when they don't have a home, or it's their parents who sold them to the den bosses in the first place.'

'Oh my God, does that actually happen?'

'I'm sad to say, Neil, yes it does. There's a lack of rehabilitation centres or safe places for kids in that situation. VHO do their best, but it's a growing problem and the numbers are increasing way too quickly.'

'Well at least when you rescue Lika Faye, you know she's got a loving family to go home to,' said Ruth.

'Ahh and therein lies the problem. Finding her and freeing her.'

'So what are you doing, Pieter? What's Ménage des Enfants' plan of action?' asked Helen.

'Well, we can't send any manpower out there just yet. And for all we know it could be like looking for a needle in a …what is it you Brits say?'

'Haystack, needle in a haystack,' laughed Helen.

'That's it,' he smiled at her.

The past few days had taken their toll on him. He looked tired, Helen thought. She had struggled with the situation and it could only have been worse for Pieter and his team. She looked at the man she was falling in love with and her heart lurched. He was rubbing his temples, his youthful looks temporarily banished from his face.

'So what can you do?' asked Neil.

"Well we know from the information Bella and Monique have given us, which chatrooms they use. We've set up profiles and over the past two nights have been posing as predators to see if we can find her.'

The other three sat forward.

'And?' Ruth asked.

'Nothing. No one using her online name has been seen. It's possible her username could have been changed. We don't know what they will do now. It could be they're not online at the moment. But we'll keep trying. Anneka is on duty tonight. She'll call if anything comes up. We're taking it in turns, but it's in addition to working all day.'

'Can I help?' asked Helen. 'I'll do some shifts if it helps. You just have to show me what to do, oh yeah and I need somewhere with an internet connection. It doesn't look like we'll be getting one here anytime soon.'

'Me too. I'll help,' said Ruth.

'Really? I'll need to speak to my boss, but I can't see her saying no. If you're serious I can arrange some training for you and you could help monitor the chatrooms after that. You do realise they work at night?'

Helen and Ruth nodded.

'Anything if it helps Izel find his little girl,' said Ruth.

Pieter checked his watch and turned to Helen. 'Shall we go? Do you guys want to join us at Guiseppe's?' he spoke to Neil and Ruth. 'That's if it's okay with you, Helen?'

'Yes, why don't you come, we can ask Ian. It's time he stopped work for the evening.'

The five of them piled into Pieter's car and headed towards Downtown Tacloban and the promise of pizza, pasta and wine.

After dinner and a few bottles of wine the conversation returned to Lika Faye and locating her.

'Isn't there a way you can trace these types of things? You know tracking emails and servers?' asked Neil. 'They make it look so easy in the movies.'

Everyone round the table nodded and looked to Pieter.

'You have to remember, we are only an NGO here and a visitor in their country. We have to go through the right channels. Our job here at the moment is only to raise awareness. We were going out on a limb going to Cebu,' he said wearily. 'Believe me, if we could do more, I would be the first to do it.'

They discussed the movies they'd seen where hackers had traced the bad guys around the world, always in the nick time to save bombs going off or people being killed. Pieter signalled for the bill.

'I'm sorry, guys. I've had a heavy few days. I'm going to go.

Dinner's on me.'

'No,' Ruth, Ian and Neil chorused.

Pieter smiled. 'Too late, already sorted,' he said as he handed money to the waiter.

'Are you coming back with me, Helen? I'm warning you, I'll be asleep in seconds.'

'I'll keep you company.' Helen said her goodnights to the rest of the WDR team and they left the restaurant.

'Are you okay, Pieter? I know you're tired, but it seems more than that to me.'

'It's the whole Lika Faye thing. It's…'

'If you'd rather not talk about it, I understand.'

'No, it's not that. I'll tell you when we get back to the room.'

Mains power had finally returned to parts of the centre of Tacloban: Pieter's hotel was lit up like a Christmas tree. The streets seemed eerily quiet without the chugging of generators.

He poured them both a whiskey and they lay on the bed in silence for a few minutes. Pieter seemed to be trying to find the right words to explain to Helen.

'You remember I told Izel about a computer we managed to bring back from the house in Cebu?'

'Yes. You said you were going to see if there was anything of interest on it. What did you find?'

'I couldn't mention it in front of the others. I can't risk it getting back to Izel.'

'I understand, I won't say a word.'

'Well, it's why I think I will have no problem getting my boss to agree to you helping us. We need to try and find Lika Faye quickly. The messages we recovered from the computer are discussing a snuff movie.'

Helen gasped and clasped a hand to her mouth. 'Bloody hell! You think they're talking about Lika Faye.'

'They refer to her as Faye, but there was a picture attached to one of the messages and it's definitely her.'

'Oh, Pieter. We have to find her. That poor child. Why would someone want to do something like that? I don't understand people.'

Pieter reached for her hand. 'I'm sure this can't be easy for you especially after losing Charlie.'

'I have to admit, when I decided to volunteer here it was to help people rebuild their lives and hopefully it would also help me come to terms with the loss of Charlie. I wasn't expecting to encounter human trafficking. I truly despair of mankind at times.' She shook her head in anger.

They discussed it for a while longer. Pieter's yawns were becoming more frequent and Helen could see he was having difficulty keeping his eyes open.

'Enough, we can talk more tomorrow. You need to sleep.' She leaned over and kissed his forehead. He was asleep before she'd turned the light out.

Helen lay in the darkness thinking about Pieter's words. Thoughts of Lika Faye swirled around her mind mixing with those of Charlie. She hadn't been able to save her boy, but somehow, if she could help rescue Izel's daughter, she felt it would help make some amends. Her thoughts turned darker, what if they were too late? No, she told herself, stop thinking like this. I won't let this happen. We will find her, we have to. She eventually dozed off, but her sleep was restless. Visions of chasing people through houses and finding rooms with blood splatters on the walls filled her nightmares.

They woke the next morning to a grey, wet day.

'Do you have any plans for today, Helen?' They were sitting in the hotel restaurant having breakfast.

'Not really. We've no new volunteers arriving for a few days. I don't think I'm needed for anything at the house, they all know what they're doing. I can give Ian a quick call to check. Why?'

'If I get approval, do you want to come to the office with me today and we can run you through some training to man the computer?'

Helen nodded as she munched on a piece of toast. Pieter gulped down his coffee and went off to make a phone call. A few minutes later he caught her eye from the door. He was still on the phone, but signalled a thumbs-up. Helen finished her breakfast and joined him.

'Yeah, yeah, we're heading in now. Hold on a minute.' He turned to Helen. 'Would you be happy to monitor the chatrooms once we've gone through everything? Susan is trying to put a rota together.'

'Sure, I'll fit in with everyone else. It might be best if I could avoid Wednesday though, with the new arrivals.'

'Susan, any night but Wednesday. Yep, okay, I'll call you later.'

They arrived at the Ménage des Enfants' headquarters. It was the first time Helen had seen the place where Pieter was based. They shared offices with another NGO above a fast food shop. Ménage des Enfants' room consisted of half a dozen desks and bookcases stuffed with folders and ring binders. What couldn't fit on the shelves was piled on the floor.

'Any luck, Anneka?' Pieter asked as they walked in.

She shook her head. 'Nothing resembling the names we were given in those chatrooms.' She yawned and stretched. 'I was just finishing off a few things, then I'm going back to the hotel to get a couple of hours sleep.'

'This is Helen. Anneka.'

The women nodded at each other.

'Her organisation employs Izel. She's offered to help monitor the chatrooms one night, so I'm going to run through some basic training.'

'That's great. We need all the help we can get.' Anneka got up, grabbed her things and headed for the door, calling a goodbye over her shoulder, before leaving Pieter and Helen alone.

'So isn't this just a matter of finding Lika Faye's alter ego in one of the chatrooms and then asking where she is?'

'It has to be a bit more subtle than that. We have to remember she is very likely supervised. We can't afford to do anything to spook her and give away the fact we're on to them. We can't take the risk of losing her again. We'll be lucky to find her this time, next time, well I doubt there will be a next time.'

'Have you done this before? Or what I mean is, is this what Ménage des Enfants do, find kids who have been trafficked?'

'Our main priority is to raise awareness. As I said last night, we are only an NGO, we have no jurisdiction, here or anywhere else. We have to work within the laws of the country we are in, particularly if we want to be able to prosecute.'

'Even if it means a child could lose his or her life?'

'Well, we're hoping to avoid that. As I said on the whole, it's about awareness programmes. We have a new project we're working on predominantly in the Philippines. It's to do with webcam sex tourism. It's still in the early stages, but is relevant to Lika Faye in a way.'

Pieter outlined the report Ménage des Enfants were working on about the prevalence of webcam sex tourism.

'So basically you're going to pose as a Filipino child in these chatrooms in the hope to get predators to expose themselves,' said Helen.

'More or less. The biggest problem is that the people watching the webcam sex can be anywhere in the world. Our thoughts behind this report are to raise the issue with agencies throughout the world, so they can recognise it as child pornography and establish ways and means of dealing with it. We can't, but maybe we can encourage those who can.'

'Wow. That's pretty ambitious.'

'Tell me about it. But for now, we are almost reversing that psychology and posing as predators to try and find Lika Faye. So, let's go through what we know and how we're hoping to locate her.'

Bella and Monique had provided Ménage des Enfants with a list of chatrooms where Phil had set up profiles for them. They had also provided Lika Faye's username. As long as the raid hadn't caused them to change their modus operandi, they should be able to locate her. When Lika Faye joined a chatroom Ménage des Enfants were monitoring, they would private message her asking her age, sex and location.

'It's abbreviated to a/s/l?' explained Pieter.

Monique had given them examples of the type of conversation which would normally follow. When a customer had found what he was looking for, fees were discussed.

'We don't want a conversation to get that far, as that's when Phil is called in to finalise payment methods and the child gets ready to perform…'

Helen rubbed her temples. The idea of people, men, thinking it was okay to ask and pay for children to perform for them made her feel sick. She knew child pornography existed, although had never come into direct contact with it before. Now she was facing it head on. And then there were people like this Phil, who provided the children, held them against their will, made them do these things. She wasn't sure which she found more abhorrent.

'Helen, are you okay?' Pieter's words cut into her thoughts.

'Yes, sorry. It's just the whole idea of people doing this to children. I don't know how you cope with it.'

He put his arm round her shoulders. 'I cope because I'm doing something about it. I wish I could wave a magic wand and stop it all, but the reality is I can't. So I do what I can.'

Helen made notes of the type of responses she should use when she made contact with what she hoped was Lika Faye. They ran through scenarios and what she should do if she managed to identify the girl.

After Pieter had sorted through some work on his desk, they left the office and went in search of some lunch. They settled for a burger and fries from the Jollibee fast food restaurant around the corner. Filled to capacity with excitable children, they took their red and white packaged fare to the RTR Plaza and ate in relative peace.

'I hope we find her. I wouldn't want to be the one to break the news to Izel if we don't,' Helen said between mouthfuls.

'Let's hope it doesn't come to that.' Pieter wiped some ketchup from the side of Helen's mouth. 'We will do everything we can.'

Pieter waited with Helen for a jeepney heading out to the V&G area.

'I'll give you a call about manning the chatrooms once the rota has been agreed, okay?'

She nodded and they kissed before she boarded the bus. Pieter waved her off and she watched him turn to head back to his office.

Helen's first shift turned out to be a couple of nights later.

'I know it's all a bit quick, but we need to be on top of this, how do you feel about it?' Pieter had asked her. 'Even if you could manage a few hours and I'll take over later, if you're a bit unsure.'

'No, it's okay, I'm sure I can cope. What time do you want me?'

They met at Pieter's hotel and walked to the Ménage des Enfants' office.

'I'll stay with you for a while, but I'm shattered, I was here all last night and only managed two hours sleep before I had meetings.'

'Don't worry, seriously I'll be fine. And I'll only disturb you if I find her. I've brought my tablet with me, so I can listen to music and read if nothing seems to be happening.'

Once she was installed in front of the computer, Pieter made to leave

'Are you sure you're going to be okay?'

'Go, go! Get some sleep.' She smiled at him.

'Okay, Good luck.' He kissed her and left, leaving Helen with a computer screen already with the relevant chatrooms open.

The first couple of hours passed quite quickly, but as it neared midnight, she started to feel weary. 'C'mon Lika Faye. Where are you?' She drummed her fingers on the desk, as she clicked the mouse on the different chatrooms and followed the inane conversations between the occupants.

By two o'clock in the morning she was struggling to keep her eyes open, despite regularly stretching her legs by crossing the length of the office a few times.

'If she's not here by now, surely she won't appear tonight,' she said to no one. Surely it wouldn't matter if I just closed my eyes for an hour, she thought. I could always set an alarm for three o'clock, but then I'd feel guilty. This was harder than she had expected. She rubbed her eyes and drank some water.

She woke with a start.

'Dammit, I can't believe I fell asleep.'

She rubbed the sleep from her eyes and stretched, feeling mortified at succumbing to sleep. She quickly flicked between the set up chatrooms. Nothing. No sign of Lika Faye's username.

CHAPTER TWENTY-SIX

The time in the van was distorted. They had no idea whether it was day or night. After months in the basement, they were used to lying around when they weren't working, but this was different. It was a confined space and tempers were short. It was also very hot and humid.

'Stop fidgeting, Lika Faye, that's the second time you've kicked me,' Lourdes kicked back at her.

'I'm trying to keep still, but my leg aches.'

'We're all in the same situation, try and keep to your space, for fuck's sake.'

Lika Faye curled up into a ball to try and keep from annoying the others.

It was so boring. Lying there, not being able to even stretch her legs. She tried to keep her mind occupied to pass the time. She thought about her family and what they would be doing at home now. She had no idea what had happened to them after the typhoon, so she visualised them how she remembered them. Mum would be talking to her Sari Sari customers. Dad and granddad would probably be at the farm, although she did admit to herself that she had no idea if it was actually daylight. But presuming it was, Grandma would be chatting to neighbours. Angelina would be at school; she wondered what lesson she might be in. Ellijah could be flying a kite or playing with his toy cars. It made her smile to think of her family busy in their everyday life. When she had exhausted that, she went through her times table. Sometimes she accidently said it aloud and that annoyed the older girls too.

Whenever they heard the scraping of the bolt on the door, they all lunged at it, desperate to gulp at some fresh air.

'Please let us out,' they begged Sam each time. 'We only want to stretch our legs and get some clean air. It stinks in here.'

'Get back, or I won't give you food and water,' he responded every time, shoving them back inside. 'I can't trust you not to run away. Then Phil would most likely kill me.'

'I promise we won't,' said Jenny. 'Let us out one at a time. Please.'

'Forget it. I don't have time to babysit you lot as you wander about.'

The only one allowed out was Marianne. She earned a pack of cigarettes each time. She shared them with the older girls and the truck filled with the smell of cigarette smoke. Phoebe, for once didn't complain about them smoking, it helped disguise the stench from the bucket.

When Sam arrived one morning, they were all waiting for him, but before they could say anything he pushed violently at them, causing them all to stumble backwards. Lika Faye looked up from the floor and saw Phil and Rosela behind him.

'Bucket!'

Jenny collected it and handed it to him. The door closed and was immediately locked. He hadn't given them any food or water. They felt the truck shake as Sam, Rosela and Phil climbed into the cab. The diesel engine grumbled into life and they moved backwards, accompanied by the beeping sensors. Then the truck lurched forward and slowly picked up speed.

'I wonder where we're off to now?' said Rebecca to no one in particular.

After a while, the truck was put into reverse and stopped suddenly. They could hear Sam and Phil's voices outside. Finally the back doors opened. The sudden glare of sunlight blinded the girls and they all lifted their hands to shade their eyes. Once they had adjusted to the light, they realised they had returned to the house.

'Phil, are you sure this is a good idea?' They could hear Rosela asking. 'If they've raided here once, who's to say they won't try again?' she continued.

'Rosela, I have already explained. Are you stupid or do you just enjoy annoying me?'

'I'm sorry, Phil. I'm worried.'

'This is what we pay protection money for. This raid will have been a token gesture. They'll go round all the other whore houses to satisfy some do-gooder's attempt to crack down, then we'll be left in peace again. Now stop your bloody whinging and get those girls and the equipment back in the house.'

Under Rosela's supervision, they unloaded the truck and replaced everything in the basement.

'Jesus, you stink,' snarled Rosela wrinkling her nose, as she organised them. 'Jenny, Lourdes, come upstairs with me to get some clean water. No customer will want to lie with you smelling like that.'

Once everything was in from the truck and back in the den, Phil lumbered down the stairs after them and disappeared inside the computer area. Making the most of the fresh water, the girls took it in turns to wash off the smell from spending time cramped up in the truck. They were sitting back on their mattresses when Phil re-emerged.

'Did you bitches take everything off the truck?'

They all nodded.

'Rosela checked,' Marianne said.

He shuffled to the basement door, unlocked it and bellowed up. 'Rosela, get your scrawny arse down here. Now!'

After a few moments she appeared at the basement door.

'Is something wrong, Phil?' she said.

'Where's my computer? Are you sure everything has been unloaded off the truck? I'll be fucking pissed off if Sam has gone off with it.'

'I double checked, there was nothing left in the back.'

'Well, it's not as if the girls could have eaten it or anything is it?' he scoffed at her. 'So where the fuck is it? Huh?'

Rosela started to shuffle a little nervously.

'I...err...I.' She stared at the floor and fiddled with her hair tucking some behind her ear. 'I don't know, Phil.'

'Well, if it isn't in the truck now, was it ever on there?' He turned to the girls. 'Which one of you carried it out when we left?'

They all looked blankly at him.

'Did any of you take my computer out to the truck?' he bellowed at them.

They all shook their heads.

'Right, so that only leaves one option, doesn't it, Rosela!' He turned back to her and poked her in the shoulder. 'I know I specifically fucking asked you when we left if you had taken everything out of the computer room and you told me you had. So you lied to me!'

'Erm...' she stuttered. 'I...erm...I thought everything was taken out. We were all in such a rush.'

Six pairs of eyes watched the exchange. The girls gasped as one as Phil punched Rosela and blood spurted from her nose.

'Get out of my sight, you stupid, incompetent bitch. Tidy up the mess those bastards have left upstairs.' He turned and started back to the den. 'And what do you cunts think you're looking at?'

Six heads bowed to the floor as he lumbered past their mattresses.

'You've had your little holiday, now you need to make up for lost time. Business as usual tonight.'

It took Phil two days to get the computers up and running for Phoebe and Lika Faye to start work again. Without his desktop, he had to wait until a computer literate friend could reset the network. By the time it was functional again, Phil was in a foul mood. With only two girls and a loss of income, his temper was worse than ever.

'Get up you lazy bitches. We've got a busy night ahead of us.'

As he kicked at Phoebe and Lika Faye's mattresses, his exposed pallid belly trembled between his navy shorts and striped tee-shirt. A six-pack of beer dangled from his left hand, while he slurped from a seventh can. Grey stubble beneath blood-shot eyes completed his unkempt appearance.

Lika Faye and Phoebe followed him to the locked den area. He thrust the unopened cans at Phoebe as he fumbled for the padlock key. Once inside she put the beers next to Phil's new computer and trudged to her workplace.

'No need to bother with chatrooms for the moment. Get over here both of you. You've been missed,' he sneered at them. 'I've a list of punters who've already paid and have been waiting for your return. Faye, let's start with you.'

Lika Faye listened to his instructions. She dressed in the requested clothes and grabbed the necessary toys.

'Hello, dear.' She recognised the middle-aged man in a red shirt in front of her as one of her regulars. His face filled the monitor in front of her and she began her performance.

Rosela appeared at one point during the night to report to Phil how the older girls were getting on. Her eyes were still swollen and black from his punch a couple of days earlier.

'Ah, good timing.' He tipped his head back and poured the remains of the last can into his mouth, crumpled it and hurled it in the direction of a waste bucket. 'Bring me some cold tinnys.'

Rosela opened her mouth to say something, but obviously thought better of it and turned and scowled at Lika Faye as she did his bidding.

CHAPTER TWENTY-SEVEN

'How was it?' Ruth asked after Helen had finished her first shift monitoring the chat rooms.

'Hard to stay awake,' she yawned. 'I can't believe I actually fell asleep, it wasn't for long, but what if I'd missed her?'

'So still no sign of her?'

Helen shook her head. 'Pieter's starting to worry they may have changed the girls' usernames after the raid. It will make it so much harder to find her if that's the case.'

'But how will they know if they do? What a nightmare. Poor Izel is beside himself. He was asking if you had any news when he turned up for work this morning.'

'It's an awful situation. I guess for now we carry on with what we're doing.'

'Are you going to do another shift? I want to help too. I've just been too busy getting this latest project up and running to get any training from Pieter. Another few days and I should have a bit more time.'

'That's okay. He understands you have a job to do here as well. I'm going to help out again in a couple of days if they still haven't found her. Once I've got the latest arrival of volunteers settled in.'

Helen checked in with Pieter every morning to see if there had been any sightings of Lika Faye the previous night. With still no news, she made her way into the Ménage des Enfants offices a few evenings later.

Anneka was waiting for her.

'It's great you helping out like this. We're all getting a bit concerned though. Pieter said he'd told you about the information we found on the confiscated computer. As we haven't seen Lika Faye in any of the chatrooms and we've been looking at others in addition to those Monique gave us, we're now a bit worried the snuff performance they were talking about has happened,' she said.

'Oh God, please no. Do you think so?'

Anneka shrugged. 'I really hope not, but given what we know…' her voice trailed off. 'I've set up all the chatrooms ready for you. Let's hope she appears soon. Good luck, Helen.'

Helen stared at the screen in front of her, horrified by what Anneka had said. How would they ever be able to tell Izel? No, this wasn't how it was going to be. She wasn't prepared to lose Lika Faye as well. She had to still be out there. Helen set up her tablet to play some music, paced up and down for a while, determined she wasn't going to fall asleep again. She sat staring at the screen, head in her hands, willing Lika Faye to appear. She leaned back in the chair and it didn't take long before she started to feel drowsy. The words on the screen in front of her started to cloud and merge together. A couple of times she jerked awake as her head rolled forward.

Suddenly she was walking up a hill. The wind was bitter and she drew her coat tighter round her. The hill was very steep and she felt as if she was walking in treacle, each step took enormous effort to lift her foot free from the dark mud. She bent her head down to shelter her face from the biting cold, concentrating on trying to move forward. It took so much energy. She didn't think she would have the strength to reach the top. When she looked up again, she could see Charlie at the hill summit grinning at her and beckoning for her to join him. He appeared to be saying something to her, but she couldn't hear him. He turned and started walking away from her.

'Charlie, Charlie. Wait.'

He disappeared from view. The treacle-like substance was getting easier to walk through. It wasn't so thick anymore and didn't suck at her feet as she walked. The hill didn't seem as steep either and suddenly she was at the top. The clouds started to clear, the sun shone in a bright blue sky and the vicious wind became a gentle breeze. She was looking at a field of bright red poppies and in the middle of it Charlie sat making a daisy chain. He turned and smiled.

She moved to join him and lay down beside him. The warmth from the sun kissed her cheeks and she closed her eyes. A feeling of tranquillity washed over her.

'Mum, mum, you have to wake up now. It's time.'

She woke with a start, blinking fast. The dream had seemed so real. She could still feel Charlie's presence, his words were still echoing in her mind.

'Charlie?' She looked around her. 'Time for what?'

She rubbed her eyes. She couldn't believe she'd fallen asleep. She wondered what Charlie's words referred to. Time to move on with her life? Take a chance with Pieter? She stood up and stretched her legs. She couldn't risk dozing off again. She sipped some water and turned to the screen on the desk in front of her. As she watched, a new user logged into the chat room. 11_f_leyte, it was Lika Faye's username. She clasped a hand over her mouth.

'Oh my God, oh my God.'

She sat back at the computer. She had to be sure it was Lika Faye and not someone else using her moniker. But in her heart, she already knew it was.

She had to be careful. Pieter had said the girls might be supervised. She had to make sure she sounded like a customer. She opened up a private message box using the name Ménage des Enfants had created and started typing.

Rob.bobby: Hi, a/s/l?

11_f_leyte: Hi, 11/f/Philippines

Rob.bobby: u a little young to be in this chatroom

11_f_leyte: u like young girl

11_f_leyte: where u from?

Rob.bobby: England

11_f_leyte: u like young girl

Rob.bobby: maybe. Where u from?

11_f_leyte: Philippines

Rob.bobby: I know Philippines, u from Leyte?

11_f_leyte: Cebu

Rob.bobby: But your name says Leyte?

11_f_leyte: Before was Leyte, Tacloban u know

Rob.bobby: Yes I know it. What's ur name

11_f_leyte: Faye

Rob.bobby: That's a pretty name.

11_f_leyte: :)

11_f_leyte: u want show? My boss getting angry

Rob.bobby: maybe later

It was her. It was definitely her. She fumbled in her bag for her mobile and with trembling fingers Helen tapped Pieter's contact details. The number rang half a dozen times before a sleepy voice answered.

'Pieter, wake up, I've found her.'

'What?' He was suddenly awake.

'It's her username and I've had a short conversation with her. Don't worry, I was very careful, I made out like I was a potential customer. It's her, Pieter. She's still alive.'

'Okay. I'm on my way.'

CHAPTER TWENTY-EIGHT

Lika Faye left the private chat. Phil had got up from his chair and staggered over to the girls. They were taking too long to find another customer and she knew he wasn't in the mood for time wasters. By the time he reached them, she was already chatting to someone more promising.

She could smell the stale beer on his breath as he bent down and slurred in her ear, spittle splattering the side of her face.

'Don't know why I bother with you good for nothings. You're all the same.' He stood up, waving his can around, slopping beer on the floor. 'Take her upstairs, she thinks I don't know she takes my money. Hides it around the house she does, bet those bitches that ran away found it too.' He took another swig of beer.

Lika Faye forced herself not to react and continued to stare at the screen.

'Don't know why I didn't put her in that truck with you lot. All she fucking did was whine the entire time. "What are we going to do, Phil? We need to find another house now."' He continued his drunken ramblings. 'Does she think I'm fucking stupid? I only married her for residency, worthless cow. I've had enough of the lot of you and this shit hole. Cause me too much trouble. Time I went back to Oz. Leave you all behind.' He bent down again and whispered in Lika Faye's ear. 'But you, you could make me a few bob before I go. The bitch upstairs may just be on to something for once.'

Lika Faye shivered despite the heavy humidity of the basement. She swallowed hard.

'Mr Phil, maybe you take me with you?' She turned to look at him with what she hoped was her cutest face.

He ruffled her hair. 'Hah! Too late for that, girl.' He shuffled off again. 'Haven't you got any more customers yet? What the fuck are you doing?' He pulled the ring on another beer and guzzled half of it down.

Phoebe and Lika Faye sneaked a look at each other. Their eyes were wide. Phoebe shook her head then spoke to Phil. 'Mr Phil, I have customer, you come.'

Eventually their shift finished and a drunken Phil pushed them out of the den and locked up.

'He was talking about that snuff thing, wasn't he,' Lika Faye whispered to Phoebe, her voice trembling. 'Rosela must have spoken to him about it and he's agreed. Oh, Phoebe, I'm so scared.'

'We don't know for sure,' Phoebe tried to reassure her friend.

'What else could it be? Why me?' She buried her head in her hands and sobbed. 'I'm going to die and I'll go to hell because of what they made me do.'

'Hush. We'll think of something.'

'Oh, Phoebe, don't you see, there's nothing we can do. I should have gone with Bella and Monique.'

'So you did know something about their escape. Why didn't you tell me?'

'I'm sorry, Phoebe, I was scared. I helped them.' She told her friend what had happened that morning.

'I can't believe they haven't come back for us, after you helped them too,' Phoebe said angrily.

They lay side-by-side in the dark, holding hands until exhaustion overcame them.

The next day passed in a blur for Lika Faye. She felt sick, her stomach turned somersaults every time she thought about Phil's words. She wondered how long she had left. She could see no way out. She became lethargic and resigned to what lay before her, it was only a matter of when. She prayed for forgiveness from Jesus, but apart from that refused to speak to any of the girls. Marianne tried to talk to her about what had happened the day the other girls had escaped. Lika Faye turned her back and curled into the foetal position, thumb in her mouth.

When Phil came for them to start work, she got up mechanically and followed him. She ignored Phoebe's attempts at conversation. She felt a bit guilty when she saw the hurt on her friend's face, but still refused to acknowledge her.

She sat at her computer and joined the usual chatrooms they used. Almost instantly the time waster from the previous day opened a private message with her. She was going to ignore it, but the opening line made her think again.

Rob.bobby: Hi Lika Faye

When they had communicated the previous day she was sure she had said her name was Faye, she always used that name online.

11_f_leyte: this Faye from Tacloban

Rob.bobby: Is your boss with you.

11_f_leyte: You want transfer money, I get him.

Rob.bobby: Wait. I want to talk a little first

11_f_leyte: OK

Rob.bobby: You close this private message if your boss comes ok?

Lika Faye frowned. That was an unusual request, what was this person wanting?

11_f_leyte: OK

Rob.bobby: You must stay calm, ok?

11_f_leyte: OK

Rob.bobby: R u Lika Faye from Palo?

She gasped and quickly shot a glance at Phil. He was busy stabbing at keys on his keyboard with two index fingers. How could this person know?

11_f_leyte: who u?

Rob.bobby: I need u to stay calm Lika Faye. We know u are working in Cebu with Phil.

Lika Faye flushed hot. Was she dreaming? She pinched her thigh and squeaked in pain, no, she was awake. She covered the noise with a cough and hunched back over her keyboard so Phil would think she was working.

11_f_leyte: How u know

Rob.bobby: We know Monique and Bella.

Lika Faye's heart beat faster and she sneaked another look at Phil to make sure he had no suspicion about what she was doing.

'What is it, Lika Faye?' Phoebe hissed at her.

Lika Faye took a deep breath and tried to act normally.

'Just chatting to a customer.' She tried to sound offhand.

'What's going on?' Phil glared at them.

'Nothing, Mr Phil,' they both mumbled and returned to their computers.

Rob.bobby: U still there?

11_f_leyte: yes here

Rob.bobby: where in Cebu are u? Same house?

11_f_leyte: yes same house

Rob.bobby: Stay brave Lika Faye. We are coming

11_f_leyte: come soon I very scared

Rob.bobby: I'm going now, I will be back later okay?

11_f_leyte: ok :)

The private chat ended and Lika Faye sat staring at her computer. She couldn't believe what had just happened. Jesus had been listening to her prayers. A slight smile crept across her face. They, who were 'they', she wondered? They said they were coming, but when? Her smile faded. What if they weren't in time? She had no way of knowing when Phil was planning for the snuff thing. The sound of a beer can crashing to the floor beside her made her jump.

'Some business sometime today would be nice,' Phil said sarcastically. 'Get on with it, you lazy bitches, you wanna bankrupt me?' He yanked at another ring tab and stared accusingly at them.

'Customer, Mr Phil,' Phoebe said.

''Bout bloody time.' He completed the money transfer and Phoebe readied herself to perform.

Lika Faye let her breath out slowly and with her heart still pounding, tried to focus on finding customers. The hours ticked by slowly and Rob.bobby hadn't reappeared. Stay calm they had said. She mustn't give anything away. She had to act normally. But what if the same thing happened as last time? Did they know the Cebu police would tip off Phil? Should she try and tell them? She found it difficult to concentrate. Phil was getting angry with her. Stay calm she kept repeating to herself.

When she returned to her computer after one of her performances a private message box was pulsating in the corner of the screen. She clicked on it, her heart in her mouth. She could barely breathe.

Rob.bobby: we're doing what we can. Don't worry

The words had been left ten minutes earlier and the user was no longer online. She closed the message box.

The rest of the night passed in a haze of performances and chatting to customers. Rob.bobby didn't make another appearance. Lika Faye decided not to say anything to the others. She knew Phoebe thought something was up, but she would say it was the snuff thing. She wanted to keep this nugget of information to herself, she didn't want to share it in case it became jinxed. She needed to hold this secret tight and safe, then it might come true, they would come for her. She let her head fill with thoughts of being rescued as she lay curled up, facing away from the others. Phoebe brought their meals over. Lika Faye ignored her pleading eyes. She took her dish and mug of water and ate in silence.

'Well if that's how you're going to be.' Phoebe flounced off back to her own bed, chatting to herself.

Lika Faye tossed and turned on her bed. It was unbearably humid. She couldn't get comfortable. When she did doze off in her dreams she was running down an endless corridor, footsteps chasing her but in the darkness she couldn't see who it was. She woke with a start. Jenny was shaking her gently.

'It's a dream, Lika Faye. Sshhh.'

Perspiration soaked her tee-shirt and her mouth was dry. Jenny handed her some water and mopped her brow.

'It's just a dream. I thought you might have a fever, but your forehead isn't hot. What were you dreaming about? You were calling a name, Ellijah I think.'

'My brother,' she croaked.

'Come on now, go back to sleep.' Jenny stroked Lika Faye's damp hair a few times before going back to her own bed. Eventually she drifted off to a more restful sleep.

The basement lights came on earlier than usual the next day, followed by Rosela hollering for Rebecca and Lourdes to come upstairs. It wasn't long before they returned carrying a roll of plastic, Rosela leading the way and heading towards the webcam sex area. The four remaining girls watched from their mattresses.

'What's going on?' asked Phoebe.

Marianne gave her a withering look.

'What?'

Jenny looked at Lika Faye then back to Phoebe with a knowing glance.

'Oh.' Phoebe looked down at the floor.

Lika Faye stay curled up on her mattress, her thumb in her mouth. 'They' were going to be too late. She had let the idea of being rescued into her head and now the inevitable was made all the worse because hope had been briefly given to her and now it was being snatched away.

All of the girls tried talking to her, even Marianne came and sat with her, trying to offer words of kindness.

Phil shuffled in as usual when the older girls were getting ready. He was equipped with the habitual cans of Red Horse beer.

'Let's go,' he growled at the younger girls.

The older girls stopped what they were doing and watched as Lika Faye walked past. She kept looking ahead and didn't acknowledge their looks of sympathy.

The night started off as usual. Phil harassed them to find

customers, the girls trawled the chatrooms, money transfers took place. Lika Faye kept an eye out for Rob.bobby. She would tell him it was too late, but he never materialised. She began to think it had all been a figment of her imagination. Maybe she was going mad.

Towards the end of the shift, Rosela appeared. She smirked at Lika Faye as she walked past.

'Are we ready?' she asked Phil.

'We?' He glared at her. 'No, missy, 'we' are not ready. This is your gig. I wasn't having anything to do with it. You organised it. It was your decision, that night when I was...err...my guts were bad.'

'You mean drunk!'

'Hey, if this was your way of getting back at me for being pissed, it's backfired. You made contact with that guy. It's your project. You carry it out.'

'But, Phil,' she pleaded. 'All that money. Only half has been transferred. You have to help me. I can't do this on my own. We won't get the rest until after...you know. ' She nodded at Lika Faye.

'I don't have to do anything. It's all yours.'

Phoebe and Lika Faye watched the exchange in silence.

'Phoebe, out!'

Before he had a chance to grab her arm, Phoebe ran to her friend and hugged her. 'I will pray for you, Lika Faye. I'll see you in heaven,' she whispered between sobs.

Lika Faye grasped her tightly until Phil dragged her away wailing.

'Bastard,' spat Rosela after him. 'I'll show him. Get over here you little bitch. We need to get you ready.'

CHAPTER TWENTY-NINE

Pieter had arrived at the Ménage des Enfants office at half past three in the morning after Helen had called him. She had been pacing up and down as he opened the door.

'Thank goodness you're here.'

'Okay, tell me what happened.'

Helen had showed him the private message conversation she had left open on the computer.

'I'll speak to VHO in the morning. We need to get the legalities moving, they'll know what to do. Then we need to find out where she is.'

'How will you do that?'

'We'll make contact with her again tomorrow night, once I know what VHO can organise.'

'What about Izel? Should I say anything to him?'

'I think it best we keep this between ourselves for the time being. I don't want to get his hopes up again. I'm not sure the poor man could cope with another disappointment.'

Helen had nodded.

'I'll run you back to the house. There's nothing more we can do tonight. You can get a few hours' sleep.'

'Seriously, you think I'll be able to sleep? Can't I come with you? I'll get a jeepney back when it's light.'

Pieter had pulled her to him and enveloped her in his arms, kissing the top of her head.

'Of course. Come on.'

They had locked up the office and driven back to his hotel.

The following morning, the house was deserted when she got back. Everyone was out at the school project they had adopted. Raul had returned to Manila for a couple of weeks to see his family. Helen wandered about the empty rooms. She couldn't concentrate on anything for more than a few minutes. Her eyes were gritty from lack of sleep. Her heart lurched every time she thought about the conversation she had had with Lika Faye. She tried for the third time to update the volunteer rota.

'Is there anything you need me to do for you this morning, Miss Helen?' Izel appeared at her side, making her jump. She hadn't heard the truck pull up in the driveway. She'd been relieved he wasn't there when she'd arrived home earlier.

'Ah, Izel. Yes. Erm, If I write a list could you go to Robinsons to get some food for tonight's dinner.'

'Are you okay, Miss Helen?'

'Yes, thank you, Izel. I'm fine, just a bit tired.'

'No news from Mr Pieter,' he asked hopefully.

'No. Sorry.' She couldn't bring herself to look at him. She hastily wrote a shopping list.

'Here you go.' She smiled quickly at him as she handed him the note paper.

She tilted her head back, closed her eyes and exhaled once Izel had left the office area. She hated having to lie to him, but understood Pieter not wanting to get his hopes up following the night's developments, especially after the last time. It was late afternoon before she heard from Pieter.

'It looks like VHO have managed to pull some strings. We're flying to Cebu tomorrow and should have the warrant first thing Friday morning.'

'What about the local police? Weren't they the reason it failed last time?'

'I don't know the details, Helen, but apparently VHO have been able to keep them out of the loop. They have a special task force appointed to go with them.'

'What time do you leave tomorrow?'

'We're on the Cebu Pacific eleven forty flight.'

'I'm coming with you.'

There was silence from the other end of the phone.

'Pieter? Are you there?'

'Yes.' After a few moments hesitation he continued, 'I'm not sure it's a good idea.'

'Maybe not, but that's not going to stop me. I have to be there. I won't get in the way, but I can't stay here and wonder what's happening over there.' She waited then went on: 'I'm going to ring the airline now and book a seat.'

Pieter sighed down the phone. 'Okay. I'll come and pick you up at nine o'clock tomorrow morning. I can see there's no point in arguing with you.'

The mood was very solemn the next morning as Helen and the two Ménage des Enfants representatives boarded the plane at Tacloban airport. Pieter had filled Helen in on the exchange with Lika Faye the night before. After which VHO had requested a communications blackout.

'So she doesn't know we're on our way?'

'We don't want to risk another tip off.'

Bad news greeted them on arrival in Cebu. Pieter received a phone call from VHO to say they were having problems getting the warrant approved.

'What's changed, Daniel? I thought...' Pieter paced the pavement outside Cebu airport. Helen only heard snatches of his conversation and her heart sank. They were so close, how could some red tape now endanger it all. Fear clutched at her heart as she thought about the young girl she had conversed with a couple of nights ago.

When Pieter returned he wore a look of exasperation on his face. He ran a hand through his hair. Helen, Anneka and Sam looked at him expectantly.

'I can't fucking believe this. There's some technical hitch to do with the warrant. Daniel is with the magistrate now and they're trying to get it sorted out. This is the bit I hate about this job. You get so close and then something like this happens.' He grabbed his overnight bag and marched towards the taxi rank. The other three followed in his wake, not daring to speak.

They booked into their rooms at the Citi Park Hotel. Pieter's phone was constantly clamped to his ear. No sooner did he end one conversation, it rang again. Helen could see he was desperately trying to keep his composure. Losing your temper in the Philippines was not regarded well and could set back the negotiations. He ended yet another frustrating call with Daniel and slumped down on the bed. 'I could do with a drink.'

Helen checked the minibar. 'Whisky, gin or vodka?'

He smiled at her and shook his head. 'As tempting as all one of those sound, I need to keep a clear head. This is all so frustrating. You would think it should be straightforward. It's a child's life, after all.'

The afternoon dragged on, until finally Pieter got the call he was waiting for.

'It's done. Signed for tomorrow morning. Thank heavens. Let's call the others and have a celebratory drink in the bar. I think we all deserve it.'

It was still dark when Pieter's alarm went off the next morning. Daniel picked them up and they drove in silence to the house where Lika Faye was being held captive.

'The house is at the end of that road.' Daniel pointed out as they continued past for a couple of blocks and parked. He took a two-way radio from the glove compartment.

'Charlie Alpha two, this is Lima Alpha one. We are in position. Over.

'Lima Alpha one. Maintain position. Over.'

Daniel turned to the others in the car. 'Once the rescue teams are ready, we can approach the house. Pieter, they've agreed you can follow the third team in. The rest of you need to stay at a safe distance. We don't know what to expect.'

After a few minutes a van parked in front of them. Daniel and Pieter got out of the car. Helen watched through the windscreen as they were introduced to a man dressed head to toe in black and holding a submachine gun. He handed Pieter a flak jacket and gestured for him to climb into the back of the vehicle. They pulled away from the kerb, turned round and headed back towards the house.

Inside the VHO car, Helen and the others listened to the radio exchanges as the teams got into position. At precisely eight o'clock they were given the command to go. Daniel gunned the car into life and they turned into the road he'd previously pointed out.

Helen's heart was thudding. She didn't know what she'd expected, but flak jackets and submachine guns weren't it. She had just watched the man she loved preparing to storm a house with a team of armed men. 'Please let him be okay,' she whispered to herself. They got out of the car and joined the small crowd of neighbours who had already started to gather, despite orders to stay back.

Minutes ticked by and nothing happened. The radio in Daniel's hand remained silent.

'What's happening?' Helen whispered.

Daniel shrugged his shoulders. 'It shouldn't be long now.'

Murmurs in the crowd grew louder and they pointed to the front door. Four girls emerged, huddled together. They were dressed in shorts and vests and were blinking in the bright sun. Armed men ushered them out into the garden. Daniel and the two Ménage des Enfants staff sprang into action. They steered them towards the VHO car, telling them they were safe now and would be taken care of. One of them was more surly than the others, she was demanding cigarettes and putting on an act of nonchalance.

Helen's attention was drawn back to the front door as a smaller girl, looking terrified, appeared. Her stomach lurched, then she realised it wasn't Lika Faye.

'Phoebe?' she called out.

The girl looked at her. Helen ran to her. 'It's okay, Phoebe, you're safe now.' The girl nodded dumbly at her. 'Where's Lika Faye?' Helen tried to keep her voice steady.

Phoebe's face crumbled as she burst into tears. Helen dropped to her knees and hugged the little girl to her as she sobbed. 'She's with Rosela.'

'It's okay, Phoebe. We're going to rescue her. Is Phil there too?'

Phoebe backed away, shaking her head. 'Phil went upstairs… Rosela hates her and… she's killing her… A snuff thing she called it.' She managed between sobs.

Helen picked her up and walked back to the VHO car. Silent tears coursed down her cheeks.

CHAPTER THIRTY

The man on the screen told Rosela to hit her again. Blood spurted from her nose and Lika Faye screamed, the force of the punch pushing her backwards.

'Please stop,' she sobbed, wiping the blood from her nose.

'That's good, really good,' he grunted. The enjoyment was plain on his face. His lips stretched across his jagged teeth in a sadistic smile.

'Now get the knife.'

Lika Faye went quiet and her eyes grew wide with fear, as much as they could. One was already starting to go puffy from the blows Rosela had dealt her.

Rosela reached behind her for the hunting knife the man on the screen had specified. It was still in its sheath.

'Cut the clothes off her.'

Lika Faye was dressed in a pink dress patterned with red and white flowers around the hem of a tulle skirt. In her hair Rosela had tied up a couple of bunches with pink ribbons. In other circumstances, Lika Faye couldn't have chosen a better outfit. A pink princess all dressed up ready to go to a party. This was not the sort of party she had ever envisaged. Blood had dripped onto the tunic of the dress, but Lika Faye couldn't take her eyes off the knife in Rosela's hand. She had unsheathed it and the blade glinted as it reflected the strip lights above them.

'Cut away the straps of the dress.'

Lika Faye stood frozen. She was terrified the knife would slip and cut her. She flinched as the cool steel touched the skin on her left shoulder. It took very little effort for Rosela to slice through the straps. The loose material of the tunic hung over the tutu skirt of the dress.

'Now cut away the skirt, down the middle, slowly now!'

Lika Faye could feel the tip of the knife catching at her belly as

Rosela sliced away the rest of the dress. As she stood naked, her hands by her side looking at the grotesque smile of her torturer on the screen, she could feel a warm trickle of blood making its way down her stomach and onto her thigh.

'Please, please stop,' she begged. 'I don't want to die.'

'Oh yes, I like the begging touch.' He leaned in closer his face filling the screen in front of Lika Faye.

She instinctively took a step back from the leering face.

'Go round behind her. Pull her head back and expose her pretty little neck.' The distorted face ordered.

As Rosela moved behind her, Lika Faye closed her eyes. She didn't want the pleasure on the man's face to be the last image she saw. A loud crash behind them to the left caused Lika Faye's eyes to fly open. Rosela turned to see armed men in black pouring in through the smashed door.

'What the fuck is going on,' yelled the man on the screen. 'What was that noise? This isn't part of the deal.'

'Drop the knife!' One of the armed men said calmly to Rosela.

Rosela looked at the man, then at the knife in her hand. She stepped behind Lika Faye and held the knife to her throat.

'Yes, yes that's it, do it, do it,' grunted the man on the screen.

'You little bitch, you've ruined everything,' Rosela hissed in Lika Faye's ear.

'Drop the knife, Rosela,' the armed man said more firmly, his submachine gun held to this right eye.

'Stay where you are or I'll do it. I'll kill the little bitch.'

'What are waiting for?' said the man on the screen, oblivious of the scene unfolding at the other end of the den. 'Get on with it, I can't wait any longer.' He continued to moan and grunt.

'This is your last warning, Rosela. Put the knife down now.' The voice of the armed man became threatening. Lika Faye could feel the tip of the knife prickling at her throat. Her eyes were wide with terror as she looked at the three armed men inside the door of the den.

'You better shoot me then, you bastards, but if I go, she goes.'

There was a deafening crack which echoed around the small den. Lika Faye felt the knife loosen from her neck and watched as it seemed to drop in slow motion from Rosela's hand and clatter to the floor. She stepped out of Rosela's grip and turned. A crimson spot grew on Rosela's forehead as she crumpled to the floor at Lika Faye's feet.

'What the fuck?' said the man on the screen. As the armed men came into view, he disappeared.

Lika Faye stood unmoving and naked, staring at Rosela's body in front of her. One of the armed men knelt and checked for a pulse. He nodded and a tall blond man appeared bedside her.

'It's okay, Lika Faye. You're safe now,' he said gently. He picked her up and strode out of the room. Lika Faye felt the rough material of the flak jacket against her bare skin. She slipped her thumb in her mouth and stared unseeing as they walked through the basement and upstairs.

'Am I in heaven?' she croaked into Pieter's hair.

'No, sweetheart. We're going to take you home,' he whispered.

She wrapped her arms around his neck tightly and felt the warm sun on her back as he walked through the front door.

'Lika Faye.' She turned her head and squinted to see Phoebe break free from a red-headed woman and run towards them.

A blanket was handed to Helen by one of the VHO members and she followed Phoebe. She draped it round Lika Faye's naked body as Pieter handed the child to her.

'You're safe now. We've got you.'

Lika Faye stared out over the woman's shoulder at the crowd which had gathered. As she scanned the people before her she saw a familiar face. A Panama hat low over his flabby face and a cigar in his mouth, she watched as he turned and shuffled from view.

'Phil…' she said.

'It's okay, sweetheart. He can't hurt you anymore.'

'But...' she pointed feebly over Helen's shoulder, but he was no longer there.

'Shhh. We're going to take you away from here now.'

Helen carried her to the waiting VHO car and handed her in to another woman before climbing in beside her. The man who had carried her out of the house sat in the front passenger seat and the car moved off. He turned round in his seat and smiled first at her, then at the woman.

'We did it. We found her.'

Lika Faye looked at the woman who smiled at him through her tears.

CHAPTER THIRTY-ONE

Helen turned to the girl sat next to her. She was barely recognisable as the same child in the photograph taped to Raul's windscreen. Her hair was longer and matted. She was a lot thinner. Before they had wrapped her in the blanket Helen had seen her ribs sticking out. The bruising around her eyes had turned a deep purple and her nose was swollen. Helen shook her head. Then she put her thoughts to one side and smiled.

'Lika Faye, I'm Helen. This is Pieter in the front. We're friends of your father.'

The girl turned to her and nodded, her face solemn. 'Where are we going?' she asked. 'And where's Phoebe?'

'Phoebe and the other girls are following behind in a couple of other cars. We're taking you to a hospital.'

Lika Faye drew up her legs and pushed herself into the back of the seat, pulling the blanket tightly round her.

'Why? I'm fine. You said you were taking me home.' She glanced out the back window to see if they were telling the truth about the other girls.

'We're taking the others too. It's just so they can make sure you're okay. Have a look at those bruises,' Helen said gently. She reached out to stroke the girl's hair, but Lika Faye jerked away.

'It's okay. I promise you, you're safe now.' She folded her hands in her lap.

Lika Faye remained clutching the blanket and staring ahead for the rest of the journey. She barely acknowledged the VHO woman when she spoke to her in Filipino.

When they arrived at the clinic, there was a wheelchair waiting. Helen gently lifted Lika Faye into it. They waited as the second car arrived. Phoebe jumped out and ran to her friend, babbling away in Filipino. Two of the older girls approached them.

'What happens now?' Rebecca asked.

'You'll stay at the clinic for a couple of days. They'll make sure you're all healthy,' said Pieter. 'Then VHO,' he pointed to the woman who had been in his car. 'Will find you somewhere to stay.'

'Hmmm. You got cigarette?'

Pieter shook his head.

The hospital staff called out to the VHO woman and after a brief exchange she nodded.

'They're ready for them. I'll go with them and we'll call you a bit later today. You can come back then and talk to them.'

Pieter nodded and opened the car door for Helen.

It was lunchtime by the time they returned to the hotel. They headed to the restaurant, shattered and hungry.

'Are you okay, Pieter? You were very quiet in the car. We found her, she's alive. I thought, I thought you would be happier. I mean, I know the past few months have been horrific, but we saved her.'

He smiled at her and took her hand across the table, as the waiter appeared with menus. He opened his mouth to say something, then thought better of it.

'What?' she asked.

'I'm just relieved we got there in time.' He hesitated. 'It was only just in time though, Helen. Rosela was about to cut Lika Faye's throat. They had to shoot her.' He removed his hand and ran his fingers through his hair.

Helen gasped.

'That poor girl. She's been through so much. What about Phil? I didn't see him come out of the house. Did they arrest him in the den?'

'He wasn't there.'

'Wait, so that woman, Rosela, she was going to kill Lika Faye on her own?' Helen lowered her voice to a whisper. 'Why...I mean, how? How can someone, especially a woman do something like that?'

She stared down at the table for a couple of moments.

'Not that it's acceptable for a man to do either, but a woman! Words fail me. So where was Phil?'

'They didn't find him at all.'

'What? He wasn't in the house?'

'No they searched everywhere, no sign.'

'Do you think he was tipped off? But it wouldn't make sense, surely he would have taken them all again like last time.'

'I don't think we'll ever know for sure, unless we find him, but the indication is he had some idea. There weren't many of his personal belongings there.'

'So it looks as if he left Rosela to take the fall for it all? And now he's free to go and do it all again?'

'We don't know for sure, Helen, but it does look that way.'

'I don't know what to say. I understand why you're not as elated as you should be. What a world we live in.'

The waiter returned to take their orders.

'Do you want something to drink?' Pieter asked her.

'A large whisky, please,' she asked the waiter.

'Make it two, thank you.'

Helen closed the menu and handed it back to the waiter. 'I've lost my appetite.'

The waiter returned with their drinks and they sat sipping them in silence for a while.

'So what will happen now? I mean, will they be looking for Phil?'

'I don't know. I expect I will learn more when I speak to VHO. But the chances are, if he was tipped off, it would have been by the police he's paid money to, so they're unlikely to 'find' him.'

Pieter's phone rang.

'It's VHO,' he said to Helen as he answered it. He listened for a couple of minutes then hung up.

'The girls are settled into the hospital. It seems apart from malnourishment and in Lika Faye's case, the bruises, they are all fine, physically that is. They've sedated her for now. She became very traumatised once she got over the shock.'

'That's understandable.'

'I'm going to be here for a few days, Helen. Make sure the girls are all okay and we can find some temporary shelter for them, if they have no family they can go to.' He took her hand across the table. 'There's not much else you can do here. Why don't you fly back to Tacloban tomorrow? You can tell Izel and his family the good news and I'll come back with Lika Faye as soon as they discharge her.'

'That sounds like a plan,' she said, suddenly very weary. 'I am neglecting my work with WDR and need to get back for that too.'

Helen caught the morning flight back to Tacloban. So much had happened in the past couple of months. It seemed like an eternity since she had left the UK. Charlie still filled so much of her thoughts, but she was able to think of him without so much pain. She knew it would never go completely, nor did she want it to, but it wasn't as raw as it had been. And she knew he would be there for her when she needed him, just like the other night. Her meeting Pieter had been a surprise. She smiled as she thought of his cheeky smile and unruly curls. Falling in love had certainly been unexpected. She wondered what their future might hold, then admonished herself.

'Let's stay in the present, Helen.'

'Sorry?' The person in the chair next to her asked.

She must stop talking aloud. She smiled and apologised to the woman.

Her thoughts turned more serious. She had had no idea of the extent of sex trafficking, even working with A21 in the UK, it hadn't prepared her for what she was seeing for herself. It overwhelmed her. Her mind wandered back to the sight of the girls emerging from the house. By the time the plane landed the germ of an idea had started to formulate in her head and she had made a list of things she needed to research.

She was met at the airport by a woman from VHO called Gabbie.

'Great news about Lika Faye. Are you ready to go and tell the family?'

'They still know nothing?'

'Pieter asked that you should be the one to tell them. I have a car waiting.'

The women climbed in and headed out to the Assumption Academy tent city.

CHAPTER THIRTY-TWO

Izel was sitting with Angelina in the tent as she explained a very convoluted conversation she and a couple of her school friends had had the previous week.

'…and then Marcie said that couldn't be right, because her mum had been there before…'

Izel nodded, feigning interest in the world of a seven year old. Behind Angelina he could see the bed they had made up for Lika Faye's return. He was still struggling with losing her a second time. He hadn't been sleeping well and when he did his nights were filled with nightmares. Adelaida refused to talk about it, so it was his father's ears he bent whenever he could. He was becoming bitter and angry. He hated himself for it, but, like a scab, he couldn't help but pick at it.

Adelaida poked her head into the tent. 'Miss Helen and another woman are here, Izel.'

Angelina stopped her babbling to look at her mother. 'But I haven't finished, I was telling daddy about…'

'You can finish your story later, sweetheart. This is daddy's work,' he smiled at her and stroked her cheek.

'Okay,' she said cheerily and turned to her doll.

'Hi, Miss Helen. What can I do for you?' He nodded to the Filipino woman with her.

'Izel, this is Gabbie, she's from VHO. Is there somewhere quiet we can sit and talk? Adelaida too.'

Izel's heart flipped. Why were they here? It had to be bad news. He couldn't bear it. He grabbed and opened out some folding chairs.

'I'm sorry, there's not much room for privacy. Will here be okay?' he indicated in front of the tent.

'Yes, yes, of course.'

'Would you like something to drink, Miss Helen, Miss Gabbie?' Adelaida smiled at them.

'No thank you. I have some water.' Helen lifted her bottle.

Gabbie shook her head.

'We have some news for you both and thought we should tell you in person.'

Izel inhaled sharply, took his wife's hand and steeled himself.

'We've got Lika Faye,' said Helen simply.

Izel's heart pounded in his ears, his mouth dropped open, but he couldn't speak. He barely heard Adelaida ask where she was.

Helen explained how they had located her and organised the raid the previous morning. She left out the details of the situation they had found there. That would be up to Lika Faye to explain if she ever wanted to.

Izel buried his head in his hands. His little girl had been rescued, she was alive.

'Where is she? When can we see her?'

'She's at a clinic in Cebu...'

Izel felt dizzy and his mouth went dry 'Why? What's happened?'

'She's okay, they're just checking her and the other girls. There were six of them in total. That's why Gabbie is here. I'll let her explain.'

'Should we go to Cebu?' Izel stood and paced. 'We should be with her.'

Helen stood and put a hand on his arm.

'It's just for a couple of days, Izel. She'll come back with Pieter.'

For the first time he started to believe everything was going to be alright.

'Oh my goodness, I can't believe it.' A grin spread over his face. 'You honestly have her this time?'

Helen smiled and nodded. 'I held her in my arms yesterday morning.'

Izel hugged Helen and embraced Adelaida, holding her tightly. 'She's safe. She's coming home.'

Angelina emerged from the tent intrigued by all the noise. She looked from her parents to Helen.

'What is it, daddy?'

Izel knelt in front of her daughter. 'Lika Faye is coming home.'

'Is she really coming this time?' A puzzled look crossed her face.

Izel nodded. 'Miss Helen saw her yesterday. She will be here in a couple of days.'

Angelina looked thoughtful. 'That's good then. She can help me decide what to do about Marcie. Can I go and play now?'

The four adults watched as she ran off to find her friends.

'Izel, Adelaida, Lika Faye has been through a lot over the past months. Gabbie here is going to tell you more.' Helen sat back as Gabbie spoke to them calmly in Filipino.

'Lika Faye has been in a very traumatic situation. I don't want to alarm you both, but we need to prepare you for how she may react. There's a good chance she will suffer from nightmares for some time. She may want to talk about what has happened to her, or she may not. Let her say what she is comfortable with. Don't push her for details. We strongly recommend she has regular contact with a psychologist, at least to begin with.'

Adelaida's face had paled. 'But she is alright, isn't she? I mean, she's not been affected...' she tapped the side of her head. 'If she has to see a psychologist...won't that be expensive?' She looked at Izel. 'How will we afford it?'

Gabbie smiled reassuringly. 'This is something VHO offer to children from these circumstances. There is no fee for you to pay. We often find in these cases, the child is ashamed of what she has had to do and doesn't like to talk about it with family. It's easier for her to verbalise it with someone neutral. It's better than her internalising it.'

Izel frowned. 'But she is okay, isn't she?'

'We will all do our best to make sure she will be. You need to show her you love her no matter what she has gone through. I also have to warn you that you may be a little shocked with her appearance.'

'Oh no, what have they done to her,' Izel jumped up again. 'I'll kill them!'

'It's nothing long term, Izel, please. She has lost weight and she has some bruising on her face. It's not serious. You can't react like that when you see her.'

'Yes, yes of course.' Izel sat back down, but inside he was raging and his feet tapped on the concrete floor. 'When will we see her?'

'Helen will stay in touch with you and as soon as the clinic is ready to discharge her, she will let you know.' Gabbie said the last sentence in English for Helen's benefit.

'Yes and I've spoken to Ian. Take next week off. Get ready for her to come home and spend some time with her.' Helen smiled at them.

'We'll be here for you,' continued Gabbie. 'If you have any questions or want to discuss how Lika Faye is getting on, anything, please call me.' She handed them a card with her contact details.

'Salamat,' Izel thanked her.

He watched Helen and Gabbie leave and turned to Adelaida.

'She's safe, she's coming home.' He burst into tears.

His relief had turned to concern. He just wanted his little girl back, to take care of her and keep her safe. He felt so racked with guilt that this had happened to her because he hasn't been able to save her on the morning Yolanda struck.

'Izel?'

'What she's been through, it's all my fault. I should have saved her.'

'Don't you dare do this, Izel. She's alive. We have to put the past behind us. For our sake, but especially for her. You have to be strong now. She will need us. Now come on. Let's find your parents and tell them the good news.'

It was Tuesday before the clinic was happy to allow Lika Faye to leave. Helen had called every day to provide Izel with updates. Now finally she had confirmed the arrival details.

'Ménage des Enfants is providing transport. We'll come and pick you up at ten thirty.'

Izel could barely contain his excitement. He paced up and down outside and told every neighbour within earshot his daughter was coming home today. Angelina had been allowed to have the day off school. Since hearing the news she had been busy making Welcome Home posters. One was pinned to the front of the tent. She was now busy discussing with her grandparents what to wear.

When Helen arrived with the cars, the five of them were standing in a row on the edge of the road outside the tented city. Angelina held Izel's hand and was chatting away. Izel didn't hear a word she was saying. He thought his chest was going to explode, his heart was thumping so hard. He tugged at the hairs on his chin and hopped from foot to foot. He grinned at Helen when she got out of the car to greet them.

'Is everything okay? Is she on her way?'

'I spoke to Pieter on the drive over. They were just boarding the plane.'

'My little girl is coming home,' his voice broke as he said the words.

Izel and Adelaida joined Helen in the first car. Angelina sat between her grandparents in the second for the forty-five minute drive. The airport was still displaying the signs of damage from Yolanda. The windows hadn't been replaced and the arrivals and departures areas were open to the elements.

A small crowd of people with cameras converged on them as they got out of the cars, taking them by surprise. Microphones were shoved in Izel's face.

'How do you feel about your daughter coming home?'

'How long have you known she was being held captive to perform sexual acts?'

'Did you know she was in Cebu?'

Panicking, his eyes wide he looked to Helen for help.

'Mr and Mrs Sombilon are relieved they are about to be reunited with their eldest daughter, after Yolanda split them up. Please allow them some privacy to welcome her home.'

She pushed a camera out of Izel's face and beckoned for the family to follow her inside.

Their attention was drawn to the sudden scream of engines and screech of rubber on tarmac as a plane landed. A few minutes later it taxied to the front of the terminal. Izel strained to see as passengers started to disembark.

'Can you see her? Dad, is that her now? I can't tell,' he said to his father and shielded his eyes squinting at the people now streaming down the steps and across the runway.

'There she is now, Izel.' Helen pointed to the top of the steps as she recognised Pieter, Lika Faye holding his hand as they descended.

Izel's hands flew to his face. He looked at Adelaida; a huge grin lit up her face as she pointed at her daughter. It seemed to take an eternity for them to make their way to the terminal. Eventually they walked into the arrivals area and she was in front of him.

'Daddy,' she said simply.

She let go of Pieter's hand and ran at her father wrapping her arms around his waist. He grabbed under her arms and drew her up to him, squeezing her tightly into his body. He buried his head in her hair. Adelaida joined the hug, stroking her daughter's hair. They stood together speechless for several moments.

Izel felt a hand tugging at his tee-shirt. He looked down to see Angelina holding up a drawing she had done for her sister. Four adults and two children, one in a pink dress, stood in a line, hand-in-hand.

'Look Lika Faye, it's all of us.'

Lika Faye turned her head to look at her younger sister. She reached down and took the offered drawing.

'Ellijah?' She looked from the drawing to her father. 'Where's Ellijah? Daddy?'

He stroked her hair.

'I'm so sorry, sweetie, he didn't make it, the typhoon took him.'

Lika Faye nodded and looked back at the drawing and then back to Angelina.

'Thank you.' She clutched it to her chest and laid her head on her father's shoulder.

'Can we go home, daddy?'

CHAPTER THIRTY-THREE

It was lunchtime several days later and Helen was waiting for Pieter to come and pick her up from the WDR house. He had suggested they had lunch at Guiseppe's, which she had thought a bit unusual. Normally they met there for dinner and she would stay over at his hotel room. Still, maybe he had plans for the afternoon, she smiled to herself. She was also keen to talk to him about the idea she had had on the flight back from Cebu, she wanted to know his thoughts on it.

Finally he arrived and they set off into town.

'I could have caught the jeepney,' she said. 'You didn't have to come and pick me up. Or is this a special occasion?'

He smiled thinly and continued to look straight ahead.

Helen shrugged and started to tell him about the new volunteers and the latest on the projects WDR were working on until they arrived at the restaurant. Pieter parked the car and they entered Guiseppe's. It was much quieter than the evenings they had eaten there, with only a few tables occupied near the cold counter. Pieter chose a table as far away from them as possible.

Helen frowned, but followed and sat opposite him.

'A bottle of Sauvignon blanc please,' Pieter told the waiter. He turned to Helen. 'Is that okay with you?'

'Yes, of course, but drinking at lunch time?' She joked.

Pieter looked down at the table, turning an empty wine glass round in his fingers.

Helen put her hand on his. 'Is something the matter, Pieter?'

He pulled his hand away and looked at her, a pained expression on his face.

'Pieter, what is it?'

'I don't know how to tell you this.'

'Tell me what?' A frown creased her forehead. 'What's going on?'

The waiter appeared with the wine, opened the bottle and poured out two glasses. Pieter snatched at his and drank half of it down in one gulp.

'Okay, you're starting to worry me. Just tell me.'

He looked at her sheepishly. 'I'm going back to Holland.'

'When? How long for?'

'Next week. For good.'

'Next week? Why so sudden. You haven't mentioned it before.' Helen could feel her heart thumping. Something wasn't right.

'Oh, fuck. I've been dreading this moment.'

'So you've known for a while? And you've not said anything to me?' Helen tried to keep her voice steady, while panic started to bubble inside her.

'It was only decided a few days ago, although the actual date of my leaving was dependent on this visit to Cebu.'

He drained the rest of his glass and poured another.

'I really like you, Helen. Actually I think I've fallen in love with you.'

'And your reaction to that is to leave as soon as possible.' Helen could feel her heart shattering into pieces like a dropped mirror.

'No. It's not like that.'

'Oh no? So what is it like?' Irritation crept into her tone.

'Please, Helen, this isn't easy for me either.' He bowed his head.

A thought occurred to her. 'Don't tell me. You're married?'

'No, no. I would never have started anything with you if that was the case. I promise you.'

Helen could see his anguish as he tried to find the right words.

'I had a Skype call last week from an ex-girlfriend of mine.' He raked his fingers through his curly hair. 'We were together for about two years. She's quite a bit younger than me. We split up about six months before I came out here.'

'Why?'

'What?'

'Why did you split up?'

'She wanted to settled down and have children. I didn't. I'm away a lot with work,' he looked at her. 'I wasn't happy. It just wasn't right, so we parted ways.'

'What's her name?'

He gave her a pained look.

'Ineke.'

'Right, so Ineke Skyped you last week.' Helen tried to remain matter-of-fact.

'Well, yes, but she wasn't alone. Lucas was with her.' He hung his head.

'Lucas?'

'Our son.'

Helen gasped. She picked up her glass and drank her wine.

'I swear, Helen, it was a shock to me too. I didn't even know she was pregnant. I couldn't tell you until we'd found Lika Faye. I've wanted to. But I didn't know how and I wasn't sure what I wanted to do.'

'And now you know?' Helen felt sick. Inside she was churning, but outside she remained calm, cold.

'He's my son. I can't abandon them. I have to do the right thing, or at least try.'

Part of Helen admired his honesty and his desire to be there for his son. The other part hated this other woman and her child. She didn't want to deal with any more emotion. The past few days had drained her.

'You have to do what you think is right, Pieter. I understand. I do. Now if you'll excuse me.'

She got up and walked away. She needed some space to let his words sink in. Outside the air-conditioned restaurant, the air was heavy. Perspiration formed on her forehead and sweat trickled down her back. She crossed the street and started walking. She didn't know or care where she was headed. She felt an enormous rush of love for the man she had left in the restaurant and at the same time a massive wave of despair swept over her.

'Why does life have to be complicated?' she asked out loud.

A car horn beeped beside her. It was Pieter.

'Please, Helen, get in. I feel so terrible about this. It's why I've put off facing it. It's a shock, I know. It was to me too. Let's talk about this.'

She gave him a brief smile.

'What's there to talk about? It seems you've already made your decision.'

'Well at least let me take you home.'

She climbed into the car and they drove in silence to the WDR house. He stopped the car outside the gates and turned to her.

'It's not how I would have chosen things.' He took her hand. 'I think we have something special, but…it's my child. It's been one of the hardest decisions I've had to make.'

'What will you do back in Holland? Will you stay with Ménage des Enfants?'

'I hope so. We're talking about an admin role I can take in Amsterdam. I'll miss the field work though.' He shrugged.

'I'll be honest, Pieter. It's not quite the ending I was hoping for.'

'But you'll be okay?' His face was filled with concern and sadness. 'I never wanted to hurt you.'

'My heart feels a little battered and I'm sad, very sad. But I'll survive. I know you're trying to do what's right' She squeezed his hand. 'Your intentions are commendable. I can't fault that.' She hesitated for a few moments and coughed. Looking him in the eye she said: 'I wish you luck and I hope it works out for you.'

'Thank you,' he said, his voice breaking.

'I hope we can stay friends, Pieter. It just might be a little bit difficult for a while, but I would hate to lose touch and I really hope I can do some work with Ménage des Enfants.'

'I'd like that.'

She leaned over, kissed his cheek and got out of the car. Her heart was breaking, but she was determined she wasn't going to cry. She walked through the gate without looking back. Once inside she sat heavily on the grass, her head in her hands.

Maybe he hadn't chosen her, but she had come a long way in the past few months. She had dealt with far worse; losing Charlie was the worst that could ever have happened to her and she had survived that. She would get over Pieter. She would be okay. She composed herself, stood and walked into the house. She had work to do.

EPILOGUE – THREE MONTHS LATER

'Phoebe, are you ready for school yet?' Helen called out from the kitchen. She smiled at the girl as she appeared in the doorway. 'Come on. You have just enough time for breakfast. Did you do all your homework?'

'Yes, Marianne helped me.'

A surprising friendship had built between the two girls since they had moved in with Helen. With the help of Ménage des Enfants, VHO and WDR, Helen had rented a house and set up a refuge for girls who had been rescued from sex trafficking.

With the departure of Pieter, she had wanted a project to fill her time and help her broken heart slowly mend. The idea of a refuge had occurred to her on the flight back from Cebu. The sight of the girls as they were rescued from the house had wrenched at her heart, filling her with anguish and a need to do something to help. She had spoken to VHO about what would happen to the girls after they were discharged from the clinic. There were so few places available and funding was stretched. VHO could only offer them temporary accommodation and there was always a concern the older girls would return to prostitution.

It had taken a month to get everything in place. She had transferred funds from England to pay the deposit and six month's rent on a house in V&G close to the WDR headquarters. VHO had been able to fast track her applications, during which time, with the help of the WDR volunteers at weekends, she had fixed up the house and prepared a safe environment for the girls. Her plan for the older ones was to assist them in finding a living outside of the sex industry. Of the four rescued from the house in Cebu, Marianne and Rebecca had accepted her offer of help. Once she had discovered Phoebe's mother had died and her father had sold her to Phil, she started proceedings to become the girl's legal guardian. Since then they had been joined by four other girls between ten and thirteen who had been recently freed from another webcam sex tourism den.

'It's just the tip of the iceberg,' she had explained on a rare Skype conversation with her four friends from England. 'But if I can help a few of these girls, it's a start. Say hello to Phoebe.'

'Hello Auntie Helen's friends.' The girl had enthusiastically waved at the four smiling faces.

'So no sign of you coming back anytime soon,' Sarah had asked. 'You're sure this is what you want to do? You're such a long way away.'

'You'll have to come and visit then.' She had said as she had ended the call.

Helen was halfway upstairs when there was a knock at the front door. She was already running late to get Phoebe to school. She was due at WDR to welcome the latest batch of volunteers, before giving a talk at a workshop in Downtown Tacloban on webcam sex tourism.

'Phoebe, can you get that, please. It's probably some of your school friends anyway.'

She was collecting all her notes together and grabbing a pair of sandals when Phoebe called up from the hallway. 'It's for you, Auntie Helen.'

'Oh for heaven's sake,' she muttered under her breath. Who on earth would be coming to the house at this time?

She started down the stairs a scowl on her face but then stopped suddenly. Her heart somersaulted and she gripped the handrail to steady herself.

'Hello, Helen,' said Pieter, a huge smile lit up his face. 'I heard you were trying to save the world!'

'Pieter!' She coughed, trying to gather her wits. They had exchanged the odd email since he had returned to Holland, but they had kept the messages brief and casual. 'What are you doing here?' She continued to stand halfway down the stairs. 'Are you here on Ménage des Enfants business? No one told me you were coming.' She couldn't believe they hadn't warned her he was coming to

Tacloban.

'Actually, no. I've come to see you.'

'Well, now's not a good time. I'm about to walk Phoebe to school.'

His smile dropped slightly. 'Do you mind if I walk with you?'

She shook her head not trusting herself to speak. Her heart was racing. She thought she had managed to put her emotions for him to one side. But seeing him here in front of her, all the feelings returned.

Phoebe came skipping out of the kitchen looking from one to the other.

'Are we going to school now?'

Helen gained her composure and walked down the remaining stairs. 'Yes, sweetie. Do you remember Pieter?'

'Yes.' She smiled at him. 'He was at the clinic in Cebu.'

'Hi, Phoebe. How are you?' said Pieter.

'Great,' she said and grinned. 'Do you like my school uniform?' She pirouetted for his approval.

'Very smart.'

'Phoebe, do you have everything, we're going to be late.'

'Yes,' she held up her school bag, then turned serious. 'You haven't forgotten Lika Faye is coming after school have you, Auntie Helen?'

'No, I haven't forgotten. Izel will drop her off and we'll take the jeepney back with her later, okay?'

Satisfied, Phoebe walked out of the house. Helen and Pieter followed her.

'How is Lika Faye?' he asked.

'Yes, okay, considering. Both the girls still have a lot of nightmares, but it's getting better. Izel is still with WDR and when he's not working is busy helping with the building of the Gawad Kalinga homes. It looks like they will be moving into one of the houses very soon. And they've started some work out on the farm too.'

When they arrived at the school gates, Helen kissed Phoebe before she ran off to join her friends.

'Work hard and I'll see you here later,' she called after her.

She turned to Pieter. 'So, what's this all about?'

He looked at the ground and kicked at some gravel.

'I tried with Ineke and Lucas. I tried to put my feelings for you to one side. To accept they were my future.' He looked up and smiled weakly at her. 'And it worked, for a little while. But all the reasons I left Ineke in the first place were still there. It wasn't long before we were bickering. It's not a good environment for a child. I don't want him growing up in a house full of resentment.' He swallowed. 'In the end Ineke realised it wasn't working. We sat down one evening and talked it through. And, well, here I am. If you'll have me back.' He grinned at her hopefully. 'I love you, Helen.'

His blond hair flopped over his forehead. She reached up and pushed it back.

'Let me think about it,' she said.

His smile faded, she could see this wasn't the response he had hoped for.

'Just kidding.' Helen laughed, moved closer and kissed him passionately. 'Oh Pieter, I missed you.'

AUTHOR'S NOTE

If you enjoyed Tindog Tacloban, I would really appreciate it if you took a couple of moments of your time to review it on Amazon, thank you.

Tindog Tacloban is a work of fiction although some of the characters and their stories were inspired by the people I met and who agreed to be interviewed during my time in Tacloban. I decided to volunteer in the Philippines following the devastation wreaked by super typhoon Yolanda on 8 November, 2013. It was the strongest storm to hit landfall in recorded history with winds gusting up to 195mph and was followed by three massive waves of five to six metres high, causing huge loss of life and extensive damage.

Ménage des Enfants, World Disaster Response and Visayas Hope Organisation (VHO) are all fictional organisations and bear no relation to any real life organisations. On the other hand, webcam child sex tourism is not fictional, it is very real and very rife in the Philippines and predators do take advantage of disaster situations to recruit vulnerable children and force them to perform sex acts directed by people watching from around the world. The Terre des Hommes International Federation is a network of ten national organisations working for the rights of children. Terre des Hommes Netherlands is attempting to raise awareness about the largely unknown, but quickly spreading industry of webcam child sex tourism which has tens of thousands of victims involved in the Philippines alone. I would like to thank them for providing me with information on the work they are undertaking and I recommend watching their Sweetie Campaign video available on their website about how they investigated the extent of webcam child sex tourism. http://www.terredeshommes.org/webcam-child-sex-tourism/ Please help them by signing their online petition to pressure governments to adopt proactive investigation policies in order to protect children against webcam child sex tourism.

I would to thank Andy Chagger from the Non-Government Organisation I volunteered with, International Disaster Volunteers (IDV), for giving me the opportunity to work with them in Tacloban. IDV works with communities worldwide which have been affected by or are vulnerable to disaster. They help survivors to achieve sustainable recovery and build more resilient communities both before and after disaster. For more information on the work they undertake and how you can help them, please visit their website: http://www.idvolunteers.org/

Raul and his feeding programme, featured in the book were inspired by the Mobile Soup Kitchen for Kids (MSKK) set up by Reynold De Vera. MSKK is saving and changing lives, one soup bowl at a time. Please support and join them as they provide much needed help, nutrition and sustenance, to the children of Tacloban, Leyte, and many other areas affected by Typhoon Haiyan (Yolanda). Their Facebook page can be found at:
https://www.facebook.com/groups/1556492901241816/?fref=ts

A couple of organisations aimed at helping to stop trafficking in the Philippines are the Viasayan Forum Foundation, Inc. and Childhope Asia / Philippines.
Visayan Forum Foundation, Inc. (VF) works for the welfare of marginalized migrants, especially those working in the invisible and informal sectors, like domestic workers, and trafficked women and children. It is licensed and accredited by the Department of Social Welfare and Development (DSWD) to provide "residential care and community-based programs and services for women and children in especially difficult circumstances."
Childhope is a Philippine NGO, which is non-profit, non-political,

non-sectarian organization whose principal purpose is to advocate for the cause of street children throughout the world.

My time volunteering in Tacloban inspired me to write Tindog Tacloban in the hope I could raise awareness of the lasting effects on survivors of a natural disaster and also prick people's conscience about child exploitation, specifically webcam child sex tourism. This is a very real issue and affecting children as young as six, please help by raising awareness of this growing problem, every child should be entitled to a childhood.

Sales of the book will benefit organisations helping disaster hit areas and raising awareness of child exploitation.

CLAIRE MORLEY
August, 2015

ACKNOWLEDGMENTS

Firstly, my thanks to my partner Steve Knight, without whom this book would never have been written. His help, encouragement, patience and suggestions have been invaluable.

Thank you to my wonderful beta readers, Barbara Morley, Marc Moss and Sandy Hewitt, who all took the time and patience to read through the emerging chapters and then the rewrite. Your encouragement and belief in my writing helped me reach the end.

To Lyndsey Blackburn at LB Designs for producing the beautiful artwork for my book cover

To Anne Hamilton, who coached me through the course at writingclasses.co.uk and my mentor through the process of editing and rewriting, also my patient proof-reader and always on hand with ideas for improvement and to hearten me when my confidence waned.

I would also like to thank all the people I volunteered with, survivors and helpers who were kind enough to let me interview them and to Fred Jaca who acted as my guide and interpreter.